To Ricky and Lincoln. You're too young to read this book now, but maybe in ten years, you'll pick it up and find something in it you like. I'm so proud of you both.

Prologue

The boy stood at the edge of the cliff, the detonator securely in his hand. He could see gray, dreary clouds, with the occasional bird soaring lazily overhead. And he could see the town. Osprey. A pathetic place filled with hateful people. It was barely a town. With less than a thousand people, it was barely a community. But it had formed because of his family, and it was where he had grown up.

He had hiked up the path and planted himself at the edge of the rock wall, peering down the hundred feet to the gravel quarry below. His great-grandfather had started this quarry in 1919, when he realized that the same ground of this area that made farming impossible was also ripe for a different harvest. Stone. Osprey was a hard, cold town, built on hard, cold ground. Fitting.

The business was profitable and people began to settle in the area. The town formed quickly as jobs needed filling and work was plentiful. For a while. The quarry passed from the great-grandfather to the grandfather, who was maybe not as good at the business side. But people still had work. When it passed again, the boy's father was even worse at business and things really took a turn. The community stopped growing.

Community. There was a laugh. A community of monsters, maybe. Selfish, ugly people living in decrepit, falling-down homes with rusted out cars sinking slowly into dirt lawns.

Here he stood, at the top of the quarry that would never be his. The stupid stepfather was driving it — and the whole town right along with it — into the ground.

The stone ground.

The immense wall of the quarry was solid and unyielding. The boy looked down at the worn out hulks of equipment below, discarded like toys in a sandbox. Bulldozers, backhoes, excavators. Each vehicle stood in at least a foot of water. He had told his stepfather that the old water pumps needed to be replaced, but the asshole had refused to spend the money. So now the site was constantly flooded with the naturally occurring groundwater that accrued as they dug deeper and deeper into the soil.

The boy opened a plastic grocery bag he had brought with him and pulled out a length of cord wound into a neat circle and held together with a bit of twine. He tossed it to the ground.

Next, he pulled out a bundle of dynamite, which he had swiped from the utility shed below. It had been easy enough lifting the key off the stupid stepfather as he slept and farted in his Easy-chair in the living room. It was Thanksgiving weekend, and he was done in on beer and turkey.

The boy bent to work, deftly rigging the explosives to the cord. He had been working at the quarry with his dad since he was six and had been working with explosives since he was twelve, so this was nothing new to him.

With the bundle of dynamite finished, he secured it with electrical tape and tossed it casually down the hundred feet to the ground below. It landed on a bulldozer with a thunk. The memories of driving the same dozer while sitting in his father's lap flooded in. They would push the gravel here and there, him squealing with delight when his dad's scruffy face nuzzled into his neck.

The dynamite settled on the hood. With that done, the boy grabbed the detonator and hooked the line to it.

With the quarry far out of his reach and with zero desire to grow up watching this horrid town dry up and die, the boy had decided to end things himself. Like putting a bullet between the eyes of a horse that's broken its leg because of the actions of a reckless rider.

He was all frigged up with nervous energy, and he didn't even feel the cold as he prepared to attach the wire to the trigger and blow the whole site to hell. He imagined his stepfather sitting behind the driver's seat of the bulldozer down below. Imagined blowing him up along with the business.

But the dozer sat empty, and the stepfather would sleep his way through the blast. The boy was only able to do it now because it was a long weekend. No one would be here for days because of the holiday.

He stepped back, his foot crunching in the semi-frozen growth that was too long to be called grass, preparing to hit the switch on the detonator. He probably should have grabbed the yellow ear muffs in the supply shed where he had grabbed the dynamite. It was going to be a loud bang.

Another step. Crunch. He glanced at the town off in the distance. He wondered how loud the explosion would be. Whether they would come running, or if they would ignore the noise and wait for the next work day. After all, everyone knew the quarry was dead, anyway.

He took another step back. But this time, no crunch of frost. His foot came down and kept going. His eyes popped wide in surprise as he felt himself begin to fall. He was still holding the length of cord and instinctively gripped it harder, as if it were a convenient lifeline. But though the six pounds of explosives was enough to blow a hole in solid rock, it was not enough to stop a one hundred and thirty pound kid from falling.

His shoulders crashed down on the soft ground. He expected that was going to be the extent of his fall. He would stand up, brush off his sore ass and finally trigger the town-fatal explosion.

But his lower back kept falling, and he quickly felt himself doubling over — being folded in half — as he slid into some dark crevice in the earth.

His shirt rucked up as he came down. His back was torn to hell as he descended into the earth. He had the crazy feeling that he was being swallowed by some mythical creature. The rock wall narrowed steadily as he slid down the monster's throat.

He wasn't sure how far he had fallen when he abruptly come to a stop — wedged into the crevice, breathing into his knees. His first thought was of the cartoon, "How the Grinch Stole Christmas."

He got stuck once or twice, for a minute or two.

Panic didn't take long to rear its ugly head as he felt himself unable to move. Blackness moved in. There was no light, except for the rip in the void far overhead.

He attempted to squirm his way into a more comfortable position. Any other position. But he was wedged in the rock with barely any wiggle room. His legs were straight up in front of him, his knees close enough to kiss, and he couldn't get any leverage. Each movement was a grating agony as the rough rock dug into his lacerated back.

"Aaaagh," he cried out in pain.

He struggled, but gave up quickly. Each time he moved, his torn back dug deeper and deeper into the jagged rock. He almost didn't feel the pain as a wave of claustrophobia took him and he frantically attempted to shift to his right, then his left.

When that proved futile, he stopped. It was hard to breathe when you were bent over almost in half. He had a difficult time filling his lungs. He breathed shallowly, trying to keep from letting that panic take over. With difficulty, he waited for it to pass.

It felt like days since he had fallen, but it likely had only been a couple of hours. Probably no more than three. But time seemed not to move at all. The gray sky above didn't help. There was no sun to mark the passage of time. But he thought it might be a bit darker.

Now he knew what a cork in a bottle felt like.

A cork. A bottle. A bottle of alcohol. A drunken stepfather. That's actually funny. He couldn't imagine his stepfather drinking something as sophisticated as wine. Beer was more his style. Cheap and plentiful. And easier to buy without having to work hard for a living.

Thinking of his stepfather reminded him why he was there to begin with. A wave of anger washed over him, fueling his determination to make it out of the literal hole he had found himself in, to show that stupid, lazy, drunken son of a—

"Aaaagh!" he cried out in pain. Not for the first or second time, but for what seemed like the ba-gillionth. "Help!" he wailed, also not for the first time. "Help me!"

But as with every other time, he knew it was hopeless. He remembered why he had come today. It was a long weekend. Thanksgiving. Nobody would be around, not for three days, at least. Maybe four.

He was awash with exhaustion and fear. He only had one cycle which he could use to keep track of time, even as it slipped through his fingers. First was anger. Then a determination to escape, which always failed. Finally, fear of starvation and death.

Anger, determination, failure, fear. Again and again.

More time passed, and he prayed for someone to come along. A hiker, maybe. Or his mother coming to check on him. But nobody knew he was there. Nobody even knew he had left the house. And it wasn't uncommon for him to spend all night in his room, keeping his distance from his stepfather. His mom probably wouldn't know he was even missing until noon tomorrow. And even then, she wouldn't think to check here. She had stopped thinking about the gravel pit at all.

The boy began to realize that he was going to die, and that terrified him. Which, of course, triggered the cycle anew.

Anger. Determination. Failure. Fear.

He broke down in tears. This, too, was not for the first time. It was because of his tears that he almost didn't hear The Voice.

The Voice that called out to him from the darkness. He didn't hear it with his ears. It felt more like an invasion in his mind. A stranger who had moved into his brain and taken control. The Voice in his mind sounded like his own thoughts. The way he sounded to himself when he thought about girls, or about going to see his favorite band in concert. Just his everyday internal voice. But it also felt foreign. Like an invader.

A thousand isn't enough, his thoughts said. I need more. His thoughts were followed by images. Words and pictures collided in his mind in an instant, and he knew what The Voice wanted. And what The Voice offered. Not just escape from this hole. But escape from his life. The life that had been given to him. Thrust upon him by his stupid stepfather.

And he was desperate for that escape. He was desperate to appease The Voice that might be able to save him — or destroy him in the worst ways imaginable. He sensed that very strongly. This was not a passive voice.

"I'll do anything," he said aloud. He said it through the tears and snot flowing down his face. His voice cracked with emotion as he spoke. "Just tell me how."

The boy listened.

Part One

CHAPTER ONE

Josh admired Amber, ignoring the dead man between them.

"You look nice," Josh said, trying to sound casual as he lay the thick plastic sheet next to the body on the ground. "New hair cut?"

Amber's queasy expression took on a slight smile. "Just a trim," she said. Then her smile faltered as her gaze returned to the body that was face down on the floor.

Josh began tucking the first inch of the sheet under the corpse of Cecil Porter, so it wouldn't shift. He worked without thinking. Cecil had been dead for over four days. Long enough that things were getting a bit ripe, but not so long that Josh needed to smear Vicks VapoRub under his nostrils to cut the smell. So he was able to enjoy the faint scent of her perfume over the reek.

"Well, it was a good trim."

Amber attempted another smile. Josh realized that the smell he considered just ripe might be a little more unpleasant to someone who wasn't as experienced around death as he was. He reached into his pocket and held out the small, round tin.

"Vicks?" he said, as if offering her a stick of gum.

She took it gratefully and began dabbing the smelly gel under her nose.

"Okay, guys," Henry burst in. "You think we can move this along? I don't wanna spend the whole day here."

"Speak for yourself, dude," Craig said, leafing through a magazine he had picked up from a musty pile in the corner. "This guy has every issue of Rolling Stone since 1972!"

Henry sneered. "They're probably all covered in black mold."

Amber stood up to move the gurney into place. Josh rolled his eyes, ever so briefly wishing officer Henry were the one on the floor decaying into the foundation. Josh moved to help Amber. Henry stood in the corner of the basement with one hand covering his nose and mouth.

"The smell's really not that bad, Henry," Josh said.

"Maybe not for you, Ghoul-boy," Henry shot back, using a nickname he had given Josh at the beginning of high school. "But some of us have a decent regard for human life."

"Really?" Amber said. "Is that why you're always bragging about your Call of Duty kill count?"

"Or complaining that you never get any bank robbers, so you can finally use your gun?" Josh added.

"Bank robbers," Craig said wistfully, and picked out a new issue of Rolling Stone.

"Whatever," Henry said. He pointed at the body on the floor with his free hand. "Why isn't he wearing pants?" He pointed at Cecil's body, which was naked from the waist down. Josh had found bodies in worse condition over his years.

"Are you seriously asking why a corpse isn't wearing pants?" Amber said. "He's an old man who died in his home. I don't see a note explaining his wardrobe choices."

"This isn't a home," Henry groused. "It's a hoarders' paradise. The city dump is a haven compared to this place." He pushed over one of the many piles of used takeout containers. They tumbled to the floor, landing beside a stack of old, yellowed newspapers and a rusty bike frame without wheels. "I feel like I need a tetanus shot just standing in here."

"We offered you gloves," Josh said.

"Yeah," he said. "To help move the body. I told you. I don't move the bodies. I'm here to, you know, collect evidence and stuff. That's my job."

"Evidence, Henry?" Josh said. "Dr. VanLakey was already here and declared the death was from natural causes. No fowl play. Therefore, no need for evidence."

"Wouldn't that be awesome if he'd been knocked off?" Craig said from behind. Josh, Amber, and Henry stopped what they were doing and looked at him.

Craig lowered the magazine and looked around at the quiet room.

"Really, dude?" Henry said.

"That's kind of sick," Amber said.

"Right, yeah, I know," Craig stammered. "I didn't mean it. I just meant, wouldn't it be cool if it was some kind of, ya know, crime thing? Angry neighbor knocked him off. Or...or like a serial killer? I'd love to catch a serial killer!"

"I'll keep praying for one, Craig," Josh said, smiling. He had been hearing about Craig's lust for action in town for as long as he could remember. It had only gotten worse since he had become a cop the year before.

"Right," Amber said. "Well, we're going to get back to OUR jobs." She turned to Josh. "This where you want the gurney?"

"A little too close," Josh replied, gesturing backward. "Yeah, that's perfect. Now come around and get ready to grab the legs."

"I can't believe this is the crap I gotta deal with," Henry said, looking dejectedly through a pile of old newspapers.

"Totally," Craig said, putting his magazine down. "This is not what I joined the force for."

Josh smiled. "The force, Craig? We're talking Osprey, here. Not New York City. What did you expect you'd be doing as a cop in this town?" He turned his focus to Amber. "You ready?" Amber kneeled at the body's feet. Josh crouched on the far side of the plastic sheet. When she was in place, he reached over and grabbed the shoulder. "On three, we start pulling." Amber nodded.

"I was hoping for something more...I don't know...exciting?" Craig said as they worked. "The occasional bank robbery or something." Both Josh and Amber laughed. "Hey, it happens!" Craig insisted. "Couple guys stole a whole ATM out of the lobby at the First National in Harlow last year. And Harlow's a way smaller town than Osprey."

Henry broke in. "Hey, how come he's not stiff? I thought bodies went into rigor mortis, or whatever."

Josh could see him peering down. "That's right, Henry!" he said, unconsciously cradling the dead man's head, so it didn't flop against the cement floor. "Three points! But rigor mortis is only temporary. It wears off after a day or so." He turned to Craig. "And it's been more than five years since the ATM was stolen."

"Really?" Amber said, amazed. "That happened? Sounds pretty intense."

"Nah," Josh said. "Some rednecks just broke the glass and pulled it out with a pickup truck. Probably drunk or high."

"Or both," Amber said.

"Aww, I hate it when old dudes have tattoos," Henry whined, ignoring the conversation. He pointed down at the body.

Josh saw a mark on the corpse's inner biceps, close to the armpit. The shape was three squiggly lines emanating from a triangle, but...

"It's not a tattoo," he said, studying it. "It looks more like..." he furrowed his brow.

"More like what?" Amber said, craning her neck to see.

"Like a brand," Josh finished.

"A brand? Like what you'd do to a cow?" she asked, doubt in her voice. "You sure?"

"I'm sure it's not a tattoo. Or at least, I'm pretty sure. This looks like a burn. It indents into the skin. Don't tattoos make the skin puff up, or something?"

"Don't ask me," Amber said, gesturing at her bare forearms. "I have absolutely no interest in getting a tattoo."

"It's probably just a scar or whatever from when he was a kid," Josh finished. "Definitely not a tattoo."

"I'd get inked," Craig said from behind them. Josh saw he was looking dreamily off into the middle distance. "Something EPIC. Like a dragon and an eagle. In a death battle."

"Anyway," Josh said, ignoring Craig and turning his attention back to the body, "we should get back to the home." He and Amber moved into position, and he counted to three. They began to pull the body onto the plastic sheet. Josh was glad it wasn't completely nude, because if it had been decomposing this long, there was a good chance that it would—

"Oh, gross!" Henry said as they had the body halfway turned.

"Uh, Josh?" Amber said, sounding panicked. He looked over just as Cecil's body settled onto the plastic sheet. Amber had her gloved hands out in front of her, looking at him in disgust. Craig and Henry were both moving toward the door. Henry actually stumbled up the narrow flight of stairs in the dungeon-like basement, looking like he was going to blow chunks.

Josh smiled as best he could. "Sorry. Should have warned you that could happen."

Amber held her hands out in front of her. Large patches of gelatinous skin were sticking to her gloves. The floor where the body had been — at least the lower half — was also covered in a couple layers of flesh. Josh always thought about the sheddings of a snake when it happened. Cecil's penis lay in the center of this mess, glued to the concrete.

Amber's face scrunched up in disgust. Which, Josh thought, made her look incredibly cute. He quickly turned his attention to the body. "Sorry," he said. Not knowing what else to say, he repeated, "Should have warned you."

"Yes, you damn well should have!" she agreed. "From now on, I'm staying where I belong. Behind my desk at the Home, filling out paperwork. Removals are all yours, buddy!" She looked around, obviously wanting to wipe her hands on something.

THEY WERE ABLE TO GET the body into the thick bag and onto the stretcher without any help. But eventually Josh had to go coax Craig back inside to help them move the body past all the piles of junk and up the rickety stairs. It was barely wide enough for the stretcher and they had to stand the body up on end — praying the straps would hold — to get it up the stairs.

Outside, it was hard to believe they were in the same place. The dank and musty inside was replaced with an immaculately landscaped exterior that looked like it belonged on the cover of a Home and Garden magazine. A wide porch extended the full length of the house, which looked freshly painted. Like most of the town, the garden out front was full and well tended. Osprey prided itself on its horticultural society, and it was clear Cecil had been a proud member.

Henry, who had stayed outside while they moved the body, was enjoying a smoke while leaning against the cruiser. He seemed to have recuperated. Josh, however, was out of breath. He bent over, gasping. He had been taking most of the weight on the way up the stairs.

Craig slapped him on the back. "You gotta start working out, man," he said. "You're going to end up like one of your clients! Take better care of yourself." Craig walked to the police cruiser and said something to Henry. They both laughed.

Josh straightened, enjoying the pops from his back as he did. Amber maneuvered the stretcher into the back of the funeral home van and shut the tailgate.

"We did it," she declared. "You need anything else before we take the body away?" Amber asked Craig.

"Nah, we're good," he responded.

"I do have one question," Henry said to Josh. "When a new body comes in, do you have to give up your coffin for the night?" He broke up in a fit of laughter, as if this were the funniest thing he had ever said. Craig chuckled but ignored Henry's attempt at a fist bump.

"Good one, Hank," Craig said.

Henry turned toward the cruiser and bent in toward Craig. Josh could just hear him say in a petulant voice, "Come on man, you know I hate being called that."

"Yes, thank you, Henry," Josh said. "Very good. I think your delivery on that joke is improving with practice." Josh slid in behind the wheel of the van.

"Love the maturity from the county's finest," Amber said, getting into the passenger seat. Josh closed his door with a sigh of relief.

"What a jerk," Amber said as he started the van.

Josh pulled the van out onto the town road. The pavement was black and the lines were a solid yellow. Like all of Osprey, it was well kept.

"Henry? Yeah, he hasn't changed much since we were kids. You can take the pot-head out of high school and make him a county cop, but at heart, he'll still be a pothead. Or something like that."

"Nice," Amber said. "Socrates?"

"I think it was Einstein," Josh replied. "So! Any big plans for tonight?" he said, turning onto main street. Cecil's house wasn't far from the home. Nothing in Osprey was far from the home. Or anywhere else, for that matter. You could drive from one end to the other in less than ten minutes. But people, especially outsiders, often took longer, enjoying the brick sidewalks and beautiful storefronts.

"Nice subject change away from your high school bully," Amber said. Josh heard the smile in her voice and glared.

"He wasn't my bully. He's just…Henry. He's a jerk to everyone."

"And they let him become a cop? Weird town you people have, here."

"It's Osprey. We take who we can get. And we like familiar faces."

She laughed. "Oh, trust me. I'm aware."

He smiled as he pumped the brakes. Dozens of people were on the street, preparing for the celebration. Josh slowed down as he drove under a banner that was being strung across main street. WELCOME TO OSPREY! 100 YEARS OF GRANDEUR, followed by the date.

The upcoming centennial was a big event. It seemed like everyone was out in their yard, tending to every last twig and unsightly dandelion in the grass.

"Give it a couple years, and you too will be a local jerk."

She brightened. "It's actually my one-year anniversary on Friday."

"Oh yeah? Since you moved in, or since you started working for dad?"

"Moved. But pretty much both."

"Huh!" He was speaking as if he hadn't already known about the anniversary. He wanted to ask her out to celebrate, but couldn't think of how to say it. A silence fell over them as he drove. He opened his mouth to speak, then shut it. Then opened. Then shut.

"We should do something to celebrate," she said.

"Yeah!" he replied, a little more forcefully than he had intended. He cleared his throat. "I mean, yeah. Cool. Did you...want to do something?"

"I think I just said that I did."

"Right. Uh...wanna get something to...eat? Maybe see a movie?" Josh asked.

"That sounds nice. How about tonight?"

He hesitated. "That...works."

"Oh, you have class, don't you?"

"Yeah, but I can—"

"No no. We can do it another night. I don't want you playing hookie. Tomorrow?"

"Done!"

"Great!" Silence. "Are you enjoying the electrician course?"

"No," Josh said, feeling embarrassed. "I'm...not doing that anymore. It was only an introductory class."

"Oh. You didn't like it?"

"Mmm. Not for me."

"So, what are you taking now?"

"Uh...still just fishing around. I'm...trying out art."

"Oh. I didn't know you drew."

"Yeah, well...not much. Just trying it out," he repeated.

"What's the class? You drawing naked people down at the college?" Amber said, laughing.

Josh stared at the road, not saying anything.

"Oh my god, you are?"

"It's an introduction to life drawing," Josh admitted.

"Oh my! Joshua! You naughty boy."

"It's a perfectly respectable form of art," he said defensively. He felt his face growing hot and hoped she couldn't see him—

"You're blushing!" she said, laughing. Josh gave her another glare.

"Was she good looking?"

"Our model was quite distinguished, yes. He had a twinkle in his eye. He was an eighty-year-old retired farmer, missing three fingers."

"Ooooo. Same hand? Or total?"

"Samsies."

"Huh. But you're enjoying it?" she asked, growing serious.

"I'm not very good. But we'll see."

"You should stick with it! I know you'll be good at it."

He laughed. "You just said you didn't even know I drew."

She nodded. "True. But I know you. You're generally good at most things you do. Much better than you or your dad gives you credit for."

"Thanks," he said with a shrug. He didn't know what else he could say. An awkward silence filled the van.

Josh drove slowly past a group of people carrying a large board down the side of the road. They were all laughing and seemed to be having a grand old time. They looked to be headed for the town center, Josh guessed. As they passed it, he could see, painted on the board, a burly farmer holding a hefty pig under one arm, with a busty woman in a checked plaid shirt on the other arm. The heads of the farmer, the woman, and the pig were missing. In their place, three holes had been cut out and people could fulfill their life's fantasy of becoming a local farmer of Osprey.

Or a pig.

Josh pulled into the driveway at the funeral home. A head poked out of the top-floor window. Josh's dad signaled to them and Josh slowed, rolling down the window.

"I'll be out in a few minutes."

"It's fine, dad. We got it covered. Just sit and relax."

"Actually, there's something I need you to do tonight. I'll come down. Just unload, and I'll meet you in the prep room." With that, he disappeared back inside.

"Oh goodie," Josh muttered. "Looks like I'll be missing class tonight after all." He pulled forward, pushing the button to the garage door, silently giving up any hope that he would ever get out of the funeral business.

Chapter Two

"Don't give up so quickly," Amber said as they pushed the gurney toward the ramp that would take them from the garage to the main floor of the home.

"I'm not giving up," Josh said.

"Uh-huh," Amber said, doubt in her voice. "It's probably just a removal. He can call Paul to do it if he needs. You should make class a priority. Unless you wanna be working here for the rest of your life. And I *know* you don't."

Josh shrugged. "Yeah, I know. I know. You're right."

They both pushed the stretcher up the steep ramp, headed for the preparation room. The funeral home was a converted house, so not everything was on the same level. The exterior was the same as every other house in Osprey. Quaint and well manicured. Landscaping was big business in town, and the home was not shy about hiring workers to keep up the appearance. Aside from a discreet sign out front, you would never know this house was dedicated to death on the inside.

"Tell you what," Amber said. "If Paul can't do it, and you can't get your dad to put it off, I'll volunteer to do it for you."

"You sure?" Josh said. "You think you're up to going solo?"

She looked uneasy as she answered. "Yeah, probably. It's most likely going to be a nursing home or something, right? They pretty much do everything for us anyway." Josh nodded. "Same with the hospital. If it's a house call…I'm sure I can get one of the family members to help me with the body."

"Thanks, Amber! You're a lifesaver."

"I know. I'm a real princess. But I'm making you take us somewhere expensive tomorrow for our date."

"Date? Who said it was a date?" Josh said.

This time, Amber was the one who blushed. She also looked like she was ready to take a swing at him. She let go of the stretcher halfway up the ramp.

"I'm kidding!" he said, straining under the increased weight. "It's a date! I want to take you on a date!"

"Oh, you are on *THIN* ice, sir," she said, reaching across and slapping his arm.

"Fine!" he said, pretending to struggle with the stretcher. "I'm a bad, bad boy! Just help me with this thing!" Eventually, she picked her end back up.

At the top of the stairs, they wheeled the body into the prep room. This was where the actual work

was done to prepare the corpse for the casket —
or for the cremation chamber in the back. From
embalming the body, to applying makeup, this was
where the "magic" happened.

Josh's dad was actually quite good at makeup,
or so Josh had been told all his life. His dad was
regularly drafted to help apply make-up to the per-
formers in the local playhouse. But it did not seem
to be a trait passed on from father to son. Amber
said Josh always made the corpses look too "easy."

Working together, they transferred the body
from the stretcher to a flat metal table. The room
was small, so they couldn't have more than two
bodies in it at a time. They broke down the stretcher
and left it at the top of the ramp. Then headed to the
office, which was in the basement.

Arthur Warlocke sat behind his large desk, filling
out paperwork. He was a thin, somber man. He
looked how you would expect a funeral director to
look. Except for his wild white hair, which made
him look like Boris Johnson.

Arthur always wore overly starched clothing,
even when he was relaxing at home. They were so
wrinkle free, Josh swore the man's clothes looked
like he cut them from a magazine every morning.

"Hey dad," Josh said, plopping down in the
chair across from the desk.

"Did you get Cecil set up properly?"

"Aye aye, captain!" Josh replied. After years
in the funeral business, his dad had developed the
habit of always referring to the corpses by their first
names, as if they were old friends. Which, given the
size of Osprey, they often were. Josh found this a

little creepy. As if the body they had just left upstairs on a metal table was a friend who had come over to take a nap. It also made for some really weird conversations.

"Joshua, hold Winnifred's head while I insert the embalming fluid."

It was a weird business.

"Good," Arthur replied. He turned to Amber, who was standing next to the desk, waiting for instructions. "I'll need you to call Cecil's next of kin to set up an appointment."

"Oh goodie," Amber said. "Do they know he's dead? I don't want a Dotty Norris repeat."

Arthur smiled. Dotty Norris was a 65-year-old woman who had died of a heart attack in bed. Her husband was a corporate auditor who was frequently out of the country on business. When Amber called Dotty's husband to set up an appointment, she not only found herself having to explain to him that his wife had passed away, but that she had died while in bed with another man. He hadn't taken it very well.

Arthur sighed. "I'm never going to hear the end of that, am I?

"Yes, Mrs. Morgan is aware of Cecil's demise," Arthur said. "I spoke with her half an hour ago. She said she wasn't available to come in today and she'd need to figure out a time in the next couple days."

"She needs to squeeze her dead brother into her schedule?" Amber said. "That's cold."

"Let's just say Cynthia wasn't on the best of terms with her brother. It's not our place to—"

"Wait," Josh interjected. "Mrs. Morgan? Cynthia Morgan?"

"Yes. Cynthia is Cecil's sister."

"Cecil Porter is Cynthia Morgan's brother?"

His dad laughed. "I think that's what I just said."

"Wow."

"Who's Cynthia Morgan?" Amber asked.

"How do you live here a year and know nothing about this town?" Josh said, smiling.

"I'm a professional ostrich," she said, then stuck her tongue out at him.

"Cynthia Morgan is the wife of Fred Morgan."

Amber shook her head. "You people seem to think I spend all my time thinking about this town."

"Fred Morgan!" Josh said. "How can you not recognize that name? It's on virtually every business in town. Morgan Hardware. Morgan Credit Union! *FRED MORGAN MEMORIAL HOSPITAL!*"

"Oh," Amber said. "Yeah, that one rings a bell. So he's, like, a big deal here?"

"I give up," Josh said, throwing his arms up in mock frustration.

Arthur smiled. "Fred Morgan was, mmm…you could say a founding father of Osprey. He was a businessman that put this town on the map." Josh knew that Fred Morgan was also a close friend of his dad. Arthur always seemed to glow when talking about the man, and loved harkening back to the "Good Old Days," when business was booming and no "damn kids" dared ran across his lawn.

"Osprey is on the map?" Amber said, smiling.

"It's in small print, but yes, we're on the map," Arthur said, smiling.

"I'm assuming by your use of the past tense that Cynthia is Fred Morgan's widow?"

"Correct," Arthur said. "She's not particularly hands on, but she's the closest thing Osprey has to royalty."

"Great. I've seen how royalty acts around the commoners. Can't wait to meet her."

"Don't worry. Cynthia is a lovely woman."

"A lovely woman who doesn't have time to grieve for her own brother."

Arthur hesitated. "There's some bad blood there. They had a falling out several years ago, from what I understand. They haven't had anything to do with each other since. Let's just say I don't think you're going to have to get the tissue box out when she comes by."

"Well, thank heavens," Amber said.

"You needed me for something?" Josh said, bracing himself. He pulled his phone out to check the time. He had class in less than two hours. He did the math, thinking if it was a removal, he probably had enough time to do both. Maybe.

"Got the word. We have a pick up."

Josh nodded. "I figured. Can it wait until after my class tonight?"

His dad didn't even try to hide his eye roll at the mention of his class. Josh chose to ignore it.

"No, you'll have to leave right away," Arthur said, shuffling around papers in a manilla folder.

"Well, I can probably make it back before I miss too much of my class," he said, glancing back at his phone.

"I highly doubt that," Arthur responded.

"What? Why? Where is it? The hospital? Or is this a home visit?"

"Up north somewhere," Arthur said, riffling through some paperwork on his desk. He pulled up a pink piece of paper with perforated edges and scanned the sheet. "Hawk Junction, Ontario."

Josh stared for a moment. "Where the hell is Hawk Junction?"

"I was told the nearest town is some place called Wawa."

"Wa-what?"

"Wawa. The town is called— look," Arthur said in frustration. "I don't know where this place is, okay? Just look it up on your gizmo."

Josh smiled as he pulled up the maps app on his phone and began typing. "'Gizmo.' It's a cell phone, Dad. You're not THAT old." The search came up on the display, and Josh nearly dropped it. "That's over half the province! It's more than a ten-hour drive!" Josh said, nearly shouting.

Amber glanced over his shoulder. "Eleven hours and six minutes, to be exact." Josh pointed at Amber with vindication.

"Why is the body so far away? And why are we picking it up? Don't they have funeral homes in Hawk Junction?"

"They don't seem to have enough people to justify it," Amber said, typing away on her own phone. "They have a total population of 190 people."

"What?" he said, pulling her phone toward him. He scanned. "That was in 2011. Who says they're still there?"

"Someone's still there," Josh's dad said. "The body was reported, and the removal order was sent to us. It's a John Doe."

"I've always wondered if they actually called people that outside of the movies," Amber said.

"Yeah, we take John Does from hospitals when nobody claims them," Josh explained. "The government pays for us to do either burials or cremations. It's all organized through the FSA."

"FSA?"

"Funeral Service Association. You've been here for a year, right?" Josh said.

"Do I look like I'm in this job for the long haul? I'm still calling the funeral coach a hearse in front of clients. I can't keep all this death stuff straight."

"Didn't you want to talk to me about a pay raise?" Arthur said to her, eyebrows raised.

"Uh..." Amber stammered, moving toward her desk. "I gotta go file...something. I'll let you two sort this out."

"There has got to be a closer home than us," Josh said.

"I'm sure there is, and I'm sure this was a big error on the FSA's part," his dad said, packing the pink paper back into the manilla folder. "But the fact is, this is a blessing in disguise. It's been slow around here lately."

"Normal folks would shout 'halleluiah' when people aren't dying," Amber yelled from her desk.

"What about Paul?" Josh tried, now getting desperate.

"I tried Paul. He's busy."

"*I'm* busy, dad!" Josh said. "I have class to-night."

Arthur rolled his eyes. "You're going to make the Home suffer so you can go ogle at naked women for four hours?"

"It's not…this isn't…it's not a strip club, dad! It's art. It's something I'm interested in."

"It's fine to have hobbies, Joshua. But right now, this is a real opportunity. Real money. I need you here. The Home isn't going to survive without you."

"Okay, fine! Can you reschedule the pick up for tomorrow night? So I can do my class and get a decent night sleep? Work with me, Dad!"

"You're twenty-five years old, Joshua. You were made for all nighters. You'll be fine missing a little sleep. Besides, if we try rescheduling, they'll recognize the error and have another home closer pick it up. We lose out on a pretty good sized commission."

Frustrated, Josh turned to Amber, who didn't make eye contact. He cleared his throat. She turned. "Yes?"

"Didn't you say something about volunteering if nobody else could do it?"

She gave a bark of laughter. "Oh, I didn't know about Hawk Junction when I said that. Sorry Joshy, but I get nervous driving bodies across town. There's no *way* I could do eleven hours through scrub brush with a corpse lying right behind me. Gives me the willies just thinking about it."

Josh sat back in his chair. He hated the funeral business, just like he knew his dad hated the idea of him leaving it. It was inevitable that his dad would find a way to sabotage his attempts, even if those attempts were as vague as taking night classes on the side.

"Fine. I'll do it! But I want twenty-five percent of the commission."

"You want a thousand dollars?" his father laughed. "I doubt it. I'll give you twelve and a half."

Josh sighed. For the John Doe cremations, they would likely make Four thousand dollars. Five hundred was a pretty good pay day. He could sock that away in his "Get the Hell out of Osprey" fund, and only have to miss one night of a class that he probably wouldn't stick with anyway. Seemed like a good deal when you put it like that.

"Fine! I'll go. But I'm using the company card to get a fancy hotel room on my way back!"

Amber laughed. "You'd be lucky to find anything better than 'Bates Motel' in a place like Hawk Junction."

Josh sighed, realizing she was right. He hated his life.

Chapter Three

As much as he didn't want to be doing this, Josh was enjoying the drive. He stopped often, just to stretch his legs. He didn't spend much money, as he didn't have much to spend. And he didn't dare use the company card for anything that wasn't absolutely essential. He knew his dad would be studying each receipt he brought home, interrogating him for information about each purchase. Acting as if Josh were a convicted felon, instead of the man's own flesh and blood.

Well, he enjoyed the first five hours of the drive, at least. The next six were pure torture. He spent half the time slapping his face just to keep awake. He had made sure to pack some caffeinated beverages for the road, and made a couple of stops for coffee along the way. Just long enough to keep him awake, but not enough for him to have to stop to pee every other rest stop.

The funeral van didn't have a CD player, let alone Bluetooth, so he had to content himself with the radio — a subpar experience to be sure. Just when he found something he liked, the static would begin creeping in, and he would have to go searching through whatever local radio station happened to be in range. Which, as he got closer to Hawk Junction, was fewer and farther between. All this in an attempt to keep himself awake. Coupled with sticking his head out of the window as he drove, it was semi-effective.

At the seven-hour mark, the radio became mostly static as there were pretty much no towers for it to connect with. Eventually, he gave up and drove in silence, occasionally filling it with his own off-key renditions of his favorite songs.

The roads became more winding, the trees became more plentiful, and the artificial light provided by buildings and streetlights disappeared for hundreds of miles at a stretch.

Still, he had been making good time until the GPS on his phone began glitching.

"What the crap?" he asked the empty van as he picked up his phone. The blue dot that represented his location disappeared from the map and didn't reappear until he got into a clearing in the trees — something that was becoming more and more rare.

"How is there no signal for GPS? I didn't think that was even possible." He continued on for another half hour, but eventually had to pull over when the directions glitched two more times. He got out some paper and began sketching out a map for himself based on the route his phone gave him. With that done, he threw the phone on the passenger seat, and traveled the way the pilgrims did hundreds of years ago - in an aging mini-van, guided by hand-written directions from a poorly functioning GPS. Yes, he was good at history.

At 6:23 am, Josh found himself pulling into The Big Bear Hotel, only to be facing a run down slat sided building. A permanent looking closed sign was taped to the outside of the front door. The tape looked yellowed from age.

"You have GOT to be kidding me," Josh muttered, getting out of the van. His shoes crunched in the gravel of the hotel parking lot. He knew there wasn't going to be a morgue, but he figured the hotel was next door to where the body would be. Like a small doctor's office. Or even a vet.

But he didn't expect to be facing a dilapidated hotel that obviously hadn't been open for years. No other buildings were in sight. "Old man, I am going to have some strong words for you when I get home," he said into the gray morning air.

If he got home, that is. He studied his surroundings and realized this was the perfect location for one of those hillbilly horror movies — where a trio of inbred hicks would capture him and slowly fillet his skin for their supper.

The squeaky sound of a vehicle door opening brought him out of his thoughts. He turned to see a man getting out of a rusted pickup truck with a gun rack in the back bed, and Josh had a moment of fright as he thought the man was going to reach around and pick up the gun. Instead, he slammed the door closed and made his way across the parking lot. He was dressed in beat up work clothes and had a long, scraggly beard which went down to his belly.

"Morning. You're here to pick up the devil," the man said. It wasn't phrased as a question, and Josh wasn't sure he had heard correctly.

"Uh, beg pardon?" he said, looking around warily.

The man grunted, which Josh guessed might have been a laugh. "Just a joke," he said as he got closer. "You're here to pick up the body."

"Yeah. How'd you know?"

"We don't get many visitors these days," he said, gesturing at the rundown hotel. He glanced at his watch. "You're late. I gotta get to work."

"Sorry," Josh said. "Long drive. GPS conked out on me. I'm with Warlocke's Funeral Home. In Osprey." He put out his hand to shake. After a moment, the stranger reached out and shook it. His hand was calloused and oil stained. It was also incredibly strong. Josh thought again about hillbilly cannibals and wondered if he could make it into the van and lock the doors before the man attacked him.

"Osprey. I have a cousin in St. Timothy," the man said, referring to a smaller town that Josh knew. As the man said this, he was studying Josh with a rough expression. "You're pretty young," he said. "I didn't think...I assumed they'd send someone with a little more...experience."

Josh was used to questions about his age and answered almost automatically. "My father owns the funeral home. I've been working for him since

I was twelve or so. That gives me over ten years' experience. There aren't many things I haven't seen when it comes to death, Mr....?"

"McTaggart," he said. "Call me Jim. And don't be offended, young man. I didn't mean to insult you. It's just..." he hesitated, and Josh got the idea that the man was struggling with exactly how to express himself. It was also when Josh realized that the man didn't look at ease. He was a big guy, and didn't look like the kind of person who would normally be jittery. But Josh thought he looked just short of terrified.

"I figured someone with more, uh, authority might be coming. You know?"

Josh didn't know. "You mean someone from the Funeral Service Association?"

"I mean someone from the government. You know, black-coat type? Guys with sunglasses and guns? Maybe some fellas in them hazmat suits? Shoot, I don't know. Maybe even a couple of them multi-star generals."

"I'm afraid I don't understand—"

"Yeah, it's okay," Jim said, cutting him off. "I've just been watching too many movies. But..." he eyed Josh again. "They at least told you what's been going on with this thing. Right?" He eyed Josh for a moment, and didn't seem to like what he saw. "Ah, hell."

Josh was thoroughly confused. "Jim," he said, holding his heads up in a surrendering gesture, "the only thing I was told was that there was a body that needed to be picked up."

Silence. "Well," he said after a moment, "I guess that's about the size of it. Long as it's out of my hair, that's all I care about. Come on. Let's get this over with."

And with that, Jim walked around the side of the building, heading for the back. For a moment, Josh considered jumping into the van and hauling ass out of there. Then he thought about explaining to his dad that he had decided to NOT pick up the body after spending hundreds of dollars on gas to get there.

He ran ahead to catch up.

"DON'T GET MUCH BUSINESS?" JOSH asked as they walked through cobweb festooned aisles. The building had apparently once been a lot of things. Hotel. Bar and grill. Laundromat and dry cleaner. Currently, they were walking through a section in the back of the building, which was apparently a local convenience store. He passed shelf after shelf of dusty food packages.

"'Not much business' is the way of life around here," Jim said. "The hotel closed down in 2017. We never had the population to support a business like this. Not ourselves. Most of our clientele were hunters. This is a good starting point during deer season. We'd get a good amount. Enough to justify the expense."

"What happened?"

Silence from Jim as they came to a door. He leafed through a ring of keys that he had been fiddling with ever since they had come in the back. He seemed terribly nervous about something and it had infected Josh, who wasn't familiar with the unlit building.

Jim found the key he was looking for and opened the door. Then he turned to look at Josh without going in. He seemed to be deciding whether to say something. "People just stopped coming," Jim said, staring at Josh. "Place just…started to feel different."

"How do you mean?"

"You ever been somewhere that people claim is haunted? People you know and trust?"

Josh shook his head, waiting for more.

Jim stared for another moment, then grunted, and said, "Come on. I've gotta get to work." He pulled a high-powered flashlight out of his back pocket, turned it on, and ducked through the door into the blackness beyond. Josh followed.

Uncomfortable with silence, Josh attempted to keep a conversation going. Something occurred to him that he probably should have asked by now. "How long have you had the body?"

"About ten years."

"Ten years!" Josh said, shocked. "Why'd you wait to report it now?" He immediately regretted the question.

"Waited?" Jim erupted in anger. "To hell with you! Are you nuts? I reported it alright. Nothing ever happened. I got stuck with the *FUCKING* thing for a *FUCKING* decade! I just got a call yesterday. Said you'd be along to pick it up. I was just happy

SOMEONE was finally coming to relieve me of the god-damned thing!"

"Sorry," Josh said, trying to think of a way to get back on the crazy man's good side. "I guess... ten years *IS* a long time to babysit a corpse. I would imagine you followed up?"

Jim stopped walking and Josh thought he had hit another sore spot. But instead, Jim sounded unsure.

"Follow up?"

"Yeah. When no one came, did you try calling again? Or...letting someone else know?"

He seemed to think for a moment. "No. Didn't seem...necessary, I guess. I reported it. Did my part. I figured someone would come, eventually."

"I thought you wanted rid of it."

"I did. I *DO*. But...I don't know."

Josh was starting to get the feeling that not all of Jim's upstairs wiring was flowing correctly. He thought silence might be better after all.

"Don't know," Jim said again without prompting. "I want it gone. Get on with my life. But... something held me back. Not like, you know, like I wasn't in control or anything, you understand."

"Of course," Josh said, not understanding in the slightest, but feeling like he needed to say something — *ANYTHING* — to get this conversation over with. "Of course you were in control."

"Woke up one morning, and something seemed to...uh...lift from me. Kind of decided it was time, I guess. That's the day I got the call. I was happy. I could move on with my life, ya know?"

"Yeah. Exactly," Josh said. As if he had any clue what the large man was talking about.

After a moment's pause, Jim began walking again. Josh let out a breath he hadn't known he had been holding and followed.

To the right, Josh could see the silhouettes of tables and chairs in the circle of light thrown by the flashlight. He realized this must be the restaurant. He followed Jim into the back of the kitchen.

It occurred to Josh to wonder why Jim hadn't been turning on any lights. Why the flashlight? The store they had entered through was all windows along one wall and the morning light had been streaming in. But here, the room was pitch black. They were walking past the metal counters of a kitchen.

"No power in here?" Josh asked, then mentally kicked himself. Why did he keep talking to this lunatic? Josh was looking at the counter tops, noting all the kitchen paraphernalia was still there, including dozens of knives of all shapes and sizes. They looked sharp, too. He once again realized that he was out of cell phone range in a remote location with a complete stranger who looked like a cannibal prospector.

"I turned off all the power in the building. Except for the essential," Jim said, stopping in front of a large metal door. He had put his hand on it at the word essential. Josh recognized it as a walk-in refrigerator. Or maybe a freezer. The latch was secured, and there was a pin and chain holding the latch shut. Josh noted that there were several more padlocks added to the door. Something he doubted was standard kitchen protocol.

"It's in here," Jim said. For a moment, Josh didn't know what "it" was the man was referring to. The question must have shown on his face.

"The body," Jim snapped. "That's why you're here, isn't it?"

"Sorry, right! Yes! The body! Of course." Why wouldn't the body of a dead man be in the freezer of a restaurant kitchen? Josh thought of some more things he wanted to say to his father. If he ever saw him again, that was.

Jim looked concerned and Josh no longer thought the man just looked terrified. Every fiber of his being seemed to be communicating extreme fright. "Are you sure you...you ARE prepared for this, right?"

Josh didn't know what to say to that. He thought he was. He thought again about just turning tail and running back to the van. Back to Osprey.

Then he looked at his empty hands and realized what Jim must have been talking about.

"Yeah, I have a stretcher in the back of my van. I just like to get the layout straight before I bring it out."

That didn't seem to satisfy Jim, who just stared at him for an uncomfortable moment. Then he reached into his back pocket. Josh tensed, but out came the ring of keys again. It seemed like there were hundreds of keys jingling.

"It's going to take me a bit to get this open," he said. "You better go get your stretcher. I should have it by the time you get back."

"Great," Josh said, looking around at the blackness beyond the glow of the flashlight beam. "Uh...

can I borrow your flashlight?" Josh said, holding out his hand.

Josh watched as the large man reflexively clutched the cylinder to his chest like a security blanket. "You got a light on you phone?" he asked.

"Yeah, of course." He pulled out his phone and turned on the flashlight in the back. It seemed weak and puny compared to the high-powered light Jim was holding. Barely good enough to see more than two feet ahead. He gestured with it to Jim. "This'll work."

"Good," Jim muttered. Then he said what Josh himself was feeling. What he probably wouldn't have been able to say out loud. It sounded too much like something a six-year-old would say.

"I don't wanna be alone back here in the dark."

Chapter Four

The Penis Bandit strikes again," Craig said as he and Aaron MacDonald leaned on fence posts, watching Aaron's cows graze in the morning dew.

"Mmmhm," Aaron said and took a sip from a travel mug with his farm logo etched on the side.

Of the two dozen cows in front of them, Craig could count about fourteen with neon green penises spray painted on their flank. He took a sip of his own coffee that he had picked up on the way over. He had responded to a call to check out a disturbance at the MacDonald farm when he got to the station that morning. He had been on a high all the drive over. Of course, he hadn't realized it was only the return of his not-so-favorite vandal.

"You know, I'm really starting to hate this kid," Craig said.

"Or kids," Aaron said matter-of-factly. "Might be a gang thing."

"You haven't been running this case for as long as I have," Craig returned. "It's the same M.O. every time. I've studied the spray pattern on storefront windows, water fountains, cars, trains, fish tanks. Tiny signs that only a trained professional would pick up on." He leaned out and pointed to a cow whose ear tag identified them as 14. "Look at the over spray on the left testicle on that one."

"Cows don't have testicles," Aaron informed him with a smile. "Those are udders."

"Not the cow! The spray-painted penis! It's always the same over spray. I find the can that has that spray pattern, I find our culprit."

"He's been at this for months now, ya say?"

"Yeah. Or she! I haven't ruled that out," Craig said seriously.

Aaron nodded his ascent. "You imagine they would have needed to switch to a new can of paint in all that time?"

Craig opened his mouth to say something, then closed it. Of course. He'd been too wrapped up in the details. Damn, this kid was good.

"Well, there are other things," Craig said quickly. "Like it's always circumcised. Always!" Craig sipped his coffee. Then his frustration boiled over and he smacked the fence post.

"Gah! What am I doing, Aaron?" Craig shouted. "I'm studying the spray pattern of some little twerp's vandalism like they're some...some mastermind villain or something."

"Like they're letters from Son of Sam," Aaron added, helpfully.

"Uh...yeah. Sure. This isn't why I signed up to be a police officer! I signed up for action. To make a difference. To stop bad guys. Not escort drunks home from the bar and break up marital disputes at two in the morning."

"I'm sure people have told you that Osprey is a small place, right?"

"Plenty," Craig muttered into his cup. "But I thought there'd be...something! Maybe one small bit of excitement per month. Instead, I'm spending my time chasing down...I don't know...friggin' taggers!"

"Banksy with sexual repression issues?" Aaron offered, gesturing at number fourteen as he reached for another clump of grass.

Craig looked perplexedly at the bovine. "Yeah... damn straight!"

"Well," Aaron said after giving Craig a moment to cool down, "if it makes you feel better, I would really appreciate you finding these kids and putting a stop to them. This is the second time they've vandalized my farm in as many weeks. I still haven't gotten around to painting over the barn, and it's right next to Janet's garden. She's been nagging me to get it taken care of it."

"What's the hold up?" Craig asked, taking the last swig of coffee and crushing the cup. "You keep reminding me how much time you have after buying that new fancy milking machine."

"I like how cute she looks when she's mildly ticked off," he said. Then he got serious. "But she ain't going to be *MILDLY* ticked off when she sees the cows. She's going to be royally pissed. Do what you can, Craig. I gotta go look up how to remove spray paint from cow hide. I'd prefer not to have to look up how to remove it from chickens and pigs in another couple days."

"Osprey county's finest are on the job, sir," Craig said morosely.

"Good. Then you can get back to hunting down the Osprey serial killer, or whatever else you expected to find in a town of less than fifteen thousand people." Aaron laughed and downed the last of his coffee. "You know," he said, as if he'd just had a thought. "You oughta set yourself up downtown. Do a little stakeout there. I'm sure those kids will be taking aim at the new banner they put up for the centennial. Doing an old-fashioned cop stakeout should put some excitement into your life, Craig!" Aaron slapped him on the back, grinning from ear to ear.

"Don't you have some cows to milk or something?" Craig groused. Although he had to admit, a stakeout might not be a bad idea.

Aaron shook his head. "I better not! Not after I just spent a quarter of a million dollars on that 'fancy milking machine', as you call it."

Craig whistled in appreciation of the money. He also thought about how much he had given up to be a cop. His own family were farmers and damn if there wasn't gold in them there rows of corn and cow shit.

"For that money," Aaron continued, "I shouldn't have to feed the hogs or collect eggs, either. But I guess I do still have some chores. I'll be seeing you, Tex," he said, and slapped Craig on the back again as he walked away. "Let me know if you find my vandals."

"Will do," Craig said over his shoulder. He continued leaning as the man walked away. When he looked ahead, he was face to face with number fourteen. They stared at each other for a moment. Then, once fourteen had gotten her point across, she moved on, cutting down patches of grass here and there, giving Craig a good look at her backside.

"This sucks!" Craig said. He turned in the direction of his squad car. He felt something smooshing beneath the rubber soles of his boots and his foot slipped from under him. He caught himself before he took a tumble.

He made a face as he inspected the cow pie that had been deposited on his side of the fence. "How did you even do that?" he yelled at the cows. They gave no response, and Craig stormed off in the direction of his squad car, stopping to wipe his boot in the grass as he went.

Chapter Five

"Stupid! Stupid!" Josh said, reprimanding himself. He was standing in the rear of the van, arms over his head, having just opened the tailgate, which was filled to the brim with NOTHING. He realized neither he nor Amber had replaced the stretcher after unloading Cecil's body last night. And had he checked before leaving? No. He had actually driven eleven hours to pick up a body without any way to get it into the van. And he didn't particularly want to carry the frozen body over his shoulders like an Antarctic firefighter.

"Idiot!"

Fortunately, there was a backup stretcher, which they had in case there were multiple bodies discovered at a location. But it was really unstable, and Josh hated using it. The "stretcher" consisted of a sheet of plywood, which was placed on a foldaway dolly. The dolly was just a frame that could accordion out to a four-wheel base. Once on top, it barely stayed in place. But it worked in a pinch. However, it was best on flat surfaces, like paved driveways or hospital halls. Not so great for gravel parking lots.

Grousing as he worked, Josh fumbled the frame open, plopped the loose board on top and started pushing it awkwardly toward the hotel. It felt like it took him three times as long to reach the door at the far end of the long building, but he got there just before realizing he probably should have just moved the van. Then it was just a matter of working it over the doorjamb and into the store, after hunting up a stone large enough to prop the door open.

Going was a little easier once he was inside, but he found himself jumping at shadows as he went through the ancient convenience store. He had to switch between holding his phone up for light and being able to steer the makeshift stretcher without banging into things. He ended up stopping every few feet, holding up the phone to see ahead, then walk forward with the phone laying on the board, pointing at the ceiling. This ended up casting some very spooky shadows, which only added to his jumpiness.

He lost his way a couple times and probably should have called out to Jim for help. But he didn't. He wasn't able to bring himself to speak aloud in the oppressive darkness of the strange building. Like there was something that would be awakened to his presence if he made too much noise.

Eventually, he was able to backtrack and find the door to the restaurant. Josh cried out in surprise when he opened the door. Jim was standing on the other side, looking pale and terrified. Terror quickly gave way to anger when he saw Josh.

"What the *HELL* is taking you so long?"

"Sorry. Trouble with the stretcher."

He looked down. "*THAT'S* your stretcher? A plywood board?"

Josh smiled sheepishly. "It's…uh…the spare. Our other stretcher is back at the home." Josh expected Jim to do some more waffling about him taking the body. But he just grunted and stomped off into the darkness of the kitchen, angrily waving Josh after him. It looked like Jim had made his decision and just wanted to get it rid of the corpse. Josh followed him, thinking how odd the man's behavior was, especially since he had been living with the body for ten years now.

Jim hesitated in front of the freezer door, his hand on the latch. Josh watched as the man seemed to be stoking himself up to opening it. Eventually, like a someone jumping out of an airplane, he pulled the latch.

The door opened. It gave a squealing sound as a rubber flap on the bottom scraped the tile floor, making them both jump. The freezer was completely dark.

"Damn," Jim said with a humorless laugh. "I cut the power to everything but the freezer to save on money. Now I wish I'd hooked the lights back up. I feel like a little kid, ya know?" Josh nodded. He sure did. Whatever paranoia this guy had, it was catching.

Josh stared into the darkness, waiting for the big man to dispel it with his flashlight. But Jim didn't move for what felt like an eternity. Josh felt exposed as they stood in front of that square of black. It didn't make sense, but the freezer seemed darker than the rest of the hotel. Like something in there was absorbing the light.

Or eating it.

Josh became sure that something was going to come reaching out of the dark and snatch them up, pulling them inside and slamming the door shut behind itself.

Unable to take the suspense, Josh pulled his phone out of his pocket with a numb hand and turned on the flashlight. He shone it into the room. Rather than helping relieve the tension, the weak light from his phone actually made it worse. The room seemed to refuse to reveal itself, as if the darkness was fighting back. He could see faint silhouettes of wire shelves. In the middle of the small room, Josh caught a faint glimpse of a form, like a person laying beneath a thick blanket. His shaking hand gave the illusion that the form was moving. Like it was breathing.

Coming to, Jim finally trained the high-powered flashlight on the interior of the freezer, dispelling the worst of the shadows — though not eliminating them completely. They clung to the corners of the room like malevolent beings.

"You said it's been here for ten years?" Josh asked. He whispered the question, like he didn't want to disturb whoever was inside.

Jim nodded.

"And you never come in here?"

"Once," he said, equally quiet. "Not long after I put it in here. Thought I'd remove some of the food inside."

Josh looked at the shelves, which were stocked full of decade old meats and frozen vegetables.

"Looks like you decided against it," Josh said.

Jim nodded again.

The walk-in freezer was longer than it was wide. The body lay along the width of the floor. It was covered in a dark green sleeping-bag in place of the usual thick rubber body-bag that Josh would normally have expected if he had been picking it up from a morgue or hospital.

Something about the room felt wrong. It was probably just Jim's obvious paranoia rubbing off on him, but that didn't make it any more bearable. There was a bad vibe about the place. He thought he understood what Jim was trying to tell him about haunted places.

Josh stepped into the room. It took more effort than he thought it would, but once done, he began to relax and realize how stupid this was. He was letting the dark and this man's fear infect him. He turned back to the door.

"I'm going to need a hand getting it onto the board," Josh said, pulling the stretcher behind him.

Jim looked down at the board, then across at the body. Obviously, the man had not considered that he might actually need to move the body himself. For the first time since entering the building, it wasn't fear Josh felt, but annoyance. "I thought you had to get to work?"

That seemed to cause Jim to snap to his senses. "Right. Yeah." But he didn't move.

Josh turned to the job at hand. He felt his old instincts taking over. This was just another body. It wasn't even his first time removing a body from a place without light. Once, someone had died during a bush party in the woods of Osprey. Josh had been sent out at one thirty in the morning to do the removal, taking it to the local morgue so an autopsy could be performed. He had to see by headlights of the trucks and cars that had driven deep into the brush.

Josh pulled the board up beside the body and gave a testing tug on the sleeping bag. He was pleasantly surprised to find that it was of high quality, which would make lifting a lot easier. He felt the body and was met with unyielding resistance.

He looked at Jim. "I'm afraid this sleeping bag isn't going to come off easily. It'll be frozen into—"

"God, I don't want the bag back," he said with disgust. "Keep it! Burn it along with the body!

Josh nodded.

This also wasn't his first time removing a frozen body. A lot of John Does were sent to them from the morgue that way. It took time to track down potential family or friends who would be able to identify someone. So the bodies were usually frozen until the FSA was satisfied that no family or friends existed. Nobody wanted to be responsible for destroying a body, then getting sued by an enraged family member down the road.

"Is it…did it…" Jim's voice drifted to him from the doorway.

Josh turned to see the large man almost cowering at the threshold of the freezer. Now that the fears he had leached from Jim had dissipated, the annoyance was growing.

"Can I get some help in here, please?" Josh said.

Jim still didn't move. "It's frozen?" he asked.

"Yeah," Josh replied. "Like a Butterball turkey. Which means it's going to be extremely heavy. I would APPRECIATE your help."

Jim looked around, and Josh half expected him to just turn and leave. Then the terrified man took a deep breath and stepped into the room, like a man walking into a body of water that he suspected hid a strong undertow.

"Move to the legs," Josh said. "I'll give a three count and we lift together. Grab the corners of the sleeping bag," he said, demonstrating with his side. "It's heavy duty, so it should be strong enough to lift him.

"I don't have to, ya know, touch it? Just the bag?"

"That's right," Josh said, as if reassuring a child. "Just the bag."

Jim didn't look entirely comfortable. He looked, in fact, like his fight-or-flight response was on a coiled spring which was pulled to full tension. And about to snap.

"Jim, I really need—"

"Okay," the man snapped, sounding now like a petulant child. He plunged ahead and moved to the body's legs, keeping his distance for as long as he could.

"Thanks," Josh said. He just wanted this over with. To get back on the road so he could find a motel and get a few hours of sleep. He realized exhaustion was probably a valid excuse for letting Jim's paranoia get to him. For most people, death is a scary, uncommon thing. Having a dead body just feet away for the past ten years had obviously done something to him.

"Lift to about here," Josh said, bringing his hand up to about his belly button. He was still keeping his voice low. He seemed incapable of talking louder. He guessed the fear wasn't completely gone. "Then we need to make sure we lower the body into the center of the board. Otherwise, the whole thing will topple over. Got it?" he asked, eyeing Jim. When the man didn't say anything, he asked again. "Got it?"

"Yeah!" he said, but Josh wondered if the man had understood, or even heard, what he had said. His eyes were glued to the sleeping bag.

Josh bent and grabbed the corners, and after a moment, Jim did the same at his end.

"One. Two. Three," Josh said, and they both lifted. With the both of them working, it was up and on the board in one swift motion. Nothing to it. Both of them sighed with relief. Jim actually gave a shaky smile.

The body was slightly off center. Josh carefully pushed with one hand, centering the torso. Jim pushed the feet on his end. It looked like a reflexive movement. Like a man who was used to neatening up his work.

The room was filled with Jim's scream, as if the body was electrified and he had received a very powerful shock. The large man jumped back, still screaming. He made to kick at the bag, whether to attack it or to leverage himself away from it, Josh didn't know. Either way, the result was the same. The board twisted, and the body began to slide.

Josh tried to grab the board and muscle the body back in the center. But that only resulted in a loud cracking sound from the plywood.

The body tumbled to the floor almost exactly where it had just been laying. It hit the concrete with a dull THUNK, landing on the head and settling like a log. Josh felt the sickening vibration through his boots.

"Look what you did!" Jim hissed. Josh looked up from the sleeping bag, surprised to see Jim suddenly twenty feet away, halfway into the kitchen, crouched behind a counter.

"It wasn't my fault!" Josh said, matching the man's hushed tone. "You let the thing…oh forget it! Get back in here and--"

"I think it moved!" Jim said, crouching lower. Josh saw the man was gearing up to scramble at the slightest provocation.

"What?" Josh said. Then he looked down at the form on the floor.

The silence in the room felt oppressive, and he felt another wave of Jim's paranoia wash over him. He kept his eyes trained on what he estimated to be the body's chest, waiting for movement, certain that he would see the fabric begin to rise and fall.

After what seemed like minutes — but was probably less than ten seconds — he tore his eyes away from the bag with an effort. That broke the spell.

"It's not going to move," he said, forcing himself to speak normally. "It's a frozen, DEAD body. Now, can you come back here and help me get it on the stretcher? Or do you want me to just leave it here? It can stay your problem for another ten years for all I care."

That seemed to get through to him. Jim stood, hesitated a moment longer, then made his way over. Josh reached out to guide Jim back to the feet. He put his hand on the man's shoulder—

And what felt like a static shock ran through Josh's hand, up to his brain. Except this static shock carried pictures and sounds. A jumble of images filled Josh's head. Jim, running, frantic. Trees and brush whipped by. A woman screaming. None of the images seemed connected. Just brief snippets of time. Another man being pulled apart, blood and gore filling Josh's vision. Then a glimpse of something dark. White teeth contrasting with a black silhouette.

Josh came to moments later, realizing he had lost some time. He became aware Jim was talking.

"...get this over with," Jim was saying. "I want this out of my fucking building!"

Fifteen minutes later, Josh pushed the board, sliding it into the back of the minivan. The wheels lined up with the height of the tailgate, so he didn't need help doing it. Which was good, because he was watching Jim's beat up truck drive down the road. The man hadn't even stopped to say goodbye.

Josh was happy to let him go, as the spooky vibe was almost instantly lifted. Now all he needed to do was find a place to get something to eat, and a hotel so he could sleep away the rest of the morning. He was going to be driving eleven hours with a frozen body in one of the hottest Mays he could remember. He thought he should be as fresh as possible.

Drive straight home, he thought. *You will be fine.*

He shook his head, thinking sleep was a safer idea.

He got in the van and grabbed his phone. He opened the browser, then hesitated. He was about to type, "how long does it take a frozen body to thaw?" He didn't want to end up on a government watch list. Rethinking, he typed, "how long does it take a frozen turkey to thaw?" Sweet.

The answer which came up was "approximately twenty-four hours per five pounds." That satisfied him. He really didn't want to be sitting in a pool of putrid corpse water when he pulled into the Home parking lot. It would likely take days for something as large as a human body to fully thaw.

He tossed the phone onto the passenger's seat and slid behind the wheel, satisfied that he would have enough time to get some sleep before heading to Osprey. He pulled out of the parking lot, leaving the Big Bear Hotel behind him.

When he braked to look for oncoming traffic — laughably unnecessary here in the middle of the wilderness of Hawk Junction — the body slid forward, bumping into the back of his chair.

Josh flinched. For the first time since he was a kid, he dreaded being alone with a dead body.

Chapter Six

J osh found a motel.

Eventually.

He ended up having to drive close to a hundred miles to find it, but it had an honest to goodness bed, so he was happy. He had been about to give up, pull off the highway and just find a safe place to sleep in the van. But this was better for two reasons.

First, considering how long he had been without sleep, he figured it was important to get the best quality of sleep possible.

Second, he wasn't exactly thrilled with the idea of sleeping next to a dead body. He was used to death, sure. He had grown up with it all his life. But that was too close to necrophilia for him to feel comfortable. Plus, Jim's paranoia was still clinging to him like a bad case of B.O.

The drive must have taken longer than he had realized, because when he finally saw the sign for the motel, it was dark out. He pulled off the road into a gravel parking lot. It wasn't until he'd gotten out that he realized where he was.

The Big Bear Hotel.

"Oh, crap," Josh said, realizing he must have gotten lost and traveled in a circle. And of course, it wasn't like there were actually any rooms available to stay in. He was either going to have to spend another few hours driving around, or sleep in the van. He turned back behind him.

"Looks like we're bunking up for the night, buddy."

The corpse didn't say anything.

He was looking around for some bushes to do his business in when he saw the light on in the front window of the building. The ancient closed sign was gone, and it appeared somebody was in there. He thought maybe Jim had come back after work and could at least tell him the closest place to stay. Josh doubted the man would be happy to see him, but if it meant the chance for a bed, Josh would give it a try.

When he walked in the front door, he stood in shock at what he was saw. He hadn't seen the front entrance when he was here, but he didn't expect to see a full lobby, like something you would find in a fancy New York hotel. And the place was busy. Apparently, there were still some rooms to let out.

The lobby was big, with much better decor than the outside led him to expect. Guests were lounging in the lobby as he strolled up to the counter. A family was walking through in their bathing suits, apparently heading out for a swim. Shocked, Josh briefly wondered if he had packed anything that could be used as swim trunks. There must be an outdoor pool behind the building he hadn't seen before. All four of them - mom, dad and two little boys - all had small tags flapping out from their sandals as they walked. There must even be a gift store! Maybe he could buy some shorts.

"Yes sir, just one?" The man behind the counter said, pulling Josh's attention away from the family.

"Yeah, my friend is staying in the van for the night," Josh replied, wondering why he said that.

"Of course," the attendant said. "He's dead to the world, right?"

The man behind the counter was a bit of a shock. His outfit also would have fit in well in a fancy New York hotel. He had a maroon vest with matching tie and white shirt.

But Josh hadn't really noticed that, because he was looking at the man himself.

It was Jim! The man with the contagious paranoia.

"It's about time you got here," Jim said. "I'll show you the way." And with that, he turned and began walking. Josh watched after. He knew Jim had said he was going to work straight from getting rid of the body, but Josh assumed the man worked in construction or something. Not concierge in his own fancy hotel.

Josh caught up, which was hard, because he was now pushing the make-shift stretcher. Strange. He didn't remember grabbing it from the van.

They went through two doors and were in the restaurant.

"You'll have to hurry. The kitchen is closing soon. Please pick your entrée."

Josh looked ahead and saw a table with two bodies on it. One lay inside a thick green sleeping bag. Someone must have brought it in from the van. Super strange.

The other was Cecil Porter, wearing only the white, stained tank top. He was nude from the waist down. His face was pulp from his fall and his crotch and legs were nothing but red gore. Josh could see the brand near the arm pit.

"Uh, this one is burned. I think I'll have the takeout bag instead."

"Excellent choice!" Jim said. "But you'll have to hurry if you want to eat. The kitchen is closing, you know."

All at once, they were in the kitchen, and Jim was holding the freezer door open. Josh looked in and there was the body, lying in the middle of the long room, a spotlight illuminating it from above. The room was much bigger than he remembered. Which was a strange thought, because he hadn't picked up the body yet.

"Now don't drop it this time," Jim said.

"I won't," Josh said, confused. "This is my first time. Isn't it?" he asked.

"Something like that," Jim said, and Josh saw they were standing beside the body, which was already on the trolley, atop the board. Panic gripped him as he realized Osprey would be closing soon, and he reached out and grabbed the board to push the body out of the freezer. As soon as his hand touched the rough wood, a loud screech startled him. He jerked back, tipping the board. The body slid off in cartoon slow motion. Josh was helpless to stop it as it tumbled to the floor.

It struck, and he heard sounds like a shattering vase. The thing inside the bag shifted, no longer rigid.

Josh looked up to see Jim's reaction. The man didn't seem to have noticed. He had changed out of his fancy hotel clothes and simply had a towel wrapped around his lower body. His feet were bare, but he saw the same price tag that the family from the lobby had on their new sandals. But now he realized they weren't actually price tags. They were toe tags. The kind that were put on bodies that came from hospitals or morgues. The kind he would always remove once the body was delivered to the home. The kind to identify the dead. Which was what Jim was. Dead.

"He must have gotten into an accident after he'd left," Josh said. "He was so nervous, he just cracked up and drove his truck into a tree, or off a ravine."

Or something caused him to drive off.

Josh looked back down at the body on the floor. The thick blanket had a strange, bent look that had not been there before.

"He broke it!" a woman from behind him said. Josh turned and saw the family from the lobby was standing at the kitchen entrance. They were also dead, based on the yellowed skin and bulging eyes that he recognized from his years growing up in a funeral home. But what he hadn't realized before was that these people weren't strangers. The man was his dad. The little girl was Amber. And the woman who had spoken, and was pointing with horror at the body on the floor, was Cynthia Morgan.

"No, it's fine!" Josh said. "It's just like dropping a frozen turkey! It's fine!"

But when he lifted the bag, it moved differently. It bent in the middle. It moved limply, not as if it had broken. It was still heavy, but definitely not frozen.

"You get what you get and you don't get upset," Jim said in a childish rhyme. The family of corpses in the back stared at him. Cynthia screamed.

"No, it wasn't my fault!" he shouted. "And besides! It's fine! It's still…still alive!"

But the faces didn't seem to believe him. He had to show them. Show them that there was no damage. Show them it was fine.

He bent down and found the zipper and pulled it down. His hand was shaking as he did.

"It's alright. The body is—"

Something shot out of the opening of the bag. It moved fast and wrapped itself around Josh's throat. Whatever it was, it *STANK!* It was a familiar smell to him, because it smelled like the death smell of the funeral home. But this was worse. Much worse. Like whatever was in there had sat rotting for months and years, decay stripping away the life of whatever it had been, but never drying out, never fully falling away. Just growing more rancid.

It sat up in the bag and Josh knew it was not human. It was a monster. A dripping mass of nightmare fuel. A line began ripping along what Josh assumed to be a head, exposing thousands of tiny teeth. But the line didn't stop where he expected it to. The slash of the mouth continued around the curve of the head, turning up and going around to the back. Teeth were visible along the entire length.

Tentacle like fingers clutched and squeezed. Josh felt his bowels spill out as a clawed hand slashed his belly. There was no pain, just a warm, flowing sensation. Like he had wet himself. But the lack of pain wasn't the comfort of knowing he was in a dream. Instead, his thought was of how spiders will fill their victims with a toxin that numbs them, even as it rips them apart.

The wide mouth opened, and the thing began an ear splitting wail that drowned out every thought in his head. The pain in his throat died away, and he forgot about his spilling entrails.

His only thought was…

Chapter Seven

CAR!!

Josh had a split second to feel the cold chill that accompanies being jerked from sleep before he became aware of the steering wheel in his hands. Milliseconds later, he saw a flash of color coming toward him. On instinct, he jerked the steering wheel to the right, avoiding a red mustang that whizzed by him, bare inches away. He caught a glimpse of the driver as he sped by, terrified and frantically yelling.

Josh turned back to the road. No coherent thought yet. Just reaction. Everything was happening so quickly. He had to get the car under control before he bled out completely from his slashed abdomen. He was also waiting for the monstrous thing to finish him from behind.

He became aware that he was drifting rather quickly toward a guardrail on the side of a highway.

His head was jerked sharply to that side as the van connected hard with the railing and he was sure the momentum was going to carry the van through the metal and into whatever lay beyond.

Miraculously, the van continued forward in a shower of sparks and the squealing of metal on metal. He was able to get control of the wheel.

Some semblance of rational thought took over, and Josh looked at the speedometer. He saw he was going twenty miles per hour above the posted speed limit. His foot was pressed down on the pedal, his leg a stiff knot of muscle. He forced himself to ease off the gas, and the van began to slow. He applied the brake, and it slowed even more. He expected to hear sirens blaring and see red and blue lights in the rearview. But apparently, he had gotten lucky.

And, of course, no monster grabbed him from behind. Still, his hand gingerly touched his stomach, hoping it wouldn't come up dripping with red.

Nothing.

Something did run into his eye, stinging it. As the adrenaline continued to wear off, he realized he was soaked in his own sweat. And he was hot. It felt like he was driving in an actual sauna. He didn't think the adrenaline could account for that.

Hot air was blowing out of the vents, and he realized the heaters were on full blast. He reached a clammy, shaking hand to adjust the nobs until the AC was pumping. Then he rolled down the window and stuck his head out. He had no idea how he had gotten here, driving the van full speed on the highway like a maniac.

He remembered drifting to sleep in the motel. A perfectly ordinary motel. He remembered seeing it an hour or two after leaving the Big Bear. It was a long, one storey building, with yellowing walls that Josh guessed were once white. But it had a bed, and Josh remembered sighing with relief that he wasn't going to be sleeping in the van.

Now, it seemed like every muscle of his body was twitching, and he had begun to shake uncontrollably. Not from the AC, but from shock. His legs felt hollow and his stomach was quivering. If he didn't pull over soon, he still might get into an accident.

Josh saw an exit and pulled off, turning into the first parking lot he came across. He braked too quickly and felt a powerful bump on the back of his seat that made him yelp out loud.

Josh got out of the van and his uneasy legs gave out on him. He hit the gravel parking lot, catching himself on his forearms.

Oh no! he thought. *I have to keep going! I need to get to Osprey!*

But he knew he couldn't trust himself. Not just yet. His heart was still pounding. He put his head back down and focused on breathing. He felt like he was going to vomit, but that feeling passed. Gradually, he got himself under control.

"What the hell?" he gasped. He kneeled in place, supporting himself on the side of the van, not yet glad to be alive, because he felt anything BUT alive. Let rational thought come later.

What time was it, anyway? He stood and reached through the open door for his phone, where he usually kept it — in a slot under the radio. It wasn't there. He glanced at the radio dash, which, of course, did not help. The clock hadn't worked when they bought the van second hand ten years ago.

He looked at the sky, trying to judge the time based on the position of the sun. But he wasn't a Boy Scout. All he could tell was the sun was pretty high up, but not all the way to the top of its arc. Which meant it was probably either side of noon. Which side? The hell he knew!

But the time didn't matter, because he remembered clearly arriving at the motel at eight and being in bed by eight thirty.

How long had he been driving? *How* had he been driving? On a regular night, he barely rolled over in his sleep, let alone taking to the wheel on a busy highway. He was surprised he wasn't as dead as the body in the—

And there it was. He had completely forgotten about his travel companion, and the cool air on his skin made him shudder.

How long had the heater been going like that? The gas tank was about three-quarters empty. He had filled it just before arriving at the motel, so that meant the van had been running the whole time. Not great for a frozen corpse.

Josh opened the sliding door in the back. The body was still there. He sighed in relief, even though he was not sure what he had expected.

PLINK. PLINK. PLINK.

He immediately knew where the sound of dripping water was coming from and found it no surprise at all that there was a good sized puddle of water forming on the floor.

Josh reached out a hand and poked the fabric of the sleeping bag. Still frozen. But there was a slight amount of give that had not been there before. Not much, but enough to be concerning. And wasn't the smell worse in here? He hadn't been aware when he was sitting in the van, but after getting a whiff of fresh air, yeah, it was definitely worse.

With apprehension, Josh closed the back door, got back inside, and headed for the nearest gas station. He filled up while trying not to think. Thinking hurt too much. His head was pounding, and his tongue felt like a wad of cotton that someone had jammed into his mouth. He bought a couple bottles of water and downed them, hoping to get rid of the feeling.

Then, carefully, he got back on the highway.

Chapter Eight

"Hello?"

Amber looked up from the paper she was doodling on — she had added a cute kitty attacking the Warlocke Funeral Home logo — and checked the time. It must be Cynthia Morgan here to view the remains of her brother. Amber glanced across the room to Arthur's office. He was on the phone, and as far as she could tell, he wasn't finishing up anytime soon.

"Is somebody here?" Mrs. Morgan said from the front entrance of the Home.

Amber jumped up from the desk and stuck her head out the door.

"One moment, please," she said, forcing a glowing smile. Which disappeared the moment she stuck her head back in the office. She had not gotten this job because she wanted to deal with the living. She didn't like dealing with the dead, either, but that seemed far more enjoyable than the moody whims of the family and friends who were left behind. She was not good with people who were grieving. She didn't know what to say or how to act.

Amber turned and knocked on Arthur's door. "Hold on, Carl," she heard him say. He looked up as she opened the door fully.

"Mr. Warlocke, someone is waiting outside," she announced, loud enough for Cynthia to hear. With her duty performed, she turned and began walking back to her desk, where she had important work to do. Waiting out the rest of her shift. Maybe the kitty could use a cute hippo friend!

"I'm afraid I'm tied up with this call," Arthur said. Amber whirled around and caught the faint hint of a smile on his face. "Amber, would you mind showing Mrs. Morgan her brother? I believe that falls under the purview of your duties."

"Oh, please no!" she whispered. "I never know what to say!"

"Then the practice will help you improve in the future," he said. "Tell her I'm on a call and I'll be with her in a minute." He made to punch the hold button, then paused. "Oh, any sign of Joshua yet?"

Amber glanced out the office window to the back parking lot, where they parked the van. The slot was empty. She shook her head.

Arthur gave a brooding nod, then went back to the call. She knew he was talking with Carl Pinofor, the director at the crematorium. The Home had its own furnace on site, but it was small, and they occasionally had to use an outside partner when the bodies started to pile up. Arthur would likely end his call with plans to meet with Carl for golf on the weekend.

Amber turned and glanced at the door to the foyer. She took a deep breath and forced herself through it.

She didn't recognize the woman outside, which was a little surprising. She had lived in Osprey for a year and was used to recognizing most people, even if only from passing them on the downtown street.

Mrs. Morgan, wearing a tasteful black dress - perfect for the mourning of kin - was seated on one of the cushioned benches nestled into some fake foliage. She rose when she saw Amber entering the room and broke into a wide grin. "Ah, I was beginning to think I was going to have to show myself my brother's corpse," she said.

"I'm sorry," Amber said, a little taken aback. "Mr. Warlocke is--"

"Oh, don't worry, my dear. I'm only teasing. I know that Arthur is a very busy man. And it's so good of him to hire someone... well, someone from out of town."

"Ooookay. Well, he is on a business call at the moment, but he'll be out soon. If you'd prefer to wait..."

"Oh nonsense. I can tell you're a bit nervous, dear. It must be difficult dealing with a lot of pesky emotional people."

Amber couldn't tell if the woman was reassuring her, or making fun of her, so she just smiled and shrugged.

"Well, don't worry. I'll be honest with you. I'm not going to be shedding any tears today. Not for my brother." She leaned in close. "We weren't very close."

Again, Amber didn't know what to say, so she just gave a polite, "Oh." She almost wished the woman WAS breaking down in tears. She still wouldn't know what to say, but she could at least understand it.

"Now," Cynthia Morgan said, "no time like the present. Show me my brother, dear."

Amber took the older woman into the back of the building, through the double doors and into the viewing room. At the far end was another set of double doors which led to the preparation room. In the middle of the viewing room was a coffin, in which Cecil Porter's body had been laid. They didn't normally display the deceased in a coffin before they had been properly prepared, but Arthur wanted to treat this as a special occasion. Amber thought he seemed a little intimidated by Mrs. Morgan, who she guessed really was some kind of town royalty.

Amber opened the lid, revealing the smashed face of the man inside, and quickly closed it. She had completely forgotten about the smashed condition of the body's face — had actually been blocking it from her memory as best she could. She hoped Mrs. Morgan hadn't seen it.

"I think maybe we'd better wait for Mr. Warlocke," she said, turning and putting her hands on the casket lid. Her back was leaning on the top, trying to barricade the woman from seeing inside.

Having turned so quickly, Amber had caught a look on Cynthia's face that she couldn't place. It seemed amused, like she was enjoying Amber's discomfort. Amber couldn't understand how someone could be so cruel.

But the look disappeared instantly and Amber thought she might have imagined it, anyway. Or the woman had thought of something funny, and it had nothing to do with her.

"My dear, I came down here today with an appointment to view the remains of my brother. I think the least you can do is open the lid."

"It's just..." Amber groped for something to say besides, "the body looks like it has been hit by a speeding semi-truck." But her mind was a blank. "The body isn't quite prepared...yet. No... uh... make up. Well...death has a way of..."

Oh! How did Arthur explain these things to people? He always seemed to know what to say in these situations. Why didn't she pay attention while he was talking? Better yet, why wasn't *HE* out here doing the bloody talking himself?!

The amused look was gone and Amber could tell Mrs. Morgan was in the land of Annoyed. "Amber, was it?"

She nodded.

"I'm a woman of almost 70 years. I've seen a dead body or two in my time. Trust me," she emphasized. "Beyond that, I'm also a *BUSY* woman. I would like to get this over with. Do you think you could open the lid, so I can get on with my day? I have the mayor coming over at three." She studied her wedding ring as she said this, as if showing off the size of the engagement diamond would remind Amber how important Cynthia was. But probably that was just Amber reading into it.

"Yes ma'am," Amber said. She turned, but still couldn't bring herself to open the coffin lid. A bizarre thought came into her head as she looked down.

The woman had already seen into the coffin when Amber had first opened it. She had been standing off to the side and Cynthia would have had a clear view. Amber thought of the amused look on the woman's face the instant she had turned. Amber had taken it as amusement at her own awkwardness. A bit of cruelty reserved for 'the help.' But now a much more sinister thought came into her head.

The woman had seen the body. And she *LIKED* what she had seen. She had enjoyed seeing the face of her brother smashed in. Enjoyed seeing the protruding cheek bone, the gore escaping from the swollen eyes. His nose bashed in like a cherry tomato.

"How about I just do it, huh?" Cynthia said, shoving Amber aside and lifting the lid. "Oh my," she said after a moment's pause.

Amber, having caught her balance, looked at the older woman, afraid of what she would see. But instead of amusement, the woman's face showed the sorrow that Amber was used to seeing, and she realized she had been mistaken. This was just an old lady who was anxious to say goodbye to her dead brother. Family was family, and even if you didn't like them much, it still affected you.

A sob escaped from Cynthia's mouth and Amber stepped back, having no idea what to say.

"Cynthia," Mr. Warlocke said, stepping into the room. Amber breathed easier. "Forgive me, I had a call." He gave the woman a short hug and stepped back. "I'm very sorry."

"He really hadn't taken care of himself at the end, had he?" she said, looking down at him. "Such a pity he'd lost his way in his later years."

Amber heard the phone ringing in the other room and had never been so glad to have work to do. She walked into Mr. Warlocke's office and picked up his phone. "Hello?" She realized after a beat she'd forgotten to say the name of the funeral home. She really was bad at her job.

A man's voice said, "I'd like to speak with—" a pause, as the man was obviously consulting a document. "Mr. Warlocke."

"He's busy with a client at the moment. Can I help you? Do you have... uh... funeral business to discuss?"

The man gave a bark of a laugh that Amber didn't understand. "Yeah, I may need some 'funeral business'. That is, if I ever see this Warlocke guy's kid again! I may be putting him in a coffin myself."

That startled a laugh out of Amber. "Excuse me?" She said. "Josh?"

"Yeah! This is the manager at the Pleasant Stay Motel in Wawa. The little twerp took the room key when he skipped out without paying his bill!"

CHAPTER NINE

Five hours later, Josh was back to slapping himself to stay awake. Apparently, sleeping while your body is autonomously driving is not conducive to quality rest. His body was sore, and he still had a headache deep in his skull.

He picked up lots of water when he stopped to get gas. He had left his wallet at the motel, along with everything else, but fortunately, they kept an emergency hundred-dollar bill in the glove box of the van. He hoped he could make it last. He had also picked up some snacks at the gas station to serve as lunch and supper. It was cold in the van now, but he had no intention of turning down the AC. Staying awake was only part of the reason.

Josh's brain kept gnawing on his dream, the way it does when you're overtired. Everything seems way more important when you are either drunk or exhausted.

"It's fine," he told the empty van. "Just a dream, right?"

"I mean, yeah," he responded. "Some of that happened. Not the dead people part, but dropping the body. That was stupid."

"Not my fault," he said, defending himself. "But stupid."

"And I didn't damage it!" he countered. "Frozen bodies are tough, right? It's not like—"

The image of him and Amber rolling the body of Cecil Porter over the day before flashed in his mind. Josh thought of the mushed nose, the battered face. He had obviously fallen face first onto the concrete floor.

"But this body was frozen," he reiterated. That didn't quell the fear that he had damaged it, though. Maybe that's why he had driven the van while sleeping. His subconscious was guilty and just wanted to get the body off his hands.

"That's stupid," he said. But he didn't believe it. Yes, it was stupid. But the human brain was stupid. Especially his brain at that moment. He wasn't exactly at his freshest. Maybe he should pull over and find a place to actually get some sleep.

Don't pull over, he thought. *Keep going. Get me to Osprey.*

"I can't pull over! I'll just end up driving this thing out of here in my sleep again. I--"

A deep rumbling shook the van, knocking him out of his personal argument. He realized he had drifted over the solid line and was headed toward a wall. He jerked the van back into his lane, over compensated and almost rammed into a metal trailer. He got hold of himself and evened out the wheel.

For the barest moment, he and the metal siding of the livestock trailer he was beside were driving together, and he was inches away from the unsettling eye of a large, hairy pig. The moment stretched out for almost half a mile. Josh felt that the pig was staring into his soul. The pig understood what Josh had done, and Josh got the feeling the pig knew that he had—

"That's it, I'm pulling over," he said aloud. "I just shared an intimate moment with a PIG. That is enough crazy time for me." He signaled carefully and pulled off the road, letting the livestock trailer drive off into the distance, headed for its designated slaughterhouse. Happy trails, porky!

He turned off the ramp and into a gravel parking lot. Josh had the fleeting thought that this was his trip for gravel parking lots. He was going to die driving into a gravel parking lot.

He was also reminded of his dream. This was the infamous Big Bear Hotel. Jim was going to get out of his beat-up pickup, and they were going to go through the whole thing again. Or Josh would just end up driving in circles. And he would continue driving in circles forever, with a frozen corpse laying behind him, thawing, becoming more and more putrescent.

Speaking of which, the body nudged his seat as he came to a stop. If the last of his nerves hadn't already frayed away, he would have said the bumping was starting to get on them.

"Okay, time to find another motel." He made to grab his phone, then cursed himself when he realized that he had left it at the motel.

"No, I'm just going to end up driving in my sleep again. Right?"

Yes, he thought. *Keep going. To Osprey.*

"It's never happened before," he said. "Why would it?"

That made sense. "Too much sense," he said aloud. "I don't know. I might have broken something," he finally admitted it. "I don't want to pull into the home, and have dad see the body with a caved in head or something."

"So just pull over and check," he said back. Perfectly reasonable.

"No, that's ridiculous! It was FROZEN solid! It's *FINE!*"

But if he didn't check, then there would be no way to make sure that this wouldn't continue to happen. He had become convinced his subconscious was jerking him around. He had to look. If he did, then his mind could rest and he could put the frickin' dream behind him. He would be free of the guilt that was being manufactured by a poorly functioning brain. He could finally get some sleep. In his current state, that thought had some kind of weird logic to it.

Thinking about sleep settled it for him. He could barely keep his eyes open. He would just unzip the sleeping bag and take a peek. Simple.

Ironically, now that the decision had been made, he didn't feel the slightest bit tired. What he felt was a fear of looking inside that sleeping bag. It almost undid his decision.

Slowly, Josh forced himself out of the van and pulled the sliding door open. His feet kicked gravel. The sound was very loud in the deserted parking lot.

He found the zipper on the bag and breathed deeply as he pulled it, bracing himself for what he would find.

The top of the body's head was gone. It was a void of black. No brains or anything, just a hole that Josh, in his sleep deprived state, thought he might get sucked into. It was a jagged line that cut the head off diagonally from the left temple down to the corner of the mouth. Josh reeled on his feet, almost losing consciousness.

Then he realized it was just hair. Long, dark hair that covered half of the face. The poor light in the back of the van had just played tricks on his overtired mind.

Now that he realized his mistake, he didn't know how he had confused it for anything other than what it was. He could see a closed eye visible in the tangle of hair. The body rested peacefully.

He had a brief moment of recognition as he looked down at the face. A fleeting memory of something. Then it was gone. What was it? He looked familiar, but how? Maybe he looked like an actor on TV? Whoever he was, he probably just had one of those faces. But the question nagged at him.

He peeked around the other side of the head and didn't see any damage there, either. With a sigh of relief, he zipped up the bag, feeling much better. No damage anywhere that he could see. It looked like his turkey theory was correct. And that his goose wasn't cooked after all.

He hopped back in the van, content that he had not caused any serious damage. He looked forward to getting some sleep.

But first, there was something he knew he needed to do. He looked at the time. He imagined his phone display filling up with calls from his dad, wondering where he was. It was time to face the music. After all, having done the difficult work of checking the body, calling home couldn't be that bad.

Right?

"No, YOU CAN'T GET A motel for another night!" Arthur yelled over the phone. "It's a ten-hour drive! You should have been there and back by now! What have you been doing? Sight-seeing?"

Josh put the phone back to his ear. At least as close to his ear as he wanted to put the greasy receiver. He had found a public pay phone at a rest stop just down the highway. It was a relic of a bygone era, complete with graffiti, and decades of ear wax.

"Please stop yelling, dad. You're going to blow your left ventricle."

"I'M NOT YELLING...*AHEM*. I am *NOT* yelling. I'm simply concerned that you're taking too long to get here. And now it's going to cost me *MORE* money."

Josh sighed. He was not surprised that his dad hadn't even bothered to ask why he was running behind. But to be honest, he was actually a little relieved. The reason was too crazy for him to get into on the phone.

"Why are you so far behind, anyway?" His father said.

Josh went blank. "Uh... sleep driving?"

"Did you say sleep driving?"

"You know, dad? Never mind! I got distracted and now I'm behind schedule. I'd love to explain this to you over the phone" - a lie - "but I really just need some sleep. Can I get another room or not?"

Josh did feel bad. Aside from the distance, a removal was a pretty straightforward thing. Something he had done a thousand times before.

"I've run into...complications. I'm exhausted and just need to sleep it off for a few hours—"

"Sleep it off? Have you been partying?" Josh felt a little relief. He knew this to be his father's idea of a joke, which meant he was starting to calm down.

"No," Josh said with a chuckle. "Bad choice of words. Look, I don't know what to say. I can explain better when I get there. Right now, I'm running the risk of falling asleep at the wheel. I just need—"

"Okay, I'm sorry. I should trust you, Joshua. I just got a little... frustrated. Of course you can get a room. Although, do me a favor and don't forget to leave the key when you check out. They called me and said they were going to have to charge me extra because you took it with you. Eighty bucks for a piece of plastic! Can you believe it? I understand mark up, but that's ridiculous."

"You wanna know the crazy part?" Josh said. "It's not even a plastic card. It's a legit key."

"Like a metal key you put in the lock? What is this, the stone ages?" Arthur said.

"I know, right?" Josh said, and they shared a pressure-relieving laugh.

"Okay dad. I'm sorry. I gotta get going now." Josh rubbed his stubbly jaw, trying to force himself awake. He didn't have the heart to tell his dad that he had left everything else at the motel, too. The motel key. Why on earth would his sleeping body grab the motel key and not his wallet or phone?

"Take care, Joshua. Get home safely." He hesitated. "But also as quickly as you safely can," he added.

"Got it," Josh sighed. He knew his dad wouldn't be able to resist getting in one last dig.

After they had hung up, Josh walked back to the van, thinking about everything he had left at the motel. His phone, which was up for renewal, anyway. No big deal. His change of clothes. He sniffed the shirt he was wearing. He could get another night out of it. His wallet. No big deal. He could cancel his cards. He would have to get a new driver's licen—

He stopped cold, realizing that if he didn't have his wallet, that meant he didn't have the funeral home credit card. How on earth was he going to pay for another motel? He had more of the emergency money, sure. But he didn't even know if there was enough for gas, let alone another motel room. He felt like shouting at the sky in frustration.

He turned back to face the phone. He thought about calling his dad back, maybe asking him to book a room for him at a motel on his route.

What finally stopped him was realizing he would have to call collect this time. He didn't have any change left, just bills. His dad would have to accept the charges, and that felt like more than Josh could handle at that moment. Not only was it like pouring acid on an already open wound to his pride, he just couldn't bring himself to do that to his dad, whose health was not great to begin with.

So, instead, he got back into the van, tilted the seat back as far as he would dare — he was careful to make sure that he wasn't touching the corpse — and settled in for a short nap.

After ten minutes, he still couldn't sleep. He couldn't shake the feeling that he was having a slumber party with the dead. That, and he was still worried that once he was asleep, he'd sit up, turn the engine, and start sleep driving. Thoughts kept swirling through his head. Fears of ending up crushed in a collision from sleeping while driving. Realization that he would need—

Stop fucking around and get this thing headed to Osprey! Josh thought. Whoa! Chill out, brain!

"Well," he said, "maybe there's something we could do to chill ourselves out." He opened the door, grabbed the keys, and quickly walked across the empty parking lot. The place was deserted, so he didn't think he had to worry about a car jacking. He walked into a wooded area, found a pretty distinctive tree, and began climbing. He selected a good sturdy twig sticking out from the branches, looped his keyring over it, then shimmied down and walked back toward the van.

There! If he was able to do all that in his sleep without waking up, then he deserved whatever he got.

Chapter Ten

Josh was roused from sleep, steering wheel in hand. He was speeding along the highway. This time, he also heard sirens and a voice shouting over a megaphone to "pull over!"

"Ah crap," he said aloud. He checked the speedometer and saw he was well over the posted limit. Fortunately, it was dark out, and there didn't seem to be much traffic on the road. And he seemed to have better control of the vehicle. Was it possible that he was actually becoming a better sleep-driver?

The heaters were blasting, and Josh was sweating. He reached over and quickly turned the heaters off.

The police kept shouting, and Josh realized he hadn't shown any sign of slowing yet. He took his foot off the gas.

No, keep going, he thought. *Get to Osprey.*

That, of course, was a ridiculous thought. He couldn't even trust his own brain because he was so tired. He wasn't going to just ignore the police. Even if he decided to — which was very tempting, when he thought of his nice comfy bed — he realized it would only be a matter of time before he was forced over.

He slowly began applying the brake. The cruiser, which had been beside him, sped up and pulled in front of the van. A second cruiser was already behind him as he pulled off to the side.

"Oh man," he said, his anxiety level rising. "Dad is going to flip out."

He pulled as far onto the shoulder of the highway as he could and turned off the engine. The only thing in the area was a strip club. The cruiser in front idled for a moment before a cop emerged and began walking toward him.

Pull out now, Josh thought. *Hit the officer and continue driving! They'll never catch you.*

"What?" he said, alarmed that he had even thought that. Sleep deprivation must have been affecting his sanity. He shook his head, trying to clear it before the cop got there. The officer tapped on his window.

"Hello," Josh said before the window was fully down.

The cop ignored the greeting and asked Josh for his license and registration. "I assume you know why I pulled you over," while Josh reached into the glove box for the vehicle information. He was trying to figure out how to tell the cop he didn't have his wallet, so the question threw him.

"Uh...speeding?" Josh guessed.

"I would say that's an understatement. You've also been driving erratically. You almost struck two vehicles coming from the other direction. One was a semi that would have flattened you."

"Right..." he said, handing over the registration.

"You were aware of the vehicle?"

"Uh... of course," Josh said.

"License," the cop said, holding out his hand.

"I, uh--" A strong beam flashed in from behind and Josh saw the other cop was approaching the back, his beam shining into the van. He leaned forward, trying to look through the tinted windows.

"Have you been drinking, sir?" the first cop asked. He was still holding out his hand for the license.

"I don't have my license," Josh said, feeling more tired and anxious than ever. He wanted to tell the cop behind him that there was a body back there, thinking maybe it would be better if he said that before the cop discovered it for himself.

"Can you unlock the back of your vehicle?" the second cop said.

"Sure," Josh said, hitting a button on the door. The locks popping open were very loud. "I should probably tell you there's—"

"I'm going to have to ask you to step out," the first cop said, cutting him off. "Have you been drinking?" he repeated.

"No sir," Josh said, feeling very behind. He started getting out while looking behind as the second cop walked to the back.

"Sir? You seem nervous," the first cop was saying. "Is there something back there you don't want us to see?" the first cop asked.

"What? No!" Josh said, and he knew he was too forceful, but couldn't control his tone. His chest felt like it was constricting his lungs, and breathing was becoming very difficult.

The back latch popped as the cop pulled the handle and the door began to lift. A moment or two later, the silence was broken by the sound of a zipper being pulled.

"Holy hell," came the second cop's surprised voice.

"What's up?" the first cop said. "Drugs?"

Grab his gun, Josh thought. He looked down as the cop was distracted by his partner. The gun on his belt was inches from his hand, and he thought he could figure out how to grab it. He had heard there was a special way cop's guns sat in their holster. You had to pull or pinch some special way to get it to release. Couldn't be too hard. *Just grab the gun, shoot them both in the head and get back on the road. Then you can sleep as long as you want back in Osprey.*

The idea was surprisingly appealing in its simplicity. He wanted to get home. Two dead cops would get him there.

"You gotta come back here," the second cop said.

The first cop turned his attention back to Josh, who quickly averted his eyes from the gun. The cop seemed to notice where Josh had been looking. His eyes narrowed a moment and Josh just looked the man in the eyes, holding his breath.

"Come on," he said after a moment. "Looks like you have something back there to explain." He gestured, guiding Josh to the back. The cop's hand was now at his side, hovering close to the gun. Josh doubted he had just made friends.

"Listen," he said. "I can explain! I work for a…"

His voice trailed off as they came around the corner, peering through the open gate of the van.

Josh looked in horror. The body was right where he expected it to be, but the floor, walls, and ceiling of the van were covered in blood. A constant flow of it was dripping from the plastic body bag.

"I'd say you have something to explain, alright," said the officer who was holding him. "You want to tell me why there's a body in the back of your vehicle?"

Josh was speechless. He tried to say something. "I-I don't…" So much blood. How could that be? Why was it everywhere back here? The walls? The ceiling? What happened?

"Alright, we can continue this down at the station. Morris, you take care of the van with our special guest," the cop said, gesturing at the body.

"Right."

"And you!" he said to Josh. "You better have your story figured out real soon."

As the officer was grabbing Josh, Morris moved toward the back, casting a shadow that blocked out the light from a red neon sign from the strip club. That broke the illusion. Josh saw that the red coating every inch of the van's interior was reflected light from the neon sign. Not blood. There was a pretty big puddle of water forming on the floor, though.

Now that the spell was broken, so was his verbal paralysis.

"Wait! I can explain," he said, struggling slightly. He was careful not to struggle too much. He didn't want to get tased or anything.

"Okay, quick," the officer said.

"I work for a funeral home! I'm delivering that body from…a morgue, to the Home I work at."

"Is there some kind of time restriction you're operating under? Let me guess. You deliver in under half an hour or the corpse is free, right?" Morris chuckled from behind them. Under different circumstances, Josh would have been laughing, too. Instead, he was trying to have a very silent panic attack.

"I…. uh…might have fallen asleep at the wheel." He shrugged.

The officer scowled. "Delivering a body, huh? Do you have paperwork to prove that?"

He sure hoped he did. He remembered the paperwork he had gotten from his dad, but couldn't remember if that was one of the things he left in his motel when he fled in his sleep.

"Should be in the front?"

"Morris?"

"Didn't see any paperwork. Lots of junk food packages and energy drinks, but no paperwork."

"Keep looking. I'm going to take him in." To Josh, he said, "I want the name and phone number for the home you work for. We'll see if we can get someone to corroborate your story."

Chapter Eleven

Bleary-eyed and exhausted, Josh turned the van into the rear parking lot of the funeral home, barely missing a group of teenagers walking on the sidewalk on their way to school. The fuel gauge was pointing at empty, and for the last 30 miles, he had been staring anxiously at the red warning light which indicated he was driving on fumes.

He tried to maneuver into one of the five spots, but ended up straddling three. He thought about readjusting, but couldn't get up the mental energy. Groaning, he put the van in park and turned off the engine. The a/c cut out and he was left in silence, which he didn't like.

He gave a quick glance back at the body. No change. He hadn't realized it until just then, but it was a habit he had begun after driving the van out of the police station parking lot. Like he expected the body to sit up.

Josh started the van up and breathed a sigh of relief when the cold air started blowing. He stared out the windshield — his hands on the steering wheel, in their own state of rigor mortis — watching the town wake up and begin going about its business. People on their way to work. Mr. Hill opening up the Hardware store across the street. The man gave Josh a salute and went inside. Groups were putting up decorations for the centennial, laughing and drinking from paper coffee cups.

Josh was watching, but not seeing. He was too busy thinking about the past several hours.

MOST OF THE TIME HE had spent at the police station, he had been locked behind bars. This turned out to be the magic answer to all his sleep traveling dilemmas. He had slept hard, even on the shockingly uncomfortable torture device that served as a bed. He didn't know what he had expected from a jail cell cot. Probably just that the conditions would be better than what was portrayed in the movies.

Later, the arresting officer had taken Josh to a desk and Josh had the pleasure of calling his dad at five in the morning to talk to the police.

"Warlocke residence. How may I be of assistance?" said the voice on the other end of the line. It sounded practiced, reserved, and understanding. Like a man who was used to getting calls from bereft family members at all hours. But Josh could hear the edge of grogginess from a man who hated being woken up before seven. His father had never subscribed to the adage of 'up at the crack of dawn.'

"Hey, dad."

"Joshua?" his father said, switching tones from calm and understanding to annoyed and tired. "What is going on now, young man?"

The scolding slipped out quite naturally. Josh smiled awkwardly at the officer, who was listening in on the speakerphone.

"Listen, dad. I'm actually...uh...needing your help. I appear to be...uh...under...arrest."

Silence on the line.

"Mr. Warlocke, this is officer Hagen. Josh is in my custody because of reckless driving and endangerment. I need you to verify something for me. We found something in the back of the mini-van he was driving. I was wondering if you could—"

"A body, yes. Joshua was performing a removal for our funeral home. He was retrieving one of our clients from...Hawk...something...I can't remember..." - a pause as his father seemed to be clearing his head - "Hawk Junction. He has been taking quite a bit of time doing it, too. I would appreciate, if at all possible, the body coming to the home soon so that we can begin the process of burial. I'm sure you understand."

"Of course I do. I'll finish up here and get the body headed back in your direction soon."

"That would be most appreciated."

As Hagen hung up the phone, Officer Morris came in. "I found the paperwork. It fell between the front seats. Checks out with his story."

"Yeah, the funeral director backed him up, too. Though it doesn't sound like your dad's too pleased with you," he said, turning to Josh with a smirk. "Might have the keys taken away for a while."

Josh gave a weak smile.

"Well, normally I would detain you for longer, but I'm going to let you go. Mostly because I don't have anywhere to store a frozen corpse while you're here. But I'm going to give you one mother of a fine for recklessness. I don't care how urgent your errand is. You don't drive while you're tired. Got it?"

"Yes, sir," Josh said. He decided not to ask what he should do if he found himself driving in his sleep without his knowledge. But he did not want to come off as crazy at this point.

"You feeling up to driving now?"

"Yeah, I got some sleep in the cell. Enough to get me home. It's only a couple of hours. I'll be fine."

"Okay, get going. And drive carefully!"

Now, sitting in the parking lot of the funeral home, Josh didn't *feel* fine. He continued staring out the wind shield, still gripping the steering wheel with both hands, his teeth chattering.

A tap on the window knocked him from his thoughts.

It was Amber. She gave him a half smile. He rolled down the window.

"Whoa!" Amber said, backing away. "It's freezing in there."

"Tell me about it," Josh said through clenched teeth. He would have stopped to buy a sweater if he'd had any money.

"Hey, are you alright? I saw you from inside. You've been sitting here for almost ten minutes."

"Oh, yeah. I'm fine. How'd dad?"

"Oh, probably how you'd expect. I heard you had a bit of a rough trip. Everything okay?"

"Eh, not really. What did he say?"

"Nothing. But he's been in a mood the past few days."

"If I wasn't his son, I don't think I'd be working here anymore."

Amber shrugged. "Honestly, I think that might be true, anyway."

"Seriously?"

She nodded. "So what happened? Your dad said you were holding out on him."

"It's..." Josh trailed off, thinking about the things he had seen and felt, all of it revolving around a dead body. "It's a little complicated. I need to get this thing inside."

"Hold up! You're not leaving it at that, are you?"

"No, I'll tell you all about it. Wanna grab lunch later?"

"Yeah, that'd be nice."

"Cool," he said, absently aware that he had just asked her on another date. Amazing how easy it was when you were low on sleep and jittery from raw terror. "Now, if you'll excuse me, I have to go face the music."

"Well, he's with Mrs. Morgan right now, so maybe—"

"Oh, good. This way he'll probably avoid yelling at m—"

"Joshua!" came a shrill voice from behind them. Mr. Warlocke was standing half out the back door to the Home. "How long have you been here?"

"I—"

"Never mind! It doesn't matter. Back the van up and let's get the body inside. He ducked back into the building, not waiting to see if Josh started moving. A moment later, the garage door to the loading area began opening, revealing rows of shelves with stretchers, wooden boxes and spare equipment. He pulled the van in and reluctantly turned off the engine, cutting off the cold air.

"You need any help?" Amber asked, looking at Josh with a mixture of concern and disgust. Her nose kept wrinkling up, as if she smelled something bad. Likely she was just smelling the thawing body in the back, but Josh imagined the dehydration, terror and exhaustion he felt were contributing to a very, very potent form of B.O.

He was about to tell her he could handle it, but then his legs gave out on him as he exited the driver's seat.

"Gah!" she cried, moving to catch him. Fortunately, he was able to get his legs under himself without hitting the pavement. He stood, swaying slightly.

"Yeah. I think I could use your help."

"It's why I'm here," she said with a sunny smile.

"Today, please!" Warlocke said from the door, cutting off their conversation. Then he quickly disappeared back inside.

Josh let out a long groan, thinking that this day would never end.

Chapter Twelve

They grabbed the stretcher Josh had neglected to put back in the van after Cecil's removal, and Amber helped him transfer the body onto it. As they crested the ramp, Josh heard laughter from inside. His dad was talking in the front room. He heard the familiar sounds of a cup and saucer clattering and knew his dad was serving tea. Which could mean only one thing. Mrs. Morgan was here to pick out a coffin for her brother, and dad was pouring on the old-lady charm. If they had owned a car dealership, this would be when his dad would probably be asking Mrs. Morgan to take the most expensive model for a test drive, just to get a feel for it.

But that wasn't really the best sales tactic for coffins.

"What do you mean you dropped it?" Amber said, keeping her voice low. They were wheeling the stretcher across the room.

"It wasn't my fault! The whacko that had the body made me do it."

"Yeah, I'll bet. Clutzo."

"It's true! Anyway, I'm really hoping the body isn't, you know, damaged."

"You said you checked?"

"Yeah…" he said, sounding about as convinced as a man who had checked to make sure the stove was off before a long trip. Nothing seemed okay at that moment.

"You still afraid it's damaged?"

He laughed. Josh was honestly more afraid HE was damaged than the body. The whole trip home had been…distressing.

"Kinda. I just…dad's already peeved at me. I don't want him noticing…I don't know. Fresh wounds?"

"Well, look again." She said.

"You'll take a look with me?" Josh said, grateful.

"*HELL NO*!" she said. "I'm goin' to step *WAAAAY* over there and you can check on your own. I've told you before! I'm not here to fraternize with the clientele!"

"What do you think about this unit?" Josh heard his dad say from the salesroom.

"It's a little ostentation, don't you think?" Cynthia said. "I'd much rather just throw him in your furnace and cremate him. Do I get a discount if I light the match myself?" she asked. He heard his dad's uncertain chuckle.

Geez, she doesn't exactly win any trophies for 'Sister of the Year.'

"Well, I'm not sure your brother would appreciate that, Cynthia. But if that is the way you would prefer to go—"

"Nobody cares what he thought when he was alive, and nobody will care now. You knew him, Arthur."

Josh continued wheeling the stretcher into the anteroom, where the bodies waited. From there, they would either be moved into the prep room to be made ready for burial, or taken to the basement, where they kept their cremation oven. A much cheaper method of internment. And one that, given the creepiness of his drive with the body, Josh would be looking forward to.

"Hurry up," Amber said, snapping Josh out of his thoughts.

"Right." He unzipped the bag and pulled it back. He was struck by that faint recognition he had seeing the face the first time. Who the hell did this guy look like? But he was no closer to remembering, and like walking into another room and forgetting why you even went there, the recognition was gone.

But he was more certain it wasn't just a celebrity. He thought this body reminded him of someone that he knew. Not just someone he had seen. There was some personal connection going on.

He didn't have time to dwell on it. He had just gotten the bag pulled back when the door burst open and in walked his father, followed by Cynthia Morgan.

"I think we have a model in gray somewhere back here. If not, we can have it here by next week — Oh, Joshua," Arthur said. "I thought you would have had, um, John there moved into the antechamber already. Are you having problems?" Josh heard the edge in his dad's voice and was about to reply, but then he glanced at Mrs. Morgan. She was staring fixedly at the body Josh was currently displaying. He quickly covered the head back up.

"No, dad. Just moving a bit slow this morning. Sorry Mrs. Morgan. I'll get out of your way."

"Perfectly okay, my dear," Cynthia said absently. But she was still looking at the sleeping bag as she spoke. She no longer had the jovial sound to her voice. He followed her gaze, to make sure there wasn't something else catching her eye. But she appeared to be transfixed by the man on the stretcher, with a look something like horror creeping into her face. It was a look, given Josh's experience with the corpse over the last three days, that he thought he could get behind. But why was she looking at it that way? He turned to look at Amber, who just shrugged at him.

Mr. Warlocke, who had been glaring at Josh, was the last to catch on to Mrs. Morgan's change in mood. "Cynthia? You look pale all of a sudden. Is everything alright?"

"Of course," she said. But Josh thought she had a bit of difficulty getting her brain going. She muttered something under her breath. Josh thought it sounded like, "I never should have—" and then she was smiling radiantly at them.

"I'm sorry," she said. "I just got to thinking about poor Cecil. We had some good times together, once. I suppose it just hit me…I'll never see him again." Her smile collapsed, and she looked around, wide eyed. Her hands were working furiously, as if she were trying to scrub them clean. She seemed unaware she was doing it — or of anything else. She kept staring at the blanket.

On cue, Josh's dad moved to her side, putting his hand on her back. "Of course. There's no rulebook on when grief should hit you, Cynthia. Come out here, and I'll get you some—"

"Could we perhaps postpone today's appointment?" she asked abruptly, cutting him off. "I just need some…some time."

"Of course," Mr. Warlocke said, practiced understanding in his voice. "Call me anytime and we'll make it work. No rush."

He escorted her toward the front door. Arthur turned back and angrily shooed Josh and Amber into the antechamber before he walked out.

"What the hell was that?" Amber said after they were gone. "Why'd she suddenly care so much about her brother? She didn't seem to care one iota for him before. I didn't think that woman…well, let's just say she seemed kind of cold, ya know?"

"I'm pretty sure she was looking at the body," Josh said. "Just as I had it uncovered."

"You think she recognized him?"

Josh shrugged. "Probably more likely she was just startled at seeing a dead body, I guess."

Amber made a face. "It's a funeral home, Josh. You go to a library, you expect to see a book or two.

Besides—" Amber stopped and looked behind her. When she could see the coast was clear, she resumed in a near silent whisper. "She seems like one cold bitch." She mouthed the last word, just to make sure neither Arthur nor Mrs. Morgan could hear. "When she viewed her brother, I think she, I don't know... Liked it! Liked seeing him that way. I don't think she has a problem with bodies."

"Whatever. Let's just get *THIS* body where it needs to go. I'm sick of being around it."

"You still haven't told me what that's all about."

"All in good time," he said with an attempt at a smile. But it felt forced, and he could tell she was aware. She opened her mouth to say something when Josh's dad came charging into the back room.

"What took you so long, Joshua?" his dad said. "This isn't like you! You should have been here two days ago! This is irresponsible! I suppose you were sight seeing, is that it?"

"Sight-seeing? In Hawk Junction. No, dad. Hear me out. It was weird, okay. The body was...well, I mean, I fell asleep but..." He trailed off. He realized there wasn't a way for him to explain what happened that didn't make the situation worse.

"And I'm not even going to mention the embarrassment of having to speak to the police! Explain that to them that, no, my employee - my *SON!* - is not a druggie, or a murderer! How do you think that made me look?"

"I don't think anybody—"

"If this is going to be a regular thing, I can't have you working at the Home anymore, Joshua. This is a place of respect and dignity."

That did it. Now Josh was angry. The last three days of emotional rollercoaster washed over him.

"Dad, I hate to break it to you, but I don't CARE if I don't get to work here anymore. I don't ever wanna to see this building again! If you haven't noticed, I've been trying to get away from here since I was a kid. It's a funeral home, dad! What sane person wants to work with dead people?"

"I didn't hear you complaining about the food I was putting on the table from these dead people."

"That's just unfortunate phrasing," Amber muttered to herself from behind them. They both ignored her.

"I didn't do anything wrong, Dad! And I'd like to think you would give me the benefit of the doubt. But I guess that's too much to ask. I'll be happy to find some place else to work." Josh stormed out of the room, headed for the front door.

Once outside, he felt elated. He had finally done it. He had quit! At least, he thought he had. He wasn't quite sure what had happened.

Either way, he was free from the home. For the first time in his life, his dad knew exactly how he felt. That he didn't want to be a part of the business — let alone take it over! As he walked, he smiled broadly to everybody that he passed.

"Josh!" Amber called from behind him. "Wait."

"Hey, what's up?" he said, turning to her with a big grin on his face. He was suddenly feeling great!

"I thought we were going to get something to eat. You know. Tell me about your weird journey back?"

Josh's smile widened. "Right. Well…" Then he thought about his diminutive bank account, which he couldn't even access without his wallet, which was in some motel in Wawa. He looked at Amber. He wasn't going to have her pay.

He gave an audible sigh.

"What's wrong?" she said.

"I…uh…got a thing right now."

Her face fell. And in that one moment, he knew he couldn't brush her off. He also knew what he had to do.

"But I'm free for supper. If you're interested? Do over for our date from the other night?"

She brightened. "That would be great!" she said. "I know a place. I can treat. I know you're—"

"No, please. I insist. I'm fine. Really. My treat."

"Okay," she said, hesitantly. "Well, I gotta get back in. Pick me up after work?"

"Sure," he said.

She turned and walked into the Home, looking back at him before the door swung shut. He watched her disappear with a goofy grin on his face.

When she was gone, he sighed. He thought about his bank account and about the five hundred dollars that his dad owed him from this last job, and realized he couldn't afford to turn down that money.

"Well, I'm not going crawling back right away," he said to no one as he walked away from the Home. He would come back that evening and talk to dad before picking up Amber. As he went, he tried to remind himself that he did love his dad. The man had his good points, too. He wasn't a complete monster.

Chapter Thirteen

Craig was in a funk as he exited the back door of his house, sliding it closed. He stood there a moment, looking at his reflection in the glass. He threw his duffle bag over his shoulder and stepped off deck into the backyard. Walking the flagstone path to his truck, Craig wondered how long his life would be on repeat.

A few steps along, his nose scented something. Was that a skunk? Craig hoped they hadn't built a den under the shed. He had just gotten rid of a family of foxes last fall.

He would have to look into it later. If he stopped, he would be late for work. More importantly, he didn't want to get sprayed in the face by a rodent. He moved on.

Now, where was he? Oh yeah.

His life should be exciting! He wanted to do more. Really help people. Stop bad guys. He didn't want vandalism to be the biggest crime he investigated.

"I'm a cop, damn it!" he said out loud, as his frustration boiled up.

"You doing okay?" someone said, breaking the morning silence. Craig stopped in mid step, caught. He looked over the fence into the neighbor's yard and saw their fifteen-year-old daughter.

"Oh," Craig said, embarrassed. "Hey Kim! Sorry."

"It's fine," she said with a laugh. She picked up a wet shirt from a hamper at her feet and began pinning it to the clothes-line. "I can take the vulgarity. I may have even said one or two bad words myself."

Craig chuckled. "Your mom got you doing chores?"

"Yeah. You still bored with cop life?" she said, grabbing a towel from the bin and shaking it out.

"Yeah. I know, it's stupid."

"You want to help people. That's not stupid. Don't worry, Craig. Something bad will happen in this town one day. You gotta be positive!"

"Yeah, I suppose," Craig said, smiling. He looked at his watch. "Hey, I'm going to be late. You take care, okay?"

"You too! Maybe you can start by busting whoever is toking up," she said.

"Huh?"

She made a show of smelling the air and waved her hand in front of her nose. "Can't you smell it?

It's like someone is burning an entire greenhouse of weed somewhere."

Craig sniffed, but all he could smell were the skunks under his shed. He shrugged. "I'll look into it!" and walked down the path as Kim picked up her hamper and went inside.

He had just reached the gate when he saw the gift someone had left on his fence.

A neon pink penis. Pink this time. Not green. They had changed their M.O. He glanced around suspiciously, as if the vandal might be lurking nearby, biding their time, waiting to gloat. He even checked his roof.

No one.

Craig gave a deep sigh and dropped his duffle bag. He was resigned to being late, but he did not want to leave this out for people to see. Especially Kim, who was young and impressionable.

Fortunately, he and Josh had painted these fences last year, and he thought he still had a can of paint in the shed. It would only take a moment to get rid of the evidence.

Evidence! He quickly pulled out his phone and took several photos of the paint from different angles. With that done, he went around, looking for foot prints, taking photos every time he saw something that might be a lead. He considered looking for fingerprints. Maybe he could use flour from the kitchen? But he decided that was going too far.

He went to the shed, glad he had decided to put his uniform on at the station, not wanting to get it covered in paint. He moved slowly, eying the ground, looking for skunks. Satisfied he wasn't going to get sprayed, Craig opened the door.

Smoke poured from the open door, followed by a shrill scream, breaking through the morning stillness. Craig joined with his own scream as Henry Ledbetter tumbled out of the shed, landing on his back, and hitting his head on the path. He cried out in pain.

"What the hell, man?" Craig yelled.

Kim and her mom both poked their heads out the back door, peering into Craig's yard with concern.

"It's okay," he said, waving to them from a bent over position. "Everything is fine." He breathed, letting the adrenaline work through his system.

Bemused, both the women went back inside, leaving Craig and Henry alone.

"What are you doing in my shed, Henry?" Craig said through deep breaths.

"Trying to chill out before my shift starts," Henry said back, rubbing the back of his head. "Help me up, man!"

Craig grabbed Henry's hand and heaved him into a standing position. Once up, Henry placed a bent cigarette in his mouth.

Wait...that wasn't a cigarette!

"Are you smoking pot?" Craig said, incredulous.

"Calm down, Sister Mary," Henry said, holding out his hand. "It's pretty much medicinal."

Craig raised his eyebrows, waiting for more.

"I got a...a neck thing," Henry explained vaguely. "Besides, last time I checked, it's legal now."

"But why in my shed?"

Henry looked around as if Craig were asking a ridiculous question. "I can't do it at the station, man. I needed a place to get center myself before work. This is nice and close. Plus, I know you never lock this thing," Henry said, patting the shed fondly. He turned and started walking toward the gate. "You got a penis on your fence," he said, pointing.

"Wait! Have you done this before?" Craig said.

"I'll never tell. But I will say your fertilizer makes a comfy seat. Now come on!" he said, opening the door. "You'll be late for your shift."

Craig gaped as Henry slid through the gate and let it slam back into place. He wondered if he should take care of the vandalism on his fence, which would make him even later for his shift. He looked at the time and decided he should get going.

He reached into his shed, grabbed a tarp, and threw it over the boards, covering the penis from view.

He took a calming breath and headed for his truck.

Chapter Fourteen

L ater that evening, Josh walked to the funeral home. He went in the front so he could avoid his dad as long as possible. At least until he was ready. Arthur only went to the front when he had business — meeting clients, accepting deliveries or getting the mail. Although, usually those were Josh's jobs. At this time of night, he was likely in the back, preparing bodies. Josh knew there were quite a few to get through. Including the newest addition.

He had crashed into his bed as soon as he had gotten home, so the sleep induced paranoia was gone. But the memories were still there. He had gotten about five hours of sleep, which was nowhere near enough time to catch up after all he had been through, but it would be enough to get him through the evening with Amber.

Now that he was feeling awake, with little to no brain fog, he was starting to feel more than a little silly about how he had been acting. Especially regarding the body. He had actually started to convince himself that it had been streaming thoughts to him. Like wanting to grab the cop's gun, or run him over. As if the body was evil and trying to sway him.

In reality, it wasn't that abnormal, especially when overtired, to dwell on the worst-case scenarios. You ask yourself what the worst thing you could do in this situation is, whether you want to or not. But that doesn't mean you ever actually do it. They're just stray thoughts.

Instead, he had done the typical superstitious thing and blamed a dead body. As if bodies actually had power, like in books or the movies. That was stuff regular people thought. Not people like him, who had grown up with death as a part of life.

As Josh approached the front door, he paused to let a couple pass, walking hand in hand. He watched them a moment, thinking of Amber and their date. When he turned back, he saw a splatter of bird poop on the front display window. He made a mental note to grab the cleaner and paper towel, then immediately forgot about that when his eyes moved to what was beside the splatter.

'WARLOCKE FUNERAL HOME IS A PROUD MEMBER OF THE OSPREY BUSINESS ALLIANCE', a white decal on the glass read. Local Business was seen in quasi-religious terms in this community. Osprey was, after all, an industry town. It had grown because of the Quarry.

Reading the sign triggered a 'eureka' moment in his mind and he remembered who the body reminded him of. The business owners in the community had regular meetings at various stores and businesses and it was at one of these meetings, many years ago, that Josh had seen the man he recognized in the sleeping bag. Or at least, that the body reminded him of. It was, of course, impossible for the body to actually be of the man himself.

But still, he would have to ask his dad if he thought so, too. It might at least be a good way to break the ice between them.

Deep in his thoughts, he walked into the darkened front foyer, bird poop completely forgotten. The room was dark, which wasn't unusual in and of itself. It was after hours. There wouldn't be any random visitors. Just late night calls for removal services, which Josh was glad to say he wouldn't have to deal with, now that he had effectively tendered his resignation.

Something brushed his neck as he walked, and he gave a spastic leap. His second thought was that a spider may have crawled into his shirt. He didn't want to give credence to his first thought, which had been ridiculous. He had imagined that the body was behind him, its yellow skinned hands reaching for him in the dark.

Josh turned to see the rustling leaves of the fake fern that stood in the corner of the lobby. He chuckled, took a breath, and walked farther into the shadow. He realized he should probably have turned on the light when he came in, but he hadn't wanted his dad to know he was there. Not yet. And now he felt silly at the idea of going back. It would mean he was scared. And why should he be scared? This was his home. He literally lived in the upstairs apartments for the first ten years of his life, before they had moved to their own house just down the block.

Something slapped down on his shoulder and his heart stopped. This wasn't the leaves from some fern. It was the creature from his dreams come to life and after him!

"Whoa!" Amber shouted as Josh stumbled away from her. "It's just me! Calm down!"

He let out a ragged breath, which ended in a laugh. "Oh man. Don't do that!"

"Sorry. I didn't think you'd freak out on me."

He shrugged. "It's dark in here."

"Yeah, it's late. What'd you expect?"

"I just...I thought you might be Dad. Where'd you come from?"

"Arthur had me upstairs all day clearing out the crawlspace. I haven't been down here since you left."

"The crawlspace? Why on earth—"

"I think he wanted to be alone," she said, answering his question before he had finished asking it. "You two had a big fight. I'm sure he's just as bothered by it as you are."

Hm. Josh thought about that. She was probably right. Fights were never one sided. He should probably remember that his leaving the business was scary for his dad. The man had spent decades of his life building this empire, and his son was threatening to just let it fall apart like a house of cards. Josh thought he had more apologizing to do than he had planned.

"Speaking of which," Amber was saying, "why are you here?"

"I, uh…just getting my last cheque."

"What happened to the big man who said he didn't need this place anymore?" she said, smiling.

He shrugged. "You know…got a pretty lady to take out."

She smiled. Then punched him in the shoulder. "I said I would pay, you doofus. Don't turn chivalrous on me!"

"Well, it won't hurt the bank account, either," he admitted. "Anyway, I won't be long. I'm sure he wants me out of here as fast as possible. I'll get the check and then we can argue about who's paying, okay?"

"Fine with me. I was captain of the debate team in high school, you know."

"That's something to brag about?"

"Oh, you did not!" she said, brandishing her fist. He cowered away.

"This is not a good foundation to build a relationship on," he said, moving away. She laughed and slapped his arm lightly instead. Then, without any pre-thought, he took her hand in his as they walked the rest of the way through the lobby. She didn't pull away. They both smiled at each other as they walked.

It was easier with another person. The terror was gone, and Josh once more felt silly for his paranoia. He just wanted his money. Then he could kiss this place goodbye. He could get another job and finally dedicate himself to college.

They pushed through the door to the back. Josh's eyes widened when he walked in.

"Dad!" he yelled.

A stretcher had overturned and was Arthur sprawled on top of it. Josh rushed forward. What is this? Heart attack? Was this because he had been attempting to transfer the body onto the gurney by himself? Something that wouldn't have happened if Josh had been there to help him. He thought if his dad died now, it would be all because of him.

Josh rolled his dad over, thinking way back in his head how many times he had done the same thing for dead bodies over the years. He just hoped...

"Is he alright?" Amber asked. Josh didn't know, but he could tell his dad was alive. The skin was warm, and it hadn't taken on the yellowish complexion he would have recognized in a lifeless body.

The older man gave a groan as Josh lifted him into a sitting position on the ground. His pulse seemed good.

Josh reached for his phone before remembering he had left it at the motel. It was hard to believe that was only yesterday. Things had happened so fast.

"Call an ambulance," he said to Amber.

"I-I don't have my phone," Amber said. "I must have left it in the attic."

"Then use the one in the office," he said, trying to keep the impatience out of his voice. She ran out.

"It's okay, son," a gruff voice said. "I'm fine." Josh's dad was awake. Groggy, but awake.

"What happened?" Josh asked. "Is it your heart?"

"I'm not sure. One second, I was rolling the stretcher into the prep room. Now, I'm waking up in your arms. You didn't whack me over the head because of our fight, did you?" he asked, with a little humor on his face.

Josh laughed. "No way, pops. If I were trying to get rid of you, I would have bundled you into the incinerator after I'd knocked you out."

"I'll try to take comfort in that."

Now that he was confident things were okay, Josh began to take stock of the situation. Had his dad had some kind of attack? Or had someone broken in? He looked at the gurney, which had been overturned, and realized something in the room was missing.

"Where's the body?"

"What body?"

"*THE* body, dad! The one I brought in this morning. It was on this stretcher when I left. Did you move it?"

His dad was catching up and looked just as upset as Josh felt. "No, I didn't move anyone. I was just doing paperwork back here. As I said, I was in the middle of moving it into the preparation room, but that's when I blacked out."

Josh surveyed the room. It wasn't big enough for anyone to be hiding. No place for a body to be laying that they couldn't see, either. It was just gone.

The door banged in the outer room, and he remembered Amber was calling for the ambulance. Things didn't seem as urgent now, but maybe it wouldn't hurt to get his dad checked out, just to be sure.

She ran into the room, looking completely freaked out.

"It's okay!" Josh said, seeing her expression and trying to calm her down. "I don't think we'll be needing an ambulance."

"Not for Arthur, maybe," she said, pointing back the way she had come. "But there's a naked guy in the office that could probably use some attention!"

Chapter Fifteen

Josh woke up when Amber came into the room. "I saw the doctor heading this way," she said. She carried a tray of coffee and a paper bag.

Josh had nodded off in one of the chairs in Arthur's hospital room. He was surprised to see his dad up out of bed already. He was standing in the middle of the room. Which, given the size, meant he was basically hovering over Josh as he slept. "Ah, coffee! Thank you, Amber," Arthur said.

"You feeling good, dad?" Josh said, getting groggily to his feet. "Shouldn't you be in bed?"

"I'm feeling fine, Joshua. I'm more curious about who our guest is than anything else."

"Yeah, well, you should probably sit down until Dr. VanLakey takes a look at you. You've got a bad bump on your head."

"Joshua, I'm fine, really! I think—"

"Hello, everyone," a cheery voice said. The doctor was another figure of the community that Josh had known for years. He had been friends with his dad since well before Josh was born. "I hear we had a pretty engaging evening."

"If you find bodies coming back to life and knocking old men unconscious to be engaging, then yeah. It was a pretty good time."

"Joshua," his dad said, scolding. "You're being rude."

"It's okay, Arthur. It sounds like it's been a pretty chaotic evening. How are you feeling?"

"Well, I--"

"He's got a pretty nasty lump on the back of his head!" Josh cut in.

"Joshua."

"Well, you do!" He turned to Dr. VanLakey. "He does."

"I don't think it's all that—" Arthur started.

"I'll be the one to decide how severe it is, Arthur," VanLakey cut in. "Sit down," he ordered. After a little grumbling, Josh's dad got into place and allowed the doctor to look at the back of his head.

"I don't see a bump," VanLakey said.

"What?" Josh said, crowding in beside the doctor. He combed through his dad's constantly disheveled hair. Sure enough, his dad's head was without blemish. "I could have sworn I saw—"

"Um, Joshua," Dr. VanLakey said with a wry smile. He gently lifted his elbow, indicating that Josh was in the way.

"Sorry," Josh said, backing up. He took a coffee cup Amber held out to him, but didn't take a sip, waiting. The examination felt like it took a year the way Josh felt, so he replayed everything that had happened the previous evening for what seemed like the thousandth time.

They had run out of the back room as soon as Amber had said there was a body out in the office. Since they were currently missing a body from the back, he had assumed to find a half frozen corpse. And although he didn't know how it could have gotten there, he figured they would be able to spend the time figuring that out.

He had not expected to see the fully naked, yet obviously alive, body of a man laying on the carpeted floor in front of his dad's desk. Josh could tell instantly that it was not a dead body. It was as obvious to him as a counterfeit bill would be to a seasoned financial investigator. He could tell almost by instinct.

The body was on its side, with its back to the door. But Josh had the uneasy feeling he recognized the long black hair.

Of course, he was being ridiculous. There's no way it was...

"You called the ambulance?" he had said to Amber.

"They're on the way."

Josh approached the body, not too quickly. His thoughts went back to the nightmare ride he had taken over the past few days, and he briefly imagined the figure jumping up and grabbing him.

He pulled the body's shoulder, and it slumped onto its back, giving them a good view of its face. The hair was shoulder length, and jet black. The features were angular, but softened from unconsciousness. Two things were obvious to Josh. Not only did he recognize this man from somewhere in his past, but he also recognized him from the brief glimpse he had gotten in the bag in the back of the van when he had brought with him from Hawk Junction.

Now, after about ten minutes of the doctor shining lights in his dad's eyes and listening to breathing, he tucked his stethoscope into his pocket and said, "I don't see a thing to be concerned about."

Josh felt almost disappointed. "Really? No concussion? No bite marks or scratches?"

"Bite marks? What are you..."

"Joshua is concerned that the man we came in with may have done this to me," Arthur said with exasperation in his voice.

"May have? Who else would it have been?" Josh asked.

"Ah, yes," the doctor said. "The mystery man. I was hoping we could talk about him."

"Did he confess?" Josh asked.

"Joshua!"

"Of course he didn't confess," Josh said, answering his own question. "Oh, did you check his fingernails for dad's skin cells? He may have--"

"He's in a coma," the doctor said, bringing Josh to a halt.

"You mean he slipped into one?"

"No, I mean, he's been in one for a while. It's not the type of thing you can pinpoint, but I'd guess he has been this way for some time. Maybe years. I think chances are good he didn't do anything to you, Arthur."

"Well, how about being frozen?"

"I'm sorry?" the doctor said.

"That's enough, Joshua," Arthur said.

"We brought a corpse to the home from out of town. It had been frozen for ten years."

"And you think that was the man you found?" the doctor said, doubtfully.

"People are cryogenically frozen, aren't they? That's a thing, right?"

"People in movies, sure," the doctor countered. "But not in the real world. Not ones that come back to life."

"Thank you, doctor," Josh's dad broke in. "My son is just a little upset."

"Well, for good reason. And I was hoping you would be able to help me identify the man, but it doesn't sound like you know any more than I do. I guess we will just have to hope he wakes up and can tell us something himself."

"Assuming he doesn't have amnesia or something," Josh added.

"You gotta stop believing everything you see in the movies," Dr. VanLakey said.

Josh looked stunned. "Amnesia...isn't a thing?"

"I'm afraid not," the doctor said. "Not the way TV writes it, anyway. It's much more mundane." Then he turned to Josh's dad. "I'll have one of the nurses come in and get you out of here soon. There's nothing I'm particularly concerned about."

"Thank you, Sven," Arthur said as the doctor left the room, tapping away on a tablet as he went.

Josh turned to his dad, about to speak. Arthur held his hand up.

"That's enough. I don't know what's gotten into you. You've never been this..." Arthur paused, obviously struggling with what to say.

"Crazy?" Amber suggested.

"I was going to say excitable," he said. "And you've never been so imaginative about the bodies before. At least not since you were a child. We both know a corpse is just muscle and bone. The person is gone. The thing you brought to the home was not alive. Has no capacity to be alive. The man that we found in our office? I don't know where he came from. Nor how he got there when he was comatose. But it is not the corpse you brought in." Josh nodded, conceding the point.

"We may never find out the truth," Arthur went on. "But of that, I can be certain. That man is not the body you brought back from Hawk Junction."

"Yeah, I know, dad," Josh admitted. He did, too. At least on one level.

But there was another, more gut-level, that told him something wasn't right about the situation. It was probably the same part of his psyche that hated putting his feet in front of the gap under his bed at night. His brain knew nothing was going to grab his ankles. But the gut part...wasn't so sure.

"But, if the mystery man isn't the body," Amber asked, "where did the body go?"

Josh shrugged. "Spontaneous combustion?"

"A frozen corpse spontaneously combusted?" Amber said. "Seriously, Josh! Do you get all your education from movies?"

"No!" he said, incredulous. "There are conspiracy theory videos on the internet, too!"

Chapter Sixteen

Officer Craig straightened in his chair, spilling coffee on his shirt. He didn't even feel it. He was too focused on the morning Osprey Edition, with the headline that read, "Body Mysteriously Disappears from Local Funeral Home."

He felt a surge of adrenaline. This was it! The 'get out of jail free' card his bored brain had needed. He looked around the room. Nobody else had the newspaper out. Nobody was scrambling to their feet.

He bent back to read the article. A missing body with no suspect? Mr. Warlocke knocked unconscious? Nude man found inside the funeral home? Comatose! This case had everything!

Casually, Craig folded the paper under his arm and stood up. Keep it cool, man. He straightened his shirt and walked to the chief of police's office, letting himself in.

"Door was closed for a reason, Craig."

"I want the missing body case!"

Chief Braden looked up from the novel he was reading. "There's coffee on your shirt."

"I want the missing body case," Craig repeated.

"What on earth are you talking about?" the chief asked, exasperated.

"The missing body case," Craig said, throwing the paper down on the desk. "I wanna take a crack at it."

"I didn't know we had a 'missing body case'," Chief Braden said, picking up the paper. He eyed Craig. "Don't you think I should be the one to decide when we have a new case?" He read the headline, then gestured at the name on the byline. "Abel will print any story just to get eyes on his paper. I haven't gotten a call on this, Craig. If the Home was missing a body, don't you think the police would find out before the paper?"

"I don't know," Craig said, deflated. "I guess. So it's not true?"

"Not that I'm--" he was cut off by the phone ringing on his desk. Craig watched him pick it up and answer.

"Arthur! We were just talking about--" he stopped talking as the other party took over the conversation. Craig recognized the name of the funeral director and realized this must be about the body. He looked up as the chief was making shooing gestures at him, pointing at the door to his office, which was open.

Craig nodded while trying to take in both sides of the conversation. He got up, closed the door, and sat back down, this time in a chair just to the right where the chief sat. Braden glared at him, then seemed to remember he was in the middle of a call.

"Yes, that's...incredible. And you don't know where it could be?" Silence.

Craig let out a small squeal of excitement. Braden clenched his fist and shook it at Craig, who ignored him.

"Okay, I'll be over as soon as I can. See you soon." He hung up the phone and started gathering his things.

"Can I come too, Chief?" Braden continued gathering his things without saying a word. "Come on, I need this! Something exciting."

"The town's troubles are not your entertainment, Craig."

"I'll just observe, sir. Learn from the best."

"I'll bet." Braden stopped and seemed to consider the request. "Okay, tell you what--"

A knock came at the door, interrupting the chief. "Aaron MacDonald just called, sir. More issues at his farm."

The chief's face brightened, and Craig knew this did not bode well for him.

"No!" Craig said in protest.

"Yes!" the chief said, brightly.

"Chief. No!"

"This is your case, Craig," Braden said with a grin. "I need my best out there. Someone who knows this thing back to front. Now get out there and find yourself some taggers!" He turned to the officer who had come in. "Sonia, I'll be down at Warlocke's if you need me."

"Yes, sir."

After Braden was gone, Craig swore. "I hate taggers," he said morosely.

"I never said it was vandalism," Sonia said, grinning. She handed him a manila folder that contained the statement she had taken when the call had come in.

"What is it? Someone tip over a cow?"

"I think you're going to like this one," she said, and walked out.

"What the hell?" Craig said. He flipped open the folder and skimmed her notes. A smile began to form on his face. He grabbed the squad car keys off the rack on his way out the door.

NARY A SPRAY-PAINTED PENIS WAS in sight when Craig pulled up in the squad car — beyond the ones already on the cows and the side of Aaron MacDonald's barn, that was. Instead, a red-faced Aaron led him into the milking barn, where he had recently taken Craig to show off his new fancy quarter million dollar milking machine. Where the machine had once stood sat an empty metal case. Most of the hoses that hooked to the cows were still there, but all the electronics had been ripped out.

"Stolen?" Craig said, repeating Aaron.

"Well, the cows didn't eat it!" Aaron said, exasperation in his voice. "Is this exciting enough for you, Craig? Someone stole my milking machine!

Hundreds of thousands of dollars of machinery and computers! I don't know what on earth someone would want with it. But I need it back!"

"Do you have any security cameras in the barn?" Craig asked, turning serious.

Aaron laughed. "Carla suggested that just the other day. Said we'd spent so much on the machine, we should probably have something watching over it. I told her I'd think about it. Guess I didn't think fast enough. I didn't expect it would actually come to this, though. I was still sore from taking out a mortgage on this damn machine," he said, slapping the metal case.

Craig looked around, trying to think like a detective. Eyeing the ground for clues.

"I mean, I'm not a lazy man," Aaron continued. "And I didn't mind spending time in the morning with the old girls. Why did I think I needed a damned automatic milking machine, Craig?"

"Anybody been in here besides you?" Craig asked.

"Just Carla. And about a few dozen royally confused cattle. And now I gotta milk all those cows by hand. By hand, Craig! I haven't milked a cow by hand in years. Not since we upgraded to the vacuum pump system in 2009. I've been at it all morning! Look at these things!" Aaron cried, holding up his bent and twisted fingers. "I've got hand cramps you wouldn't believe!"

"Geez, didn't you have insurance?" Craig asked.

"Of course. But that'll take weeks to pay out. I got cows that need milking now."

"How do you think the thieves got in here without being seen? It's a lot of equipment."

"Oh, there are back roads along the fields someone could take if they knew what they were doing. They could come up behind the barn and never be seen. And the barn isn't really visible from the house, anyway. Plus, Carla and I were out last night."

"If they knew what they were doing," Craig repeated to himself, stroking his chin and looking into the distance.

Aaron glared at him. "I hate that you're enjoying this," he said. "No, I take it back. Enjoy it all you want! Just as long as that helps you find my MACHINE!

"Now if you'll excuse me," he said. "I need to milk about two dozen more cows before their udders start exploding."

Craig perked up at that. "Do they really explo--"

"NO!" Aaron yelled back, and stalked off towards the fields, a bucket in one hand, and a three-legged stool in the other.

Chapter Seventeen

After his dad was discharged from the hospital, life pretty much went back to normal. Josh quickly forgot about the stranger they had found in the Home as life became busy.

There were more Tuesday night business meetings at the Home. They usually discussed the upcoming centennial celebration, discussing how their local businesses could help out (and maximize potential revenue, of course). The town was in the throes of setup, and Josh and Amber were roped into decorating the outside of the Home.

And as for the events that took place on that long drive from Hawk Junction to the Home, neither he nor his dad ever brought them up. Josh figured Arthur wanted to let the water go under the bridge and Josh's momentary resignation was ignored. And as for Josh himself, he only thought of the strange ride at night, when he had trouble falling asleep.

But those were quickly forgotten, with the hub-bub of daily activity. It was a hot year, and old people always seem to die quicker in the heat. Josh was called out almost every day for the month of June, either to do removals at private residences, old folks' homes, or hospitals.

A few deaths were of the more tragic variety. Collisions, suicides and the death of kids. Those were the days Josh dragged himself to the couch after work and put on "The Naked Gun", or another screwball comedy; anything that would help him remove the memories from his psyche. With a lifetime of practice, he was getting quite good at it, too.

Another thing that kept Josh busy over the next few weeks was the government. Specifically, a new rebate program that had been issued to all funeral homes in the region. A few days after their trip to the hospital, Arthur came into the office and announced that the government was returning up to $500 to each of their clients who had purchased a plot of land in the last ten years. He explained it was something to do with encouraging people to get their affairs in order.

This, of course, meant that Amber and Josh were busy calling and booking appointments so everyone could meet with Arthur to issue the rebate.

Josh thought that they should just mail out the checks, but his dad explained that they needed to get signatures. Josh thought it more likely that his dad sensed an opportunity to put into practice his favorite word. Upselling. And his dad was an old pro. If Josh knew his dad, those folks would walk in to collect a $500 rebate, but would walk out with upgraded silk lining in their coffins, or a new industrial strength vault — to keep all those creepy crawlies from getting near their earthly remains under ground.

Weeks passed without a day off. It was time he and Amber finally had their date.

"Hey dad," Josh said, tapping on the office door late one night. He had just come back from a removal and had safely deposited the body in the preparation room.

"Your mother would not like us working so hard, Joshua," his dad said, setting his phone down in the cradle. He stood, cracking his back and sighing.

Josh was surprised into a laugh. His dad never talked about his mom. Not in the two years since her death. But he had to admit, she was always complaining when they didn't seem to have time for each other.

"Yeah, she would be on your case to slow down, that's for sure. Speaking of which—"

"You should take a night off, Joshua. Tomorrow, maybe?"

Josh was silent. His dad had never voluntarily given him a night off. It just wasn't part of his makeup.

"For real?"

"Yeah, of course. You've been working hard. Both of you have."

"Both of us?"

"You and Amber. You know, pretty girl that sits at that desk and takes our crap all day? I assume you've noticed her."

Josh laughed. It also wasn't like his dad to take an interest in Josh's romantic life. Though, in Arthur's defense, it wasn't like Josh ever really had a romantic life to take an interest in.

Still, the man had been acting differently since their trip to the hospital. Obviously, the experience had more of an impact on him than Josh had thought. It hadn't been a near death thing, but maybe just the hospital visit had put some things in perspective for his normally closed off father.

"Yeah, I've noticed her," Josh said awkwardly. He wasn't sure how to have this conversation. Not with his dad. "We actually had a date scheduled a few weeks ago. But, uh—"

"I believe a certain hospital visit probably put the kibosh on those plans?"

"Something like that," Josh said.

"Well, I'm sorry," Arthur said. "And I'm sorry that I haven't always encouraged you the way I should, Joshua. You deserve better than that."

Josh's jaw felt like it dropped to the floor. Had his dad just apologized? Unprompted?

"I've been meaning to talk to you. I know this isn't what you want to be doing with your life. Running a funeral home, I mean. It's just not part of who you are. Am I right?"

Josh nodded. "Yeah, dad. I don't want to be ungrateful, but I think I need to, you know, find my own way. Even if I don't know what that is."

"And you'll find it, son. I have faith in you. And...I'm proud of you." His dad put his arms out for a hug. Josh put his arms out, too. Mostly in shock. His dad also wasn't a hugger. Or much of one to share his feelings, let alone start a deep conversation. If this was the result, maybe more people could use a trip to the hospital now and then.

Josh could feel his dad trembling with emotion as they hugged. He felt a little choked up himself.

"Oh!" came a shocked voice from behind them. They jumped apart. "Sorry," Amber said, still standing in the doorway. "Should have knocked."

Arthur cleared his throat. "Don't be ridiculous. You've never been expected to knock to enter the office before. Why would you need to start now? Just a father and son moment."

She nodded approvingly and made eye contact with Josh while Arthur went back to his desk. She mouthed the words, "what the crap?" All Josh could do was shrug and twirl his finger at the sides of his head.

"He's gone crazy," Josh mouthed.

"You know, I CAN see both of you, right?" Arthur said.

"Need anything else from us, pop?" Josh asked. He looked at the time and saw it was past seven.

"No. Go home and get some rest. Busy day tomorrow. Probably be the last big push of rebates." He paused, seeming to be thinking. "I would like to speak to both of you. Individually. You've been doing a lot of hard work, and the Home wants to show its appreciation."

"Oh," they both said. This sounded like bonus talk to Josh. Add it to the pile of strange behavior from his dad. Will miracles never cease? "Thanks, dad."

Arthur nodded. "Let's make you two the last appointments tomorrow. Okay?"

"Sounds good, Arthur," Amber said. "Not sure what's gotten into you, but I kinda like it."

"You make me sound like I'm normally an old grump," he said. "Anyway, get out of here. But be in all the earlier tomorrow!"

"Yes, Mr. Scrooge," they both said in unison, and the three of them burst into laughter.

Part Two

Chapter Eighteen

It was almost time for supper on the following day when Josh pulled into the Home parking lot. He was returning with Mrs. Popov, who had passed away while on the toilet. The elderly woman's daughter kept apologizing to him, and nothing he said would convince her that it was okay. The fact was, dying on the toilet was far more common than most people realized. Besides, Josh had found people in much worse situations over the years. All part of the family business. Some kids grew up making and delivering pizzas. Some kids grew up removing dead bodies from stranger's homes. It was a crazy world.

He drove to the back and hit the button to engage the garage door. Nothing happened. He hit the button a second time. Nothing.

"Huh," he said, examining the opener.

Concluding the batteries must bead dead, he sighed and got out. He made his way to the front entrance. At the door, he saw the bird bullet streaking the glass of the front display. After the excitement of finding his dad unconscious, he had never actually gotten back out to clean it up. And things had been so busy the past few weeks, he hadn't even come in through the front entrance.

His eye caught the decal 'WARLOCKE FUNERAL HOME IS A PROUD MEMBER OF THE OSPREY BUSINESS ALLIANCE' and terror spiked in him. He remembered the body he had transported from Hawk Junction, and a cold chill ran down his spine before his rational mind squashed it back.

He remembered who the body reminded him of. Josh stepped inside, determined that this time he would not only clean up that bird poop, but that he would also finally ask his father if he had also seen the resemblance.

He knew his dad still had a few appointments, and he had been insisting on having them in the back showroom. He claimed it was because he didn't want to hold up operations by having a constant flow of people coming in and out of his office. But Josh knew his dad just wanted them in the showroom so he could upgrade them into the Cadillac of coffins, or a more extravagant (and expensive) headstone.

Josh rounded the corner into the office and saw Amber at her desk, filling out paperwork.

"Did you find out if it was Popov or Popof?"

"V as in victory," Josh said, grinning while holding up his first two fingers to demonstrate. He had been pretty confident he would be right.

"Crap!" she said, and grabbed the white out from her desk. "Everything go okay?"

"Yup. Textbook removal. You ready for our date?"

"Not until I've had my meeting with your dad," she said with greedy eyes.

"You think you're finally getting your raise?" Josh asked. "I admit dad has loosened up some, but he's still frugal at his core."

"Well, when you have a stellar employee like yours truly, you gotta know when to pay up."

"Uh-huh," Josh said, sounding dubious. "I'd like to hear you explain that to him."

"Knock knock," said a gruff voice from behind. They turned to see a tall, white-haired man at the door to the office.

"Hi, Mr. Hill!" Amber said.

"I told you, young lady. Call me Reg."

"I'll try to remember," she said, smiling.

"How's it going, Reg?" Josh said.

"That's Mr. Hill to you, Joshua," the old man said, coming into the room and applying a vigorous noogie to Josh's scalp. This was something he had been doing since before Josh could remember. Reg Hill owned the town hardware store and was a regular around the Home. Especially at the monthly Osprey Business meetings. Josh was reminded to ask his dad about the resemblance of the body. He would have asked Mr. Hill, but the man hadn't even seen it before it disappeared.

"Where's your dad? I have an appointment."

"He should be finishing up with his last appointment, Mr. Hill—uh, Reg."

"Good girl," he said, smiling.

"He's meeting in the show room."

"I'll bet he is," Reg said, shaking his head. "The old crook's trying to steal every penny, isn't he?"

"You know dad."

"What are you gonna to do with your five hundred dollars, Reg?" Amber asked.

"If I know Arthur, I'll be upgrading all the hardware on my coffin from brass to silver."

"Ah, Reg!" said Arthur from behind them. He was sticking his head through the office doors. "Glad to hear you're going with Silver! Would you like to add a burial vault?"

"I'm using that rebate money to upgrade my damn fishing boat, you old grave robber!"

"We'll see about that. Step into my office," Arthur said with a wicked grin, gesturing into the show room. Reg walked in, grumbling, as Arthur held the door for him. "Who do we have left?" Arthur asked Amber.

"Just your favorite person ever," she said with a sunny smile. "Followed by your son."

"Good. It's been a long day. I'll get you two in a minute." And with that, he ducked out.

Josh, who had been mulling over the body for the first time in weeks, heard all this in the back of his brain. He finally came to when the room was quiet and Amber was staring at him.

"Deep thoughts?" she asked.

"Not really," he said.

"Thinking about a certain pretty lady?" she asked, clearing off her desk.

"No. About a certain corpse."

"Oh, well, don't you know how to kill the mood?" she said, glaring.

He smiled. "Remember me saying that the body I picked up a while ago looked like someone I knew?"

"Which one? This is a funeral home, Josh."

"*THE* body. The disappearing corpse."

"Oh! That one. No. Did you say that?"

"Pretty sure. But yeah, it was…familiar. It looked like…well, I wanna check with dad to confirm. It's been so long, I don't think I can trust my memory."

"Well, who was it?"

"Someone who was part of the business owners' association."

"Oh, with Mr. Hill?" she asked.

"Yeah," Josh said. "Maybe I should actually bring it up with him, too. He might be interested. Even though he didn't actually see the body. I think I'll go in and ask them now."

"I don't know. Your dad might get upset if you interrupt him mid spiel."

Josh headed to the door, with Amber following. "Meh, no. I think it'll be fine. Mr. Hill is practically family, so I doubt I'll be interruptin—"

Josh stopped cold when he opened the door and looked in. The show room had a large table in the middle of the room where various displays were kept. Mr. Hill was laying flat on the table. Josh's dad, whose back was to them, was on top. Both men were panting deeply.

"Dad?" Josh said, dumbfounded.

"Uh…" Amber said. "I think they might want to be left alone, Josh. Come on," she said, tugging at his shirt.

"Oh, Joshua," his dad said, turning to look at them. "Yes, not really a great time, son."

Mr. Hill was doing more than just panting. He was also making muffled sounds. When Arthur turned, Josh could see that his dad's hand was over Mr. Hill's mouth, preventing the man from talking.

Wait, no. His dad's hand wasn't just over the man's mouth. The fingers and palms were actually sinking into Mr. Hill's skin. Mr. Hill's eyes were wide, and Josh didn't think he had ever seen a more terrified expression on someone's face that wasn't on a movie screen.

"Dad, what are you doing? What's going on?"

Amber, who didn't have the angle that Josh did, tugged at his shoulder more, trying to pull him out of the room and whispered. "Come on, Josh. I'll explain it when you're older."

"Ah well," Arthur said. "I guess I've been found out. Why don't you two come in and close the door?"

And with that, he let out an ear-piercing shriek that tore through Josh's head. He and Amber were forced to their knees from the pain.

That's when Arthur's face began to split down the center. Josh watched in horror as the line continued down his chin, neck, and then disappeared behind the collar of his shirt. Then, with an explosion of fabric and buttons, his body split in a star pattern. Arthur's face, chest and limbs now formed a kind of hideous mouth. It pulled apart with sticky veins of mucus separating and splattering to the floor. The hand holding Mr. Hill's head to the table flexed, crushing the man's skull. Mr. Hill's body slid limply to the floor. It didn't stay still, however. Josh saw it quivering and shaking, as if it were sitting on a powerful massage chair.

Amber let out a scream. Josh couldn't scream. Or move. Shock held him in place. He stood, inventorying with his eyes what was happening, unable to look away.

The star shape of his dad's body began to sprout teeth, becoming some kind of grotesque human Venus Fly Trap — though Josh didn't think the word human applied to whatever this was.

The body reared up on an elongating stalk of tendrils behind it. All the while shrieking the same terrible sound. Josh and Amber were still on their knees, covering their ears.

The thing lashed out at them, lightning quick. Josh saw its body growing taunt and anticipated the strike. His paralysis broke in time for him to push Amber to the side. He rolled in the other direction, using the momentum from the push. Whatever it was chomped down close enough for Josh to feel the rushing wind.

"Run!" Josh said to Amber as he scrambled to his feet. They stood separated by the trunk of the huge creature.

"Okay!" she said, immediately getting up and heading for the door. Josh watched after her.

Josh tried to follow suit, but before he got moving, the thing flipped around and was back in front of him. It closed its mouth and his dad's body reformed.

"Joshua," Arthur said, reaching out to him. "Don't leave me, son! I…I need you. Help me!"

"Dad," Josh said. His reaction was involuntary and immediate. He reached out, preparing to grab his father, as if the man were flailing on the edge of falling down the stairs.

At the last moment, his sanity took over, and he flinched back. The jaws snapped down where his hands had been.

Josh doubled back as the seams reappeared, revealing the teeth lined void that formed the throat of this monstrous thing.

Something grabbed Josh's foot, and he stumbled backward. He looked and saw Mr. Hill lying on the floor behind him. The man was whole. No crushed skull. He was somehow back to normal.

Normal was the word Josh was thinking when Mr. Hill's mouth ripped open to his ears, revealing his own set of jagged, yellowed teeth. Hundreds of teeth.

Hill lunged. Josh didn't think. His body reacted on its own; a wonderful self preservation mechanism. Josh dropped. No thought for cushioning his fall. He just wanted to get low. His head hit the tile floor hard. His visioned blackened.

He heard a collision above him. Felt it more than saw it happen. When he opened his eyes, he saw the two animal forces that were once his dad and Mr. Hill battling furiously over his inert body on the floor. It was like watching a snake and a badger who stumbled upon the same food and were fighting over who would get it. Tendons sprouting from his father's body whipped wildly and wrapped around the body of Mr. Hill. Josh was transfixed, and he would have gone on staring that way until both creatures had finished with each other and turned their attention to him.

"Josh!" Amber yelled. He turned to see her standing at the back door that led out into the alley behind the Home. She was waving to him.

He did a backward scuttle out from under the two monsters, then turned and sprinted in her direction. He didn't give the two fighting forces a second look. He could hear them going at each other, but who knew how long it would take them to turn back to him? He dove for the door, slamming it into place behind him, closing off the carnage in the showroom.

Chapter Nineteen

Amber was already on the street when Josh caught up to her. She was waving frantically and Josh saw she was flagging down a police cruiser. He was amazed that one was passing by just then. He only hoped it wasn't Henry.

"Where the hell's the fire?" Henry said as he rolled down the window of the cruiser as he slowed to a stop in front of the Home.

Of course it would be Henry.

But Josh figured it really didn't matter. With what was going on inside the Home, Henry could call someone higher up just as easily as anyone else. They might need to call a swat team. Or the army.

Amber leaned in, and Josh watched Henry steal a look at her breasts — being a funeral home assistant, they weren't exactly exposed. But that didn't stop Henry.

"There's trouble inside!" she said.

He didn't catch on to her terror. He looked at the building. "The Home? What's wrong? Did you guys lose another body?" Henry laughed, then stopped laughing when he saw their faces. "What's going on?" he said, turning serious.

"You just need to see it," Josh said, knowing that explaining would be the worst thing they could do. No crazy talk out here. Just get him inside, and the mayhem could explain itself.

"I just need to see it? Look, if there's a problem, tell me about right here. I just got started on my patrol. I got the seat adjusted the way I like it. I'm not leaving this car for, 'You just need to see it.'"

"You were right," Amber broke it. "Someone stole a body." Josh liked where she was going.

"Yeah! Broke in and took it," he added.

"Are you kidding me?" Henry said. "Another body? What kind of place are you people running?"

"It doesn't matter, Henry! Come on! Don't you need to, I don't know, look for evidence?"

"What happened to you, anyway?"

Josh looked down at himself. His clothes were ripped and torn in places. He felt a pretty good sized gash on his forehead and there were small scratches everywhere else.

"I fought the guy," he said.

"So you saw him?"

"Come on! Just come in and we can explain everything," Amber said, opening the cruiser door. Josh knew they couldn't explain any of the crazy story they had just concocted on the spot, but he also knew that one look inside the home would send Henry running back to the patrol car to call for backup.

Eventually, with enough prodding, Henry exited the vehicle. They walked up the steps to the front of the building, as Josh didn't want to take them in the back and have the thing grab Henry before he could get some help. He would consider letting it get Henry after he had been helpful, but not before.

"Where'd it happen?" Henry asked as they stepped into the foyer.

"In the back," Josh answered, stepping slowly in the direction of the show room. He was scanning the room, frantically looking behind them as they went. He saw Amber was doing the same thing. They crept forward, barely faster than a crawl. Josh's eyes couldn't dart around the room fast enough for his liking.

"You two wanna stop that," Henry said. "You're starting to freak me out."

"Oh," Josh said while still scanning. "You'll get plenty freaked out in a minute. I think you'll—

"Hello, officer." Josh and Amber jumped as Arthur stepped out the swinging door and into the foyer. Henry looked at them with disgust, then turned to accept the handshake of the other man.

"Afternoon, sir," he said, taking on a very un-Henry-like tone of authority. Something he reserved for the regular patrons of the town. "I understand there's been a disturbance?"

Henry had phrased it as a question, as if he doubted the word of Josh and Amber could be reliable. Josh didn't care. He was busy inspecting the thing that had taken over his dad's body. The funeral director looked…normal! Completely normal. No strange tendrils coming out of his back. No skin shifting or seams down his body. He looked like he always had.

Josh's dad — or the thing that was impersonating Josh's dad — looked taken aback. "Disturbance? No, not that I'm aware of." He turned to Josh and Amber. "Joshua, is this your doing? Stop wasting Officer Henry's time with this foolishness. Nothing is going on here. Now, I'm sure officer Henry here would like to get back to his job."

Josh was about to say something when Mr. Hill exited the back room.

"Everything okay out here?" he said.

"Evening, Mr. Hill," Henry said, and shook the store owner's hand.

Arthur nodded and turned to Josh. "Are we ready to get back to work?"

Josh and Amber stood staring at the two men. Josh knew there was something sinister hiding in these two normal looking bodies, but he also knew there wasn't anything he could say to convince Henry of that fact.

"Well, if you don't need anything, sir," Henry said, "I'll be on my way." He turned and glared at Josh and Amber on his way out. He gave Josh a bit of a shove as he passed. Josh barely felt it. He was transfixed by the two figures in front of him.

"Uh…I think we'll pass, dad. Something's, um… something's come up. I…"

He and Amber began backing slowly toward the front door where Henry had just exited. Josh didn't want to take his eyes off the two figures in front of them.

"Yeah," Amber said. "Gotta get going myself."

The two men stood there, smirking slightly, as Josh and Amber backed toward the door.

Josh didn't allow his eyes off them until the door closed, shutting them from view.

Chapter Twenty

Josh woke from a daze. He didn't remember walking from the funeral home to the park, but that's where he found himself, not twenty minutes later. About thirty minutes after being attacked by a weird creature that took the form of his father. Sitting on a log that separated the grass from the rubber cement of the playground, staring at nothing and understanding about as much.

Half a dozen kids were playing on the colorful equipment. Their squeals of delight grated on Josh's nerves as he and Amber stared into the distance.

"I'm a monster!" yelled a small boy from the top of the jungle gym. Three girls screamed in delicious terror and began running away, laughing, as the boy chased them. A three-year-old also screamed, but his tiny cries were followed by tears, and he fled to his mother. Josh watched the boy's progress across the grass and into the arms of his protector. His tears quieting as she comforted him.

"Lucky kid," Josh said.

"What?" Amber asked.

He hadn't planned on speaking aloud. "Nothing." They went back to staring.

"That didn't happen," Amber said. "Right?"

"It seems pretty crazy," Josh agreed. "But it happened."

"How can you be sure?" she asked.

"Because I saw it. *WE* saw it. We remember it. We can't be crazy if we both saw the same thing… right?"

"I don't know. How do you know we saw the same thing?"

"Did you see my dad split into a giant teeth monster and try to kill us?"

"…yes," she said. "Did you see Mr. Hill being controlled like a puppet from hell?"

"All puppets are from hell," Josh corrected. "But yes. I did."

"Great!" she said. "I honestly wish we were crazy. Then I wouldn't feel so insane."

"I can't argue with your logic."

"So what are we talking about, then? If we're not crazy, what the *FUCK* did we just see? Aliens or something?"

"I have no idea. I don't think it matters what it is at this point. What do we do about it? That's probably a better question."

"Is that our job?" Amber asked. "I mean, this is a little above the pay grade of a funeral home assistant."

"I don't know. Hell, I don't know what to think. I just saw my dad ripped in half in front of me. You think I have answers for that?"

Amber was silent for a moment. When she spoke, she sounded a little calmer. "I'm sorry, Josh. You're right. How are you doing? It's not every day you discover your dad is a—"

"It wasn't my dad," he snapped. "I don't know what it was, but it wasn't my dad."

"But," Amber said hesitantly, "obviously it must have…you know…done something to him, right?"

"NO!" Josh said, much too sharply. "Not obvious at all. He might be fine somewhere. That thing might just be impersonating him."

"Josh," Amber said. "We saw it take Mr. Hill. It took his body. It didn't make a copy of him. It—"

"We don't know that's what happened to dad!" Josh said.

"Okay. Calm down. I'm sorry."

Josh took a deep, shaky breath. "No. I'm sorry. I mean, what I said is true! We don't know what happened to dad. We don't know anything. But I shouldn't be yelling at you. I'm just…"

"Yeah," she said. "Me too. Frigged up. This isn't the kind of thing that…I mean, schools don't exactly prepare you for this kind of stuff."

He smiled. "Yeah. You'd expect this to be up there with sex-ed. '*Monster Spotting 101*' or something."

"Sooo," Amber said. "What do we do?"

"I think it's safe to assume that whatever this is has to do with the body I brought back from Hawk Junction."

"Yeah, I think that's a safe assumption," Amber agreed.

"Well, clearly Henry didn't catch on to anything back at the Home," Josh said. "Which means we're the only ones that saw something happen in there. We're the only ones who know...dad... isn't actually dad. We're the only ones who know a strange creature disguised as a corpse—"

"Brought into town by the funeral director's son..."

"An irrelevant detail," Josh said. "A creature that can... what? Meld with people? Take them over? Impersonate them?"

"That was pretty freaky. If I didn't know that wasn't...you know...your dad. I would have bought it. How did it talk like him?"

Josh thought. "I think that's the wrong question. The only how that matters is *HOW* do we stop it?"

"We can't," Amber said. "I don't want anything to do with this!"

"It's okay. We just need to get some evidence to the police, and—"

"We tried that!" she said, raising her voice. "We tried that and nothing happened! Officer Jackass brushed us off and now we're sitting in the park while some monster is going around town taking over more people until...it has the entire town under its control? Or until every fucking person in town is freaking dead!?"

Across the park, the little boy in his mother's arms burst into fresh tears. The woman glared at Amber and Josh, gathered her things and stormed off.

"Sorry," Amber called after her. "Just acting out a play." She sat back down.

Josh was deep in thought. "You're right. We tried, and we failed. But we can't give up. We just need to get it into the hands of someone who can do something about it."

"But if it can become a perfect version of any-one—"

"No one said it was perfect," Josh countered.

"Good enough," she said. "So why is it doing this? Oh, sorry. We're only asking how questions."

He paused, thinking. "No, you're right. Why? Why did it need to come HERE? Why couldn't it just take me over when it thawed and start its weird people collection party in any town it happened to come across?"

Amber just shrugged and shook her head.

Josh thought, then had an idea. "I think it's time we called the source of all this."

"What the hell does that mean?" Amber asked.

Josh reached for his phone. It was a move he did about a thousand times a day since he had forgotten it in the motel on his drive back with the corpse from hell. Each time, he reminded himself he really needed to get down to the mall to get a new one. But things had been so busy the past few weeks... which didn't seem very coincidental, now that he was thinking about it.

"Government mandated rebates," he said out loud.

"What? Can you start making sense?" Amber asked.

"Probably not. Can I use your phone?"

"Sure," she said. She unlocked it and handed it over. Then she sat silently as he tapped away at the screen. Eventually, she said, "What the heck, man? Are you just going to leave me in suspense?"

"I'm giving our friend Jim a call," Josh said, then went back to tapping at the phone, ignoring Amber's confused expression. He wasn't sure he would find what he was looking for. The Big Bear Inn had been closed down for years. But he was surprised to find that the phone number was still listed. He tapped and waited, expecting a message to tell him the number was no longer in service.

Amazingly, it began to ring. After two more rings, someone picked up. Josh was immediately assaulted by the sounds of saws and hammers.

A woman came on the line. "Hello. Uh, crap. I mean, Big Bear Inn. Grand Re-Opening coming soon. How can I help you?"

Josh pictured the dilapidated exterior of the hotel that he had visited just a few weeks ago.

Hell, had it only been a few weeks?

Josh pictured the cracked glass of the display window out front. The overgrown garden. The siding that was falling off in places and in dire need of a new paint job.

And most of all, he pictured the terrified owner who seemed unable to keep from peeing his pants when inside the old building. Had he sold the place already?

"Hi…is Jim there?"

Hesitation on the line. "Uh…hang on, I'll check. We're pretty busy. He might've gone out to get…no, he's here. Just a second." There were sounds of the phone being set down and muffled shouts over the raging power tools in the background. Josh waited, rehearsing in his head what he might say when Jim came on the line. Josh watched as the group of kids ran around playing a game of tag. A girl tugged at a boy, and they split off, hiding together in a large bush off to the side of the playground.

Moments later, the phone was picked back up.

"Jim here. Grand Re-Opening coming soon," he said.

"I told them that!" the woman shouted from the background.

"Well, it never hurts to repeat. Hello?" he said into the phone.

He sounded...chipper. Like a completely different person. Josh recognized the deep voice of the man, but he found it difficult to believe this was the same man who had cowered behind a kitchen counter from a frozen body in the freezer.

"Hello?" Jim repeated. "I think you hung up on them, Dotty!"

"Hi!" Josh said, jumping in before Jim could hang up. "I'm here! I was hoping to get some information from you, Jim."

"Sure can!" came the reply, which was twice as happy as before. "It'll be awhile till we're fully operational. Just got renovations under way this week. We won't be booking rooms until September, but we hope to have the restaurant and store open in the next couple of months. Are you local? Or hoping to get some hunting in?"

"Neither," Josh said into the phone. He looked at Amber, who was straining to hear both sides of the conversation. She seemed concerned by Josh's reactions and Josh realized he must be making some pretty odd faces. He pulled the phone from his ear and put it on speaker so she could listen in.

"Hello?"

"Hi," Josh said. "Sorry. Neither local nor hunter. Jim, I'm actually calling about the body."

Silence. Josh didn't have to wonder if the line had gone dead. He could still hear the work going on in the background. But the silence from Jim sounded more like the man Josh remembered than anything else he had said so far.

"Jim, are you—"

"What body?" Jim said. "You talking about the deer out front? Is this the p-Peg—I mean park ranger? 'Cause yeah, I'm hoping you can get rid of it before it starts to stink." He laughed and was all of a sudden talking much too loud. His voice had taken on a bit of an edge.

"No, Jim. Not a deer. This is Josh. From Warlocke Funeral Home. Last month, I picked up a frozen body that was in your freezer. The body you said you had been in there for ten years." Josh waited, wondering if the man was just going to hang up on him.

"Uh-huh," Jim said in a guarded tone. Josh could hear the man bracing on the other end.

"Jim," Josh said, hesitating, not sure how he should proceed. "There's some weird stuff going on in town. Like killer monster stuff. I need you to tell me what it is you passed on to my town."

"Nothin'!" Jim said abruptly. "I didn't pass on nothin'! You came to me, remember? I didn't even report…whatever it is. So it wasn't my doing! You hear me?" He stopped and Josh could hear the man breathing. "I didn't say nothing to nobody! I did what I was told, but he knew about it! He knew! So I figured he could take it, ya know? Not my fault."

"What, Jim?" Josh said. He didn't understand what the man was saying, but he also didn't get the idea Jim was exactly talking to him at that moment.

"Nothin'! I'm not…why are you calling me? This is what you do, okay? You're a funeral home! I thought you were going to burn the sucker. Why didn't you fucking torch that thing? Don't you have a cremation oven, or whatever? Why are you talking to me? That thing should be toast!"

"Well, let's just say we didn't have it long enough for us to—"

"WHAT?!" This time Jim did yell. "Escaped? You let it escape? You piece of shit! How could you—" There were a series of loud bangs, and both he and Amber winced. Josh had to put the phone to his chest to muffle the noise. He eventually placed the sound. Jim was pounding the landline receiver onto a table or door frame. The man was having a full-blown temper-tantrum.

Josh waited for it to end. The kids had abandoned their game and were playing on the equipment, taking turns on the slide. Josh spied the girl and boy coming out from the bushes. The girl ran to join the rest of the group. The boy stumbled after her.

When Josh lifted the phone, he could hear Jim muttering. Josh noted the hammering and power tools in the background were silent, so the workers must have been equally shocked on their end.

"It's okay," Jim was saying. "Osprey is really far away. Like, to the moon. It's too far away. Not my problem. Not going to—"

"Jim, we need your help here. Just some information—"

"Don't you bring it back here! Okay?! You just better not! Or...or I'll sue. You hear me? I'll sue you. No! I'll *KILL* you! Yeah. Just...deal with it yourself."

"It's taking the shape of people, Jim! Is that what you saw? Was it replacing people?"

That silenced the man. "What? Replacing? No. It just...just ate. All of them. I...escaped. How could you let it...?"

"Jim, we need your—"

"Leave me alone! You hear me? Leave...don't call again!"

The line went dead.

Josh turned to Amber. "He's going to think about it and call back," he said, handing her the phone.

"Yeah, sounds like it," she said. "Any other ideas?"

"I'm tapped out," he said. "But open to suggestions."

"Leave town?" she said. Josh thought that sounded like a very good idea. At least put some distance between them and the town, so they could think. He found coherent thought pretty difficult at the moment. Probably not surprising, considering their conception of what was possible and impossible had been radically changed in the past forty-five minutes.

But he couldn't bring himself to abandon his dad, who might very well still be alive. It wasn't like he knew his dad was dead. Sure, that thing seemed to consume Mr. Hill, but maybe it could either consume someone or just mimic them without actually killing them.

Josh shook his head. "No, I can't leave. Not without trying to find dad." He paused. "You should go."

"And let you have all the fun around here?" she said, giving a failing attempt at a smirk. "Not likely. So what do we do?"

Josh smiled, touched by her lack of hesitation about staying with him. "I wonder...maybe if... maybe the body is still at the hospital?" he said.

Amber nodded. "Yeah," she said, standing. "We should check. See if it's gotten up and started eating any nurses."

CHAPTER TWENTY-ONE

Craig opened the glass door of the university entrance, heading for his cruiser. He absently looked back, pausing to hold the door open for anybody behind him. Nobody was there.

He walked down the university steps, deep in thought. The past several weeks had definitely brought some much needed spice to his daily routine. Too much spice. Like how he always forgot to ask for the mild wings at Dell's Grill and he had to order a glass of milk to go with his meal instead of a beer. Milk! Like a kid.

The thefts had started off pretty small. Nothing more than teenagers taking cell phones and game consoles. But it had quickly gotten out of hand. Within the first week of the thefts, larger, more exotic items had begun to disappear. Whole sections of wiring from the local hardware store had disappeared a few weeks ago. Next, steel support beams from construction yards. It seemed like everything was being taken.

Tools started disappearing next. Power tools from garages and stores. Welding equipment from shops.

Aaron McDonald's milking machine was just the beginning of the large electronic thefts. As odd as that one seemed, that machine contained a lot of expensive computer equipment and parts.

Now, Morgan University was missing something called an Infrared Spectroscope, along with a Computer Cluster...whatever the hell that was.

The odd thing about these last ones was that nobody seemed to agree on what had happened. Oh, they all agreed that something wasn't where it should be. But the stories didn't line up.

The head of the science lab, who was a friend of Craig's and who had called him in to begin with, said it was stolen. The University president said that the equipment had just been "misplaced." The head of shipping and receiving said the equipment had been shipped out the day before, but couldn't say where it was headed. Just that it was signed by the University President, who denied signing anything.

The whole thing was a mess.

So now Craig had his big interesting case, but he didn't know what to do with it. He didn't know what half the missing stuff even looked like. How was he supposed to know if he had found the Infrared something-or-other?

Chief was acting weird, too. Like, everything else was more important than the growing crime wave!

The call to come to the university was just one example. Craig had been sitting at his desk, filling out a report — which always seemed to take him ten times longer than everyone else — when Sonia called him over.

"Craig," Sonia said from her position at the call center. "Your buddy Sharon just called. Got some missing equipment at the university you should check out."

"The university?" Craig said, shocked. "Okay. I'm on it." He had crossed to the key rack, looking for cruiser five. He loved Five. He had the auto adjust seats just the way he liked them, and all his favorite station presets on the radio. He grabbed the keys and headed for the door.

"Philips!" Police Chief Braden shouted from his office door.

Craig turned back. "Yeah chief?"

"Where are you heading?"

"University. More stolen equipment. Chief, this is starting to get pretty serious. I think maybe I should, I don't know, bring someone along. We might need to put some serious manpower into this."

"Mmmhmm. I'll think about it. Have you put any 'manpower' into the vandalisms lately? Doesn't seem like there's been much focus there. I'm still seeing penises popping up all over town."

Sonia tried to stifle a chuckle. Chief Braden looked at her quizzically.

Craig ignored her and moved closer. "Chief, that's kid's stuff. This is serious. Major stuff is disappearing all over town. Big stuff. Expensive stuff. I don't think some taggers compare to—"

"Every crime against this town matters, officer," Braden said sternly.

"Yes, chief," Craig said, reluctantly taking the rebuke. "But I got a call that I gotta check out."

"Hm…okay, get going."

"Thanks," Craig said.

"But I'm going up to meet with the mayor now. I'll be taking car five." Chief held out his hands for the keys.

"Aww, chief! I got everything—"

"The way you like it. I know. You're a regular Raymond Babbit. You'll survive in car three." He continued holding out his hand for the keys. Craig reluctantly gave in.

"Yes sir." He watched the chief go out the door, then begrudgingly went to the key rack. He hated car three. It was always breaking down and out for—

The key rack was empty. He turned back to Sonia.

"Where's car three?"

Sonia didn't look up from the novel she was reading. "The usual. Out for repairs."

Craig sighed in exasperation. Now he would have to take his truck, which was all kinds of humiliating. He hated driving around in a civilian vehicle when in uniform. He always felt like he was playing dress-up, or trick or treating at Halloween. Which, to be fair, he still did. He used his niece and nephew as an excuse. Just to get free candy.

But this wasn't Halloween!

Now, sliding behind the wheel of his truck outside the university, Sonia's voice came over the CB radio attached to his shoulder.

"Hello. Calling Craig's dirty Dodge Ram. Come in, dirty Dodge Ram."

Craig grabbed the radio. "It's a Ford F-150, Sonia! And you know it!"

"Whatever you say, Craigels," she said deadpan. Craig glared at the receiver. Two months ago, he had said he was going to start doing kegels as his new exercise routine. Sonia had laughed so hard, she'd spewed her mouth full of coffee across her desk and all over Craig's uniform. To this day, she refused to tell him what a kegel was.

"What is it, Sonia?"

"Get yourself down to the hospital. More thefts."

That got his attention. "Really? The hospital?"

"Yup. They didn't get into specifics, but something big is missing there, too."

"Roger. I'm on my way."

"Good. And Craig?"

"Yeah?"

"Don't forget to keep up your exercises on the drive over. It'll keep you from wetting the bed."

"Okay?" he said, confused. "Over and out, Sonia."

Chapter Twenty-Two

I really don't think this was a good idea," Amber said as they walked into the hospital lobby. The light coming in through the floor to ceiling windows was fading, and the strong white halogen lights of the lobby were almost blinding in comparison.

A few people were eating at the coffee shop inside the lobby, and several more were sitting in chairs in the waiting area, but far fewer people than Josh expected to see in a normally busy hospital at this time of day. It looked more like two in the morning than early evening.

"I feel like it's my duty to remind you that this WAS your idea," Josh said.

"Well, then I had a damn stupid idea," Amber shot back. "Any one of these people could be a monster!" she said, eyeballing a passing nurse.

"Would you stop saying stuff like that?" Josh said. The nurse gave them both a wary look, then walked down a side hallway.

"Why? Aren't you, like, terrified right now?" Amber asked.

"Of course I am. But you're starting to sound like a crazy person!"

"Oh."

"Besides," Josh went on, keeping his voice low, "if there is something in here — hiding in these people — then we don't want it to know that we know. Ya know?"

"Yeah, I know," she said.

They reached the elevator, and Josh pressed the button. And waited. There were more people now than when they had first walked in. Hospital staff in uniforms, patients in gowns, weary people who looked like they had spent sleepless nights in chairs next to sick loved ones.

But that was on the outside. Josh wondered who they were on the inside. Were they who they looked like? Or were they hiding something?

Josh was forced to step back to let two women in hospital scrubs pass. Amber jerked back, bumping into the wall. She eyed the two women as they walked by. Neither of the women seemed to notice them.

"Easy," Josh said, putting a hand on her shoulder to calm her.

His touch seemed to have the opposite effect. She jerked out from under his hand and looked around, seemingly ready to run. Then she made eye contact with him, and she seemed to calm.

"Sorry," she said.

"Just take a deep breath," he said, checking to make sure the button was lit up. The elevator was taking forever. He moved to let more people by.

"I don't know how you're so calm," she said, eyeing each person that passed.

"Oh, I'm freaking out on the inside, believe me." And he was. Especially now. The crowd walking through the hallway had almost reached the point of being a mob. Nobody was paying them any attention, but Josh felt like they were under a microscope. He kept seeing fleeting glances their way, but he wasn't sure if they were really being watched, or if it was just paranoia.

DING!

The elevator doors opened, and both Josh and Amber backed their way onto it, watching as each person walked by on their way to...wherever it was they were going. Josh was certain that any second, the crowd in the hall would all turn in their direction and—

Amber screamed. As she did, Josh felt something on his shoulder. Something was behind him. He jumped, adding his own small scream to hers.

"It's okay, folks," said a cheery voice. "Just getting off here." Josh turned and saw an older man with a gray mustache trying to get off the elevator. He had a mop handle and was pushing a yellow bucket of water in front of him.

Josh took a deep breath. "Sorry," he said, stepping aside and letting the janitor off. He chuckled as he went. He walked across the hall, opening a door and stepping inside. Josh could see shelves of cleaning products, more mop and broom handles, and a sink on the floor where the custodial crew could dump their buckets.

Josh tried to calm himself down. He was going to blow a gasket.

"What floor is it on?" Amber said. She was studying the buttons. "It's been a while since we were here.

Josh searched his memory. "I think he was on the eighth," he said. She pushed the button.

The elevator doors began to slide shut. As they did, Josh watched a nurse walk casually into the janitor's closet. The custodian's back was to her as he poured the used water from the bucket into the sink on the floor.

Before the elevator closed, Josh saw her shut the door behind them.

The elevator doors opened onto a deserted hallway. The nurses' station ahead of them was empty. Absolutely no one was on the floor. A single florescent bulb in the hall stuttered on and off, occasionally casting eerie shadows.

They stood in the elevator staring at the hall so long that the door began to close. Josh put his hand out and stopped the door. It opened, and they still didn't move.

"Are we going, or what?" Amber said.

"Ladies first," Josh said, gesturing out.

"I don't think so, Joshua! When it comes to being eaten by a monster, I'm equal opportunity!"

The elevator door began to close.

"Fine. Let's go," and he began to move, catching the door.

They walked slowly down the hall. Without someone at the nurses' station, they had to check every room. Neither one had actually seen him in the hospital.

They poked their heads into the first room. An older man lay in a bed, unconscious, breathing tubes sticking out of his mouth. A machine beeped a steady rhythm. The other bed in the room was empty. They moved on.

In the next room, a woman sat in bed, desultorily eating from a tray, watching Jeopardy on a small TV hanging from the ceiling.

"This is going to take forever," Amber said, frustrated. "And what prize do we get if we finally find him? Getting eaten. Not my type of game show."

Josh smiled and continued down the hall, his smile quickly fading as he peered through another door. Empty.

They made their way through each room without seeing the stranger from the Home. They reached the door to the last room in the hall. It was partly closed. Josh could see another flickering bulb inside.

"This must be it," Josh said.

"Yeah, it's got the vibe for sure," Amber agreed.

Hesitantly, Josh reached his hand out and gave the door a gentle push. It swung slowly open. Equally slowly, they peeked their heads around the corner.

On the left side of the room, the bed was empty. The divider sheet on the right was pulled around, covering whatever was on the other side.

"Great!" Amber said as they both ducked back into the hall. "This is where we pull back the sheet and find a pulsing green cocoon that sprouts tentacles and pulls us into it, right?"

Josh nodded. "Best part of the movie," he said, smiling. Then led the way in.

Slowly, Josh reached the hanging sheet that was supposed to give a sense of privacy in this building that seemed designed to make you uncomfortable, and searched for the opening. He found it, and slowly peeked inside.

The bed was empty.

"He's not here," Josh said, pulling back the sheet to show her.

"You sure he was on the eighth floor?" Amber asked.

Josh didn't know. He had expected a couple of things. The Thing posing as a man would be in the bed, still in a coma. Or it would be awake, hanging from the ceiling like a demonic bat, skewering hospital staff on forearms made of barbed wire. But he had expected they would find something.

"Are we going to have to check every floor?" Amber asked as they checked the bathroom. Also empty.

Josh thought. He really didn't want to do that. But they had to do something.

"I don't know. But whatever happened to dad — whatever was impersonating dad! — this guy was at the center of it. I don't buy this coma thing. It's too coincidental, this body showing up, and all this weird stuff happening."

"Sure, he probably caused it," Amber said. "But maybe it's good we didn't find him. If we go looking for him, we'll probably just end up like your da— end up monsters, too." She turned back the bedsheet as she spoke. Nothing on the mattress.

Josh shook his head. "No, I can't just give up."

"We're not giving up. We're just... hedging our survival."

"But we still don't know what happened to dad. He might still be alive somewhere. Maybe this thing can just change forms at will. Ya know? It's a shapeshifter. No one said it has to absorb people to take their shape."

"If that's true, then there were two of them," Amber said. "The thing taking the form of Arthur and the unconscious body in the office.

"Okay, then it can split itself in multiples, then change forms!" Josh could hear how defensive he was sounding, but he couldn't stand to admit that maybe his dad was gone.

"Josh, I hate to be the one to say this, but if that wasn't your dad, then where is he? I doubt the thing that crushed Mr. Hill's skull would just set him up in a fancy hotel while it ate the rest of the town."

Josh turned away, not replying.

"Can I help you?" a voice said from behind them. They spun, as if caught doing something wrong. A nurse stood in the doorway.

"Sorry," Josh said. "We were looking for someone. We must be on the wrong floor."

"What's his name?" she asked.

"No idea. We didn't know him. He was found in the funeral home, comatose."

The nurse smiled. "Oh, him. He came out of it shortly after being admitted. He stayed with us for a few weeks, then left. Dr. VanLakey discharged him just this morning." She had entered the room. She smoothed the bedspread out where Amber had disturbed it. Both Josh and Amber were slowly making their way to the door, not wanting to take their eyes off the nurse.

A voice came from behind, startling Josh as he backed up. "Hello, Joshua." Josh turned to see Dr. VanLakey watching them back into the hall. There was a smile on his face, as if the two of them looked ridiculous. Looking at themselves now, Josh had to agree. They probably did look ridiculous.

"I assume you've come to check on our mystery guest?" he said.

"Yeah, just, uh, wanted to make sure he had everything he needed." Josh knew Dr. VanLakey fairly well. The thing that absolutely scared the crap out of Josh was how much this man in front of him seemed to be Dr. VanLakey. Though Josh honestly couldn't say that it wasn't. Nothing seemed to be different about him. But if anyone in the hospital had also been turned, VanLakey would be one of them.

"I'm afraid you missed him," the doctor was saying.

"Yeah, so we heard," Amber said. "Glad to hear he was feeling better."

"He, uh, never said who he was? Did he?" Josh asked, hoping he sounded casual.

That seemed to catch the doctor off guard. "Oh… no, I suppose he didn't. That is to say, not that I can share. Doctor, patient confidentiality."

"Right," Josh said. "Well, we should get going. Got...got dead people to collect." They both walked down the hall. Josh glanced back and saw both the nurse and Dr. VanLakey watching after them.

Amber called for the elevator. Josh stared ahead at the door, waiting impatiently for it to open. He thought he heard footsteps approaching from behind, but when he took another glance back — expecting to see the nurse and Dr. VanLakey bearing down on them in some monster form — he saw an empty hallway.

DING! Josh heard the doors slide open, and he stepped on, still watching the spot where the doctor and nurse had been.

He turned just in time to keep from bumping into the small mustachioed janitor they had seen in the lobby.

"Ah!" he said, giving a short cry of surprise. It wasn't quite a scream.

"Jumpy, aren't you folks?" the older man said.

"It's been a long day," Amber said, smiling. She pushed for the lobby, and they settled as the elevator began to descend, the janitor standing between them. Josh looked down. The man was once more holding his mop handle, but the yellow bucket he was pushing around was empty. As if he had just forgotten to fill it. Josh went back to staring at the elevator doors.

Moments later, the three of them stepped off, the janitor going back into his closet as he had before. As the door closed, Josh watched the back of the man as he stood in the center of the tiny room, staring forward. Possibly studying the bottles of chemicals on the shelves in front of him.

"They seemed a little off, didn't they?" Amber said as they walked into the mostly deserted lobby.

Josh shrugged. "I guess. Not strange enough for me to feel comfortable bashing them in the head with a baseball bat."

"Is that your normal litmus test for peculiarity?" Amber asked, smiling.

"In this case, yeah."

"Well, where to?" Amber asked.

Josh was about to say he had no idea when he saw Craig coming out of a door marked CT Scans. Josh waved him over.

"What brings you to the hospital?" Josh said. "Let me guess. They did a brain scan, and didn't find anything?"

"Why are you people always so mean to Craig?" Amber asked.

"Hey, he dishes it out worse than we do. Right, Craig?" That's when Josh noticed Craig's demeanor. "What's wrong?" he asked. "More missing stuff?" The few times Josh had seen him — either on the streets or at a few body pickups — the thefts had been all Craig could talk about. But usually he was bubbling over with joy at having a case to solve. Now he looked like someone had run over his dog. Craig let out a deep sigh.

"Yeah. The hospital is missing a CT Scanner." That got Josh's attention.

"What? An entire scanner? Aren't those things, like, huge?"

"Yeah. Room sized. But that's not the weirdest."

"The milking machine was the weirdest," Amber said.

"Nah," Craig said. "Two expensive things from the university are gone, too. And nobody seems to agree on where they went, or if they're even missing."

"Hm, that is weird," Josh said. "Sorry Craig. But glad you finally got that interesting case."

"Yeah, but now I don't know what to do with it."

"Well, we've got something even weirder for you, if you're interested. Maybe we could talk to you after your shift today? Meet you at Dell's?"

"Yeah, I could do that. But I can't imagine it's any more interesting than this."

"Oh, I think we might want to put money on that," Amber said.

They watched Craig walk away. As he did, Josh looked around at the few people in the hospital lobby — a man asleep in some chairs in the waiting area. The staff at the coffee shop. He couldn't be sure, but he felt that the majority of the people in this building were now a part of whatever was going on. They were now some monstrous thing that impersonated people. Some insect-like hive of creatures that were just multiplying until—

"It's your dad," Amber said.

He looked up and saw his father coming into the hospital entrance. Arthur brushed past Craig without a second look. He hadn't seen Josh and Amber.

Josh was transfixed. He studied the man who looked like his father. Maybe this actually was him, not whatever was impersonating him. He should—

"Turn around," Amber said, pulling him back. He realized he had been on the verge of rushing forward to talk to his father. "I don't think he saw us." She grabbed him and turned him forcefully. They both turned to face a display case. He pretended to study it.

"Thanks," Josh said, realizing she had probably just saved his life. He observed the framed photos in the display case. One photo in particular caught his attention.

"Don't mention it."

Arthur — or the creature that only looked like him — got on the elevator and disappeared from view.

"I bet he's going to see Dr. VanLakey," Amber said.

Josh barely heard her. He was distracted by the image of a man he hadn't seen for more than fifteen years. The man that had made the town what it was. The man who had died and left that town to carry on without him.

"I know who the body is!" Josh said, turning to Amber.

Amber jerked, wide eyed. "What? How?"

"Cause I'm looking right at him."

Amber looked around the lobby, then out into the front parking area of the hospital. "Where?"

"There," Josh said, pointing not out into the parking lot, but through the glass of the display case. He pointed to a very old photograph of a man cutting the ribbon at the grand opening of the hospital they were standing in. The man was tall, well built, and very handsome.

"The frozen body I brought to Osprey! It's Fred Morgan," Josh said.

Chapter Twenty-Three

Who's Fred Morgan?" Amber asked as they walked.

They were on a residential street, passing beautiful houses with perfectly manicured lawns and gardens. Neither of them wanted to stick around the hospital, knowing that anyone they saw might be hiding a monster inside.

"'Who's Fred Morgan?'" Josh said, incredulous. "Are you serious? Again with this question?"

"I know you and your dad had some kind of love-fest chat with me about the GREAT Fred Morgan! But come on! That was weeks ago! Do you really think I hang on your every word? Remind me who Fred Morgan is. Is that better? Your dad said he was some kind of town founder?"

"Ehhh…not so much a town founder, since he wasn't actually around when the town started. Maybe you would call him a town resurrector? Is that a thing?"

"Resurrector?" Amber repeated.

"Yeah. The town was in pretty bad shape when he was young. "Dying" was how my dad put it." Josh paused, a flood of memories of his father invading his mind. He wondered if his father was still alive.

Josh tried to push past his feelings and continued talking. "They only had a couple hundred residents, and the quarry was the only business in town that was half way profitable.

"Dad was…*is* a big history nerd. He's also a big Osprey nerd. Dad grew up here, and he used to tell me all about the man who single-handedly brought this town out of its own little depression. The town was dying and Fred Morgan is the man who brought it back from the brink."

"How?" she asked.

"I don't know! I said my dad was the history buff."

"You said he told you all about it."

"I said he told me. I didn't say I was listening."

"Josh!" Amber scolded.

"Okay! I may recall a detail or two. Fred Morgan's father started the quarry."

"What quarry?" Amber asked with a blank expression.

"Seriously?" Josh said. "The quarry. *THE* quarry. This town was built around it! It's why there's a stone quarry in the town logo."

"The town has a logo?" Amber asked, this time with a smile on her face.

"If I wasn't a gentleman, I'd—"

"You'd what?" she said, stopping and putting her hands on her hips.

"I'd…well, it's just a good thing for you I'm a gentleman." She smiled, and they resumed walking. "Anyway, the quarry was failing. I think his father died or something, and his mom remarried. The step-father took over and almost killed the whole business. Then, the step father skipped town and left Fred holding the bag. Fred fought to keep the whole thing going. Took it over and brought it back to being productive. Voila! The town was suddenly rolling in dough."

"Okay, that was fifty years ago. And now you think our mystery man is Fred Morgan. But I'm looking at the body you brought back, and in my head, he barely looks older than we are. Are you seriously telling me that was the body of Fred Morgan?"

"Now, I never said he was Fred Morgan," Josh said.

"You're kidding me, right? In the hospital, you were looking in that glass case like an idiot in a trance and you literally said the words, "the mystery man is Fred Morgan."I've pretty much got a photographic memory, so I should know!"

"Okay, okay, yes. Point taken. I did—"

"Then you walked out the front door, down this street without saying a word, and I finally asked you who Fred Morgan was, and you—"

"I don't need a recap of two minutes ago! Yes, I said that. But if I'd known I was going to be graded for accuracy, I guess I would have said, "the mystery man looks like Fred Morgan." At least how I remember him."

"You knew him?"

"Yeah. He lived here up until fifteen years ago. I think he was one of dad's best friends. At least dad said so. He was a fixture of the town. Everybody knew him. He came to the Home a lot. He was part of the business alliance meetings."

She looked at him blankly.

He sighed. "The meetings that happen in our office the first Tuesday of every month."

"Don't you talk to me like I'm stupid, Joshua. I know what meetings you're referring to. I just don't care. There's a difference."

"Okay, I'm sorry. Yes, he was a regular around our place. I didn't know him well, but he was a nice guy."

"And his wife? Cynthia Morgan, right?"

"Yeah. I didn't see her often. She was a bit more reclusive."

"Or probably she just had a life of her own that didn't involve her husband's business," Amber said.

"Point taken," Josh admitted.

"Okay," Amber said. "We have a guy that saved the town and everyone loved him. How'd he end up back in town inside a funeral home van?"

"Like I said, I don't think it's him. Just like I don't think that is actually my dad. But Fred Morgan has been dead for, like, fifteen years now."

"How'd he die?"

"Boating accident, I think. Out with his wife. I don't remember the details. I was just a kid. I think the boat tipped, and he got sucked under or something."

"I thought maybe he could have just walked on water back to the shore. With the way you're talking about him," Amber said.

"Ha ha. Anyway, it was a major blow to everyone. The town had a special ceremony, like when royalty die. All the businesses closed down and people gave speeches in the town square. Most of the town showed up and lined the streets. It looked like a parade." Josh laughed. "I remember being disappointed that there were no clowns giving out candy."

"So, now something has come to town and… what? Is taking the form of this guy who pretty much saved the town? Why?"

Josh shrugged. "I don't know. But we don't exactly have anything else to go on. Whatever this is, we can't call for help. Nobody would believe us. And if they come to investigate, they would just end up getting consumed by whatever this thing is, anyway. We need to look into this ourselves."

"I don't like that. Why's it our job to solve this? I still think we should leave town. We don't know what this thing is!"

Josh was silent. He could see her point, but couldn't bring himself to agree. He obviously had more invested in Osprey than she did.

"What if it's some kind of alien creature?" she said. "It's going around mindlessly infecting people as some kind of evolutionary defense mechanism. That's not the kind of thing we can really stop, is it?"

"No, probably not. But it isn't working mindlessly," Josh said.

"Oh? And how do you know that?"

"Because of the rebates," Josh replied.

"Rebates?"

"That thing came to us as dad with a story about government rebates for clients. That was obviously a front to draw people in so it could easily infect them — or whatever it does. That tells us two things."

Amber was nodding her head. "It's smart. You're right, that is crafty. Easier to have people come to it than for it to go out and collect people individually."

"Right. That's a pretty clever story for... a mindless space-spore."

"What's the other reason?"

"This thing isn't just grabbing people randomly. At no point did that dad-creature assimilate anybody when we were looking. It did it one by one. You and I were actually next. If we hadn't interrupted the meeting, dad said he wanted to speak to me."

"Right," Amber said, dawning realization on her face. "He said he wanted to tell us some good news. That thing is clever."

"And it likes to hide."

"It sure didn't hide from us," Amber said.

Josh nodded. "Yeah, but we didn't give it much choice. I think bears only attack when you startle them. Come around a corner and surprise them. This thing probably felt cornered—"

"So don't corner anybody into trying to kill us," she said, nodding. "Where are we going, anyway?"

"I'm not the only person who recognized Fred Morgan."

"Oh yeah? Who else? Nobody said anything. The doctor didn't seem to know who he was."

"Remember the day I brought the body back? The day dad and I had the fight about me running so late from picking it up?"

"Yeah."

"That was also the day Cynthia Morgan came by."

Excitement lit Amber's face. "Right! I got a good look at her when she started freaking out! She wasn't reacting to her brother's death! She was looking at the half-frozen corpse of her dead husband. That's why she broke down! So we're headed to see her?"

Josh shrugged. "I'm up for other suggestions. I mean, I guess it's not likely she would—"

"Are you kidding? What do you want, a loaded gun? You're right, we need to go see her. Lead the way. I knew there was something about that old bitch I didn't like."

Chapter Twenty-Four

Amber and Josh stood staring up at the beautiful house on Cherry Lane in Osprey. It was large. Not quite a mansion. A mansion would have been too gaudy to be allowed in Osprey. But still magnificent.

The house was an asymmetrical wonder of straights and curves. The second floor was made up of large windows. Jutting out from the main roof was a large dormer peak that was almost all glass. Below this was a large porch that looked more like someone had stuck a modern style living room outside, with comfortable furniture, and a beautiful monster of a barbecue. The front lawn indicated that Cynthia either loved gardening and spent many hours each day up keeping the property, or that Fred Morgan left her enough money to pay a landscaping company to do regular upkeep. The latter was most likely, as Osprey's unofficial second industry was a glut of landscaping businesses.

As beautiful as the house was, to Josh, the large windows above the extravagantly decorated porch gave the appearance of a cyclopean eye seated over a gapping mouth, daring them to step inside so it could chomp them to mush. Enforcing the image in his mind were the series of triangular banners that had been strung up over the porch steps. Each triangle had the phrase, '*100 YEARS OF GRANDEUR*' printed on it.

"I think this is a bad idea," Amber said, still staring at the large window overhead.

"Once again, I would like to remind you that this was your idea," Josh said.

"I wish you'd stop reminding me when I have bad ideas. I'm the girl who thought it would be smart to apply for a job at a funeral home after moving into town."

"True," Josh admitted. "But if you hadn't done that, you would be missing out on all this fun we're having."

"I think we should leave. I really don't want to get eaten."

Josh couldn't have agreed more. What kept him from turning around and sulking out of town wasn't just his father, but every single man, woman and child of Osprey that hadn't yet been turned into one of these creatures. If he left town now, he didn't know how he would live with himself.

Not that he would live long. Something like this would eventually spread out into the surrounding towns, and that would just grow and grow until eventually—

But he really didn't want to think about that. Instead, he turned his attention to the door, and put his foot on the first porch step.

Amber grabbed his arm, seeming almost frantic. "Don't!" she hissed. "Let's go, Josh!"

"We can't just leave the town to die," he said. "Not without trying something."

"We won't be much good if she turns us into the new crowd!" Amber said.

"We won't go in," Josh said. "We'll just talk to her through the door. I don't think these things will attack us in broad daylight."

"Josh, it's nighttime," Amber said.

"You know what I mean. They won't attack out in the open. I think. Remember, this thing lived with me for two weeks as my dad without ever turning me."

She was silent at that and Josh took her silence as acceptance. He continued up the steps. Amber reluctantly followed, but she trailed back several paces.

The large white door loomed up ahead of them. In the center was a porthole, which looked to Josh like another monster's eye staring down at them.

He put out his hand, but Amber grabbed him from behind.

"You promise we won't go in?" she asked. Her voice was small and timid, like a scared little girl.

"Not a chance," he said in his most reassuring voice. She nodded, and he pushed the button on the faceplate to the right of the door. A series of chimes sounded from deep inside the house. He stepped back.

Moments passed, and nothing happened.

"Well, we tried," Amber said, turning to leave.

That's when they heard the door open. Cynthia Morgan stuck her face into the gap. Josh saw a chain was still attached, keeping the door from opening all the way. She peered out.

"Yes?"

She was a small woman — small by nature, not shrunken by age — and Josh looked down on her as she stood cowering behind the mostly closed door. On the few occasions he had interacted with her, she had seemed strong and virile — full of energy. Even lately, in her seventies. Josh had always thought she was more energetic than he had ever felt in his life.

But now, she seemed like a gentle breeze would blow her over. He could tell she was terrified.

"Mrs. Morgan? It's Josh, from the funeral home."

She stared at them and Josh was reminded of the way rabbits will become stuck in place by a bright light. That's how she looked. Frightened and shivering, like they were a large semi-truck bearing down on her.

Josh continued, keeping his tone measured and gentle. "Mrs. Morgan, we need to talk to you."

"What? NO! No, I'm not seeing visitors today. I...well, I'm still in my bathrobe," she said, looking down at herself. Josh saw that this was true, but he also recognized the tones of desperation. She was scared. And Josh thought he had a pretty good idea why.

"Mrs. Morgan — Cynthia? We don't want to come in. We just want to talk." He struggled with what to say next. How could he get her to trust them? To open up? "We're not a part of what's going on," he said. "That body you saw at the funeral home—"

"That wasn't my husband!" she blurted out. "My husband's been dead for fifteen years."

Josh glanced at Amber. Well, that was one theory confirmed. He hadn't just imagined it. "Yes, that's what we thought," Josh said. "We were hoping—"

"He died in a boating accident," she blurted, cutting him off. "There was nothing I could do. I--"

"Mrs. Morgan, can we talk to you about what you saw? We're hoping we can...we're hoping you can help us."

"I don't want anybody coming in my home," she said, preparing to shut the door. "I don't want any of that business. No, sir!"

That business? What did that mean? Josh was starting to think maybe Cynthia really did know more about what was going on than he had guessed. Josh pressed further.

"What business is that? Do you know about the...well...what's been infecting people?"

She looked startled. "No! No sir! I want none of that in my home. You get away, you hear me?!" She gave a shooing gesture, and began to close the door the rest of the way.

"No!" Josh said. By instinct, he put his foot in the gap before the door could fully close. If she knew what was going on, they had to talk to her.

She began kicking at his foot, trying to get the door closed.

"Josh!" Amber said with concern in her voice.

"Mrs. Morgan, we're not one of them!" he said, frantic. "We're not a part of that thing! We just want help. We need help! Dad might be dead, or maybe just trapped somewhere. I don't know. But we need someone to help us because we're in over our heads!"

"That doesn't mean nothin' to me! Now get off. I don't want you bringing him to me!"

"Nobody knows we're here!" he said. That seemed to get through. Just like that, she stopped fighting. She paused in thought.

"We didn't tell anybody we were coming to see you," he said. "Nobody saw us coming here." He glanced back at Amber. She was starting to look as terrified as Cynthia Morgan. He wanted to reassure her, too, but things were moving too quickly. He had to get them out from the gaze of prying eyes. It suddenly occurred to him that anybody on this street could be one of the Things they were running from. Obviously, Cynthia Morgan knew something, and that meant she could help them.

"You're alone?" the old woman said through the crack in the door.

"Completely. We came straight here from the hospital. I think whatever is happening has turned everyone there. Nobody saw us," Josh repeated. "And we didn't tell anyone where we were going. We're safe!"

More silence and this time Josh didn't try to break it. He just let her process. He started to study the door frame. If she ended up shutting them out anyway, he wondered if he should force his way in. This was too real for them to just leave. It might be for her own good, too.

"Alright," she said. She looked down at Josh's foot, which was still keeping the door open.

"Okay," Josh said, removing his foot. She closed the door. Josh was just wondering if he had been tricked. He might need to force the door after all. That's when the chain began to rattle. A moment later, the door opened. Cynthia still looked terrified as they came in. She glanced around outside as he stepped into the entryway, which gave into a sitting room.

"It's okay, my dear," Cynthia said from behind him. Josh turned to see Amber outside the door. "I'm not going to bite."

"I...uh..." Amber stood on the other side of the door, looking unsure. "I wasn't going to...uh... Josh!" she said with a little foot stomp. She glanced toward Mrs. Morgan, then back at him.

"It's fine," he said, trying to tell her everything was okay with his eyes. "She's going to help us!"

Amber looked down at the older woman and gave a very tentative smile. The smaller woman looked up at Amber and gave her own smile. But she was still glancing furtively outside, making sure nobody was seeing them.

"Come in," Josh said. "It's okay."

Finally, Amber stepped inside. Cynthia Morgan closed the door behind her, bolted it, and slid the chain in place. That didn't seem to settle Amber. She glared daggers at Josh.

"It's okay," he mouthed to her, trying to reassure her. But the fact was, he was anything but sure of the situation himself. He hoped he wasn't leading both of them to their doom. But he had a feeling that Cynthia Morgan was exactly who she appeared to be.

"If you'll excuse me," Cynthia said, gesturing at herself as she spoke. "I'd like to get out of this bathrobe and into something more presentable." She walked out of the sitting area and into the main part of the house.

As soon as she was out of sight, Amber slapped Josh's shoulder from behind.

"Are you insane!" she said in a whispering tone. "You said we wouldn't go inside! She could be one of those things!"

"Would you calm down? I think I know what I'm doing!"

"You think? You *THINK!?*" she said and slapped him again. "I think you just trapped us in a house with a monster!"

"Would you let me explain? I don't think she's one of those...creatures!"

"Why? How can you tell? Your own dad was one of those things for weeks and he seemed fine and dandy!"

"Exactly!" Josh said. "He seemed exactly the same as he always did. Does Cynthia Morgan seem to be acting like a normal person?"

Amber paused. "No. She's definitely scared of something."

"Exactly. If she was a monster pretending to be Cynthia Morgan, don't you think she'd be acting like Cynthia Morgan?"

Amber thought some more. Her body started to relax a bit. "Yeah, I guess. But try to keep me in the loop next time you go off script," she said, holding a threatening finger in his face. He held up his hands in surrender.

"Promise!" he said.

"Yeah, like those are any good from you," she said. "She really does seem, like, terrified of something," Amber added.

"Obviously, she knows something about what's going on in town. She might be able to tell us what's going on. Maybe she'll be able to tell us what to do. Or who to call. She's a powerful woman."

Amber cocked her eyebrow at him. "Powerful? Really? 'Cause she's the widow of the great Fred Morgan?"

"Well, yeah, he was a powerful man. In this town, at least. I'm sure she has some of his connections or something."

"Grasping at straws, much?" Amber said.

"Of course I'm grasping at straws, okay? We have very few straws, so I'm working with what I've got."

"Okay," Cynthia called. "I'm ready for you, dears."

Josh gestured toward the interior of the house. Amber looked back at the front door, seeming to consider bolting for it anyway. Then she turned back.

"Okay, I think you're right. She's not one of those things. But that does not mean she's going to be able to help us. I mean, she's just a little old lady, Josh. What could she possibly know about these monsters?"

"Let's find out," Josh said, walking further into the house. After a moment's hesitation, Amber began to follow.

Josh went through an arched door frame, exiting the sitting room into an elegant living room.

"This is a very lovely home," Amber said, walking across the cushion soft carpet. The room was bare of what Josh thought of as "old lady decorations." No spice racks of porcelain animals, decorative plates hanging on the walls, and other cluttered knick-knacks. It was very modern, with minimal touches of color that popped.

"Would you like something to drink?" she called from the other room. "Tea? Coffee?"

"No, thank you," Josh said. "We just want to talk. I figure I should tell you about the body I brought back into town. It's what's started all this. I was in a town called Hawk Junction—"

"That's nice, dear," she said, cutting him off. "Can you grab the tea for me, please? I'm dying for a cup."

"Oh, sure. Where is it?"

"Straight ahead, to the right of the fireplace."

Josh looked toward the large mantled fireplace. It was big enough for both him and Amber to stand up inside. And it looked clean enough, too. There was a small pile of logs, obviously only there for show.

He doubted this thing was ever used for something as pedestrian as keeping the house warm at night.

To the right of the fireplace was an open door. He could see shelves of canned goods, preserves, and other grocery items. Josh walked inside and saw the whole room was neatly organized. At the far end was another wooden door. Beside that, he saw an entire shelf of assorted teas.

"What flavor?" he called out. He saw Amber had followed him in. She was studying the wall of cookies with great interest and he felt his stomach rumble. He realized he hadn't eaten since lunch, and it must be past seven in the evening by now. Maybe something to eat wouldn't be a bad idea.

"Surprise me," she called back.

"Will do. So, uh, this Hawk Junction place," he said, trying to pick up where he started. "It was a weird place. Not the usual removal. I..." Josh stopped. He realized he had been hearing a hissing sound since he had come in. He looked back. Amber's nose was twitching, as if she smelled something unappealing.

Josh sniffed the air. There was a definite odor in the room, like something had turned. Some of the jars of preserves must have cracked. He smelled a rotten egg smell, for sure. Suddenly, he didn't want to be in this room. He grabbed a box of tea at random, meaning to take it and leave. The hissing sound got louder. He saw the box had been hiding a small vent.

He leaned in close and the rotten egg smell hit him full in the face. His head fogged up instantly.

His vision blurred, and he thought his legs were going to give out.

"Josh?" Amber said. He turned, and he saw her eyes closing. A box of Oreo cookies dropped from her hand, hitting the wooden floor of the pantry.

"I think we'd better..." he stammered. He had to get them out of there. Something was not right. He grabbed her hand and made for the door.

Cynthia Morgan appeared, blocking his way. He made to push past her. There was some kind of gas leak, and he had to get all three of them to safety.

Something hot and hard punched him in the gut when he went to move past her. Josh looked down to see a large carving knife sticking about two inches into his abdomen. Blood began to spray out of the wound. Josh didn't feel any pain, either because of the effects of the gas, or because of the complete surprise.

The other end of the knife was being held by Cynthia. Josh saw her face had been transformed from the timid old woman who had answered the door a moment ago to the energetic, virile woman he had known. A wide, maniacal grin had turned her into some kind of malevolent elf. She seemed more alive than ever.

"I'm afraid you're not going to be leaving here, my dear." She gave him a push, and he stumbled back, his legs giving out. He hit Amber, and they both fell to the floor. Josh watched Cynthia Morgan leave the small room, closing the door behind her.

Then the world went black.

Chapter Twenty-Five

Officer Henry Ledbetter walked toward the Warlocke Funeral Home. He guzzled the last of the coffee he had picked up on the way over and tossed the disposable cup at a trashcan. The cup bounced off the rim of the can and into the bushes beyond. Henry looked around, didn't see anybody, and kept walking. He wasn't in any particular hurry. After all, it was probably just Josh and Amber with another prank.

He walked under the banner for the centennial that had been strung over the street. It had a noticeable sag to it. It was a bit of an eyesore in a town that normally prided itself on its neat and clean streets. But it wasn't his business. His shift was almost over. He just had to deal with this last-minute call before he could knock off for the day. He reached into his pocket and felt the five joints there. He had taken them from a stack they had confiscated from the Davenport kid the other day. Nobody would miss them, and Henry was practically salivating to light one up.

He reached the funeral home and opened the front door. Mr. Warlocke was waiting in the darkened foyer.

"Henry! Thank you for coming," Arthur said, grabbing his hand and shaking it.

"Not a problem, Mr. Warlocke."

"Before I get to why I called you here, I wanted to apologize for Josh's behavior earlier tonight. That must have been incredibly embarrassing for you. You are, after all, a pillar of this community."

Henry shrugged. "Yeah, it was a bit of a douche move. But he's always been a bit of a weirdo. Ya know? Even in high school."

Arthur nodded sagely. "Yes, I agree. Too much coddling from his mother, I believe."

"Oh, I'd believe that," Henry agreed. Then remembered who he was talking to and added, "Not that I think any of that was from you, sir. I would imagine the apple just, you know, fell from the wrong tree."

Arthur put his hand to his heart, as if Henry had just soothed a long burning ache. "That is so kind, Officer Henry. I'm happy that Osprey has such understanding men on the force."

Henry nodded agreement. "How can I help, Mr. Warlocke?"

"I asked for you specifically when I called the station. I didn't mention this earlier — I think you'll understand once you see it. Wouldn't have been possible, not with Joshua still here. Come with me," Arthur said and walked toward a set of stairs. Intrigued, Henry followed.

"I discovered this just before Josh's little, uh, inappropriate tomfoolery," Arthur said, leading them toward a door at the top of the stairs. Henry had been here a few times when he was a kid. Usually when Josh had to invite him over for a birthday party or something. Henry knew he was only invited because he was in the same class as Josh, and everyone in the class was invited. He knew Josh never wanted him there, just like Henry never wanted to go. Who wanted to go to some creepy funeral home for a party? He couldn't believe the family actually used to live in a place where dead people were just downstairs. So sick.

Arthur opened a door and stepped inside.

Henry recognized Josh's room, and it looked pretty much the same. He even remembered a few posters on the wall. On the bed in the middle of the room, Henry saw something that definitely wasn't there when they were kids. A pile of computers and cell phones.

"I wasn't sure what to do," Arthur said. "I knew there had been some thefts going on in town the past few weeks, but I didn't pay them much attention. I never suspected that Joshua...well..."

The old man trailed off, but Henry was looking around with growing excitement. Yes! He knew it! Everyone seemed to like this little shit, but Henry had always known Josh was a bit of a psychopath. All this time, Josh had been behind the thefts!

Henry tried to hide a smile as something else occurred to him. He could scoop the case from Craig! He had always hated that smug moron and was sick of hearing him moan and complain about the lack of excitement in town. Well, now there was excitement, and Henry was going to be the one to solve it. He just had to make sure Sonia didn't tell that he'd been tipped off by the dad. And she would, that bitch.

"I can take it from here, Mr. Warlocke," Henry said. "And don't worry. I'll be as lenient on Josh as I'm able to."

"I know you will," Arthur agreed. "But of course, the law must be upheld."

You bet it would be. That little bastard was going to pay for embarrassing him. But how the heck was he going to find him? Josh probably knew his dad was going to see all this stuff. He might have even skipped town by now.

Henry looked down at his watch. He only had a half an hour left on his shift. No time left to find Josh today. And Henry had the next two days off. Plus, he started thinking about all the paperwork that would be involved in a find like this. Maybe he would just leave Craig—

"We just got a tip off," a voice said from behind him. Henry whirled.

"Chief!" he said as Chief Braden walked into the room.

"Josh was seen heading into Cynthia Morgan's home not twenty minutes ago."

"Cynthia Morgan?" Henry said. "Why would he—"

"You don't suppose he's trying to steal from that little old woman, do you?" Mr. Warlocke asked.

Braden nodded. "Yes, that would be my guess." He turned to face Henry. "I'm glad you're here, son. Get over there and arrest Joshua Warlocke."

Henry looked back down at his watch. "Eh...I mean, Chief, my shift is almost—"

"You're the best man I have, Henry. I need you on this."

"Yeah, okay chief. I'll head there right away. But what do I do? We can't, you know, go in without just cause, right?"

"Just go there and wait for back up. Don't engage until...well...I suspect you'll know when the right time is. You have good instincts for this kind of work."

Henry nodded. Yeah, he had always thought so, too. He headed out the door, reminding himself how sweet it was going to be lording this over Craig's head. But maybe he would still share credit. That smug pretty boy would probably get a hard-on doing all the paperwork on a case like this.

ARTHUR AND CHIEF BRADEN WATCHED Henry go out the door. Arthur was giving a half-raised wave goodbye, and chief Braden had a smile on his face, showing how proud he was of one of his best men on the force.

After the kid had gone down the stairs and out of sight, a man stepped out of the bedroom at the end of the hall and watched to make sure the idiot wasn't going to come back for more instructions.

Arthur stood like a statue in mid wave, and chief Braden was smiling at the empty door frame, also statue still.

"Relax, gentlemen," the man said, a grin on his face. Every thought in the cop's head was some kind of complaint or whining, but the man knew he would follow the orders. Braden stopped smiling and Arthur put his hand down. Beyond that, neither moved.

He was getting tired of this behavior. He could control the creatures, but it was tiring. And it grew harder with each person he infected. But, if there was even one normal person around, well, the whole process seemed to work almost on autopilot. It was like a real person's mental wave lengths were what powered them. The man didn't want to think about what would happen once the takeover was complete, as it almost was. Controlling so many people was a power trip, but he also needed a break. Maybe a vacation to Hawaii when this was done.

"The bitch will take care of the kid and his girlfriend by the time the cop arrives," the man said. "And the cop will put the bitch in a cage where she belongs."

"Two birds with one stone," Arthur said in a monotone.

"Yes, couldn't have said it better myself," the man agreed.

"But what if the cop gets there before she's done?" Chief Braden asked.

"She's good at what she does," he answered himself. This wasn't an actual conversation. It was more like masturbation than human interaction. But it was better than the blue-balls that of internal thinking. And he absolutely hated talking to himself. So this was better than nothing.

"I'm sure she's cutting into them as we speak," Arthur agreed.

"But I'll get you over there as soon as we're done here," the figure said to Chief Braden. "The cop will need some babysitting to make sure everything is taken care of.

"What's more concerning to me is how close the other one is getting to the truth," he continued. "What's his name?"

"Craig," Braden said. "Officer Craig. Been working on the thefts case for weeks. Just before you turned me. But he hasn't been made aware of..."

"Us," Arther finishes the man's thought. "So what's the worst that could happen?"

"Still," he said, pondering. "I would very much like to get him alone, so we can take him out of the game all together."

"Yes, it won't be much longer till everything is... finished," Arthur says. Then stands silently.

The man sighed, then looked at the bed of electronics. "Well, we had better get this shit to the quarry."

"Waste not—" Braden began.

"—want not," Arthur finished.

The man walked to the window and peered out at the town while Arthur and Braden began taking armloads full of electronics out. They piled them into the back of the funeral van. The two of them would need to take several trips to grab it all, but he wasn't exactly sure how much more equipment they were going to need. So, better to make sure they got it all.

Outside, a man helped Warlocke and Braden as they were struggling through the front door. The man and his son held it open while the men finished up. Arthur and Braden come to life in a way they hadn't since Henry left on his assignment. The man gave a sigh of relief as the mental burden of controlling the two men was lifted from his shoulders.

"Thank you," the man said to the dad holding the door.

"No problem, Arthur," the dad said back as Arthur placed his arm load of gadgets into the back of the van.

Chapter Twenty-Six

Josh woke in the dark. He had no idea where he was. He was lying at the foot of a set of old, wooden stairs. He could see to the top, where a door stood open. The door looked vaguely familiar, but he couldn't quite place it. He could just make out the tops of what looked like pantry shelves.

That brought everything home. The door at the top of the stairs was the door he had seen in the pantry of Cynthia Morgan's house. He remembered going in, the hissing sound, the smell of rotten eggs. He remembered trying to leave and getting stabbed. Then he woke up here.

He didn't know how long he had been unconscious. His arm was pinned down behind him. He felt pressure on his back and turned his head far enough to see Amber butted up against him. She was either unconscious or dead. He couldn't tell. He tried to move to get a better look, but severe pain forced him to put his head back down. Pain from his face, arms, legs. You name it. It felt like every nerve in his body was crying out for attention. The inside of his mouth tasted like copper, and his tongue was covered in what felt like large bits of sand. He spit onto the cold concrete of the basement floor. The splatter it made was dark red. He had slid his tongue around his teeth and felt jagged edges.

"Sorry about that," Cynthia said as she stepped into the room. She was holding a thick rope in her hands. "I'm not as young as I used to be. In my prime, I could have carried you and your girl down the stairs all by myself. But now," she said, and put a hand to her back in a dramatic fashion. "Well, I figured it would be best to just roll you down the stairs and let gravity do the work for me." She chuckled to herself. "I let you tumble to my workshop. I'm glad you didn't break your neck on the way down. It would have been a shame for you to die — or even worse! Lose feeling in your body — before I'd had my chance to...well, you'll find out. I don't want to ruin all the fun. What is it you kids say these days? No spoilers?" She tittered again. Josh noted she seemed to be high as a kite. He didn't know if she was actually on drugs, or was just really excited about pushing him down the stairs.

The basement was nothing like the rest of the house. Calling it unfinished was an insult to dark and dingy basements everywhere. The walls were the exposed foundation of the house. Any interior walls were only partially boarded up, leaving gaps to the rest of the room. Cynthia Morgan grabbed him by the legs and dragged him deeper. She didn't seem to have any issues with her back that Josh could tell.

She moved him into place, hoisted him up, and plunked him down on a wooden chair. He was in the middle of some kind of storage room. The pain of the movement forced a scream out of him. She smiled, picked up a rope and got to work tying him up.

He didn't put up a fight. He didn't think he would have even been able to if he wanted. His body was screaming in pain, and his mind felt incredibly foggy. He figured whatever she had gassed them with was still at work in his system.

"Ow!" Josh yelled as Cynthia Morgan pulled the cords tight around his wrists. "You are really good at tying knots!" he said.

"Thank you," Cynthia said. "I've had a lot of practice. Though I'm feeling a little rusty. It's been a while. You'll go easy on me, won't you, dear?" She chuckled to herself and continued checking the ropes. Then she moved behind him. He had just enough range of motion that he could see her placing Amber on a chair directly behind him. He lost sight of her, but he felt something bump him from behind, and gathered she had just been placed back-to-back with him.

Cynthia repeated the process with Amber. Josh was left to check out his surroundings, which was difficult. His vision was blurry and the room wouldn't stop spinning. He guessed this was some kind of scrap booking room. Papers and binders were stacked helter skelter on a counter. Bottles of rubber cement and old photographs were scattered among the binders and papers were spilling onto the floor. Yellowed newspaper clippings hung from almost every surface, including the exposed two by fours of the walls of this small room within the basement. Most clippings had a small baggie pinned to it. Josh saw various items in the bags. Earrings. A gold watch. Some neon scrunchies. A naked baby-doll. None of it made any sense to his drugged brain, which was struggling to take it all in.

"Wha-ma…ooooh, men," came Amber's groggy voice. Then he felt a jerk and a thump from behind as Cynthia pulled the rope tight.

"OW!" Amber cried.

"Oh, how lovely!" Cynthia squealed. "I wasn't sure if you were going to join us. I haven't done a two-fer in over fifteen years!"

"Glad we could help," Amber said, slurring most of her words.

Cynthia just danced around them, checking her handiwork, making sure the ropes holding him and Amber to the chairs were secure. Satisfied that neither of them could move, Cynthia went to the outer room. Josh heard a clatter, as if she were searching for something.

"Are you okay?" Josh said.

"I guess," Amber replied. "I'm not the one that got stabbed. How are you?"

He had forgotten about the knife, but the reminder brought the throbbing pain in his abdomen to the forefront. He winced as he looked down.

"Doesn't look like it's gushing blood at the moment. I guess that means she didn't hit anything vital. Or I'm out of blood. Either one is possible."

"I don't think you're out of blood. At least not yet. Do you see any way out of here?" she asked. He felt movement and guessed she was looking around. She didn't speak for a moment.

"Oh god," she finally said. "This is the creepiest place I have ever seen in my life."

"Why is she tying us up?" Josh asked. "You'd think she would have just transformed, like the other creatures at the Home. Bitten our heads off and gotten it over with."

"Uh, Josh," Amber said. "I don't think she's one of them."

"Well, obviously she is. Normal little old ladies don't go around stabbing people and throwing them down stairs, Amber." Josh said.

"Yyyyyyes," Amber said slowly. "I would agree with your assessment, Joshua. But I think you're missing my point. She isn't a normal old lady."

"Right. So my question is, why didn't she transform into a monster? She—"

"Oh please!" Amber hissed. "How dense are you? We're tied up in a creepy basement, surrounded by newspaper clippings and bags filled with creepy death mementos. She's obviously a *SERIAL KILLER!*"

Oh man. Amber must have hit her head harder than he had thought. She wasn't making any sense.

The room was still wavering, but things were starting to come into focus. He read some of the headlines of the yellowed newspaper clippings.

*C*OUPLE *G*RIEVE FOR *T*HEIR *M*ISSING *C*HILD.

*S*EVEN *D*EAD IN *H*ORRIFIC *F*IRE.

*P*OLICE *C*ALL *O*FF *S*EARCH FOR *L*ORI *N*UNIS.

"I'm so confused," Josh finally said.

"Dude! There's a plastic baggie hanging on the wall with either beef jerky, or a human thumb. I think it's safe to say she's a serial killer."

Josh looked around and saw where Amber was looking. "I don't think that's a thumb," Josh said.

A moment of silence passed. Then Amber said, "Oh, gross!"

Josh scoffed. "No way! I've known this woman my whole life! She's not a serial killer! She's got to be one of those things."

"If she were a serial killer, she wouldn't go around advertising it!" Amber shot back. "Now stop talking and try to get us out of here." Josh felt her moving around.

"Well, don't worry," he said. "Fortunately for you, two summers ago, I thought I wanted to become a magician."

Silence. "Joshua…why the HELL would I care about that right now?!"

"Would you calm down!" he said. "I'm getting to that. I did a lot of research on Harry Houdini and learned the secret to all his tricks. Including how to escape being tied up!"

"Oh brother. I'm supposed to feel better because you know how to use Wikipedia?"

He ignored her. "The trick to getting out of being tied up is to let your muscles go limp as the ropes are being tied. Then, when you want to get out, you just tighten up your muscles, and—Gah!!!" he cried in agony as every major muscle in his body failed against the unyielding rope.

"And you scream like a little girl?" Amber said. "Good trick, Josh. What's the next step? Drip tears onto the knots to loosen them?"

"Not exactly," he said, breathing in. The sudden pain cleared away the remaining fog in his head and he could think clearly for the first time since waking up.

"That doesn't make any sense," Amber said from behind him. "Shouldn't you tighten your muscles as the rope is being tied, then relax when you want to get out? That way you create slack in the rope when you—"

"Yeah, yeah!" Josh said angrily. "You're right! I got it mixed up, okay?" He brooded as more clanging came from outside.

"Oh drat!" Cynthia said. "Where is it?"

"Do you need help out there, Mrs. M?" Josh said. "If you wanted to untie me, I'm sure I could—"

"Oh shut up!" Amber hissed.

"I'm sorry for the delay," Cynthia sing-songed. "I've misplaced some of my favorite tools. It's probably buried in the garden. I'll have to go grab it. Do hang in there, won't you? This will all be worth it in the end!" Josh heard footsteps going up the wooden stairs, followed by a door closing.

"What are the odds on this?" Amber said after Cynthia was gone.

"I'd say fifty-fifty that she's getting some kind of large knife," Josh said.

"No. I mean, what are the odds that this Creature shows up in our town taking the form of Fred Morgan?"

"What's so weird about that?" Josh asked, then realized the ridiculousness of the question. "I mean, this whole situation is bonkers. But what does it matter who it disguised itself as?"

"Well, it's a little coincidental that the man it impersonated just happened to be married to a serial killer, isn't it? I mean, who could have seen that coming?"

"Well, I can tell you Fred Morgan didn't see it coming. First, it turns out he married an ax murderer. Now, some intergalactic space being is impersonating him to take over the town he built. Poor guy."

"Oh, boo-hoo. He's been dead for fifteen years," Amber said. "I'm alive now! And I have no interest in ending up just another headline pinned up in Cynthia Morgan's murder bunker! Have you found a way out of here yet?"

Josh looked around for something within reach. He didn't see anything. But then again, even if there was something he could grab, the way she had tied them up, he wouldn't have been able to reach it, anyway. "Nothing yet. How about you?"

"Nope. Do you see anything that can cut this rope on your side?"

Josh looked down and saw a drainage grate beneath their chairs with a very suspicious looking brown stain on the floor. Obviously dried blood. He decided that probably wouldn't be useful information to share. He kept looking.

He followed the brown stain, which moved along the floor. It led to a part of the wall where there was no boarding. Just exposed studs with criss-crossing electrical wires and pipes. Then he saw something that he thought he recognized, but it certainly didn't belong in a normal basement. He studied it for a moment longer to be sure.

Josh had only attended four life drawing classes. One of them was using oil clay to create quick life studies in 3D. The instructor, some art hippie, had brought in his own homemade hot cutting wire. As Josh understood it, you used an electrical charge to super heat the thin steel wire, and you could use it to cut all sorts of things, like foam, clay—

Or human flesh. All in a fun and exciting way. Especially appealing to psychotic old ladies...apparently.

"I think I might have a way out. But I need to get down on the floor somehow," he said.

Seconds later, he heard Amber's chair scraping the floor. Then he saw a blur of movement to his right as the backs of her chair legs smacked him in the head and shoulders. He tipped, toppled for a moment, then crashed to the cold concrete floor. The tip of his nose was less than two inches from the length of steel wire strung between the studs. His landing kicked up a puff of residue from the brown stain on the floor. He heard a hissing and saw smoke drifting up from the wire. He didn't move.

"That work?" Amber said. Josh glanced her way and saw that she was still tied to her chair, but she had managed to get on her feet and was balancing in a hunched over position.

"There was, like, no hesitation for you to smack me to the ground with a chair," Josh said softly, not moving for fear that he would slice off his nose. No sense getting things started before Cynthia got there.

"Hey, you tell me you have an idea to get us out of here alive that involves you being on the floor? I'm going to put you on the floor, my friend. So what's the plan?"

"This wire in the wall is used for cutting," he said, carefully gesturing at it with his chin.

"Weird," she said.

"It's heated. I think we might be able to cut through my ropes," Josh said, grunting. He was trying to maneuver his chair up and closer to the wire without cutting off any of his precious body parts. "I need to get closer to—"

He felt his chair being pushed from behind. Amber was still balanced on her feet and was using the legs to slide him toward the wall with the death wire.

"WHOA! WHOA! WHOA!" he yelled as his shoulder came into contact with the wire. "Too close! Too close! BACK ME UP! BACK ME UP!"

"Then start giving me better instruction!" she shouted back.

The two of them managed to slide him away from the wire before his shirt caught on fire. After a brief pause to make sure they didn't hear Cynthia returning, they got back to work.

"Slowly," Josh said, speaking very deliberately, "push the legs of my chair counter clockwise. That should spin the rope into the wire."

"Now those were good instructions, Joshua!" Amber said.

They got the chair rotated, spinning Josh's back within reach of where he wanted to be. He was just able to lift his arms enough to make contact with the thick rope holding his wrists.

"I think I'm almost there," Josh said. He couldn't see the wire, so he was going slowly — he didn't particularly want to slice his arm off while he was at it.

"Uh, Josh," Amber said. He ignored her. He needed to concentrate to get this done. He thought he was making some progress. He couldn't be sure, but it felt like the tension on the rope had given slightly.

"Josh, I think you should see this," Amber persisted.

He felt a bit more slack as the cords in the rope continued giving way. Then he remembered where he was and that there was a psychopathic killer in the house with them. Carefully, he allowed his focus to shift from the burning hot wire near his wrists. He looked down.

His heart stopped at the sight of the darkened floor; a shadow cast by someone behind them.

CHAPTER TWENTY-SEVEN

Henry stood on the sidewalk outside the Morgan house, pacing back and forth. It was now twenty minutes past the end of his shift, and he could practically taste the joints he still had in his pocket. He considered for the thousandth time calling in for back-up and just leaving before they got there. It wasn't like he wouldn't be justified. He had been working since eight that morning — more like eight forty-five, but nobody saw him come in late, so he wasn't counting that as missing work.

"This sucks," he said aloud as he continued walking back and forth beside the squad car.

He didn't call in because he knew as soon as he did, Chief would show up, see he wasn't there, and then Henry would get another write up for insubordination. That and he was more and more picturing

Craig's face when he told him he had caught the guy Craig was after. It was going to be great!

But his chest was starting to tighten up. He really needed to blaze. It wasn't any different from people who needed an aspirator, right? When he had gone too long without toking up, he had difficulty breathing. It's a thing. Sonia was allowed to use her inhaler while on duty. Why should this be any different?

Henry looked around for approaching squad cars and didn't see anything.

"Screw it!" he said. He looked around for a secluded spot where he could keep an eye on the house without being seen.

Nothing on the street. But there was a neatly trimmed bush that wrapped around Cynthia Morgan's house, and Henry decided he could probably stay out of sight there. He walked to the side and peered around the corner.

A wooden fence with a gate blocked off access to the backyard. But there was a gap between the fence and the bushes — he could crouch down out of sight. And if the chief showed up, Henry could just claim he was scoping out the perimeter.

With the decision made, he made his way next to the bush, placing the joint between his teeth as he walked. He had gotten his lighter out and was pulling in smoke before his back had even touched the brick of the old woman's house. His chest relaxed with the first exhale, and he began to mellow out.

Ten minutes and two joints later, Henry put his hand on the lawn to push himself up. He had been there long enough. He still had two more joints, but he thought he shouldn't push his luck any more.

The small window behind him broke upon with a crash. The ax head that had broken through grazed him from midway up his forearm to his wrist. Henry squealed and tumbled to the side, rolling away from the house. At first, he thought he had been attacked by a swarm of bees. Then he saw the blood flowing from the tattered remains of his uniform.

He continued screaming incoherently.

Josh turned his head as far back as he could, expecting to see Cynthia Morgan hovering over them with an ax.

But nobody was there. Then where was this shadow coming from?

"There's an ass out the window," Amber said.

Josh looked up and saw a small window near the basement ceiling. Someone was outside, leaning on the side of the house. They didn't appear to be aware of the small window just behind them.

"Someone's out there!" he said. "Did you see who it is?"

"Yeah. I already said I see an ass!" Amber said. "It's Henry."

"Right. Get his attention!"

"Oh, okay. And how do you expect me to do that?"

That's when Josh felt the rope give way. His arms broke free, and he could breathe again. He pulled himself free of the rope and scrambled away from the burning wire. He had signed himself on it, but he suspected he would live — as long as he could get Amber and himself out of this godforsaken basement in one piece.

He began untying Amber's knots, which were tight. But five minutes later, she and Josh were both standing. He had considered using the wire to speed things up, but with the way his hands were shaking, he had been afraid he would end up slicing her forearm off or something.

So far, no sign of Cynthia.

"Henry!" Amber shouted. She had run over to just below the window. The basement had remarkably high ceilings — probably twelve feet, Josh guessed. Amber continued shouting Henry's name, but he didn't seem to hear. Little wonder. This basement was some kind of killing zone for Cynthia Morgan. Josh imagined it was very well soundproofed to keep the noise from reaching the outside world. This fact was also working in their favor, as Cynthia hopefully wouldn't be aware they were calling for help.

Josh made to jump, but apparently taking a tumble down a flight of stairs hadn't made him very agile. He couldn't even touch the bottom of the glass. His hand just slapped concrete.

"Get out of the way," Amber said from behind him. He turned just in time to see her rushing at him with a rusty old ax. The kind he pictured a serial killer would have in a creepy dungeon of death.

He quickly dodged out of the way as she took a running leap at the window, the axe held high over her head.. Henry was to the left. Josh saw she was aiming for an empty spot to the right of him. But at the last second, Henry put his hand down. The ax shattered the glass. A few splatters of blood rained down on Josh's face as he looked up. He shielded his eyes as glass tinkled down on him.

Henry's falsetto screaming actually hurt Josh's ear drums.

"Shut up, you moron!" Amber shouted. There was no way Cynthia had missed that. Sure enough, Josh heard pounding as someone came running down the stairs.

Cynthia Morgan burst through the basement door, carrying a black toolbox in one hand and a large machete in her other hand.

"Large knife!" Josh called deliriously. "Called it!"

"What's going on here?" Cynthia bellowed. She gasped when she saw they were free, the toolbox dropping free from her hand. "You get back in those ropes, you two," she yelled, as if they were toddlers who had left their beds after lights out.

"Henry!" Josh shouted. "Gun! Now, please!"

The screaming continued from up above as Henry tried to find the source of what had attacked him.

"Move!" Amber shouted. Josh turned just in time to see Cynthia Morgan lunging at him with the biggest knife he had ever seen in real life. On instinct, he moved to the side and sparks flew in the dark space as the machete struck the concrete foundation behind him.

Josh saw Amber push the old woman from behind with the handle of the ax. He was surprised when she barely stumbled. Cynthia must be strong as an ox!

"Henry! Little help!" he shouted to the window above. The screaming had stopped, but now he didn't hear anything. Hopefully, the idiot hadn't run away. If he had, their goose was cooked.

He dodged another blow just in time to avoid having his skull cracked open like a coconut.

"He's not back!" Cynthia screamed. "I don't care what you say! He's dead! I killed him! I don't care what you saw! He's gone!" She was flailing the blade around wildly, which for the moment meant she was easier to avoid. But soon enough, she would get hold of herself and would start hacking at him with more precision.

"Amber!" Josh yelled, looking behind her at the top of the stairs. "The door is open! Get out of here!" That's when he heard a loud noise, followed by a bright flash of light. Then darkness flowed in.

"Josh!" Amber scream. The darkness lifted, and he was on the floor again. At first, he thought Henry had finally gotten his gun out and had only managed to shoot Josh. But he looked up to see Cynthia Morgan standing over him. She must have hit him in the back of the head with the handle of her machete. He had only been unconscious for the time it took him to fall. Now she held the blade up over her head, ready to bring it down on him like an executioner. Amber stood behind her, still holding the ax. But she seemed to be frozen in place. No help there.

A *BANG* sounded in the enclosed space. Cynthia Morgan's body bucked, tripping over him and sprawling onto the floor behind. The blade went flying out of her hand.

Josh looked up to see a shaking hand holding a gun through the broken window.

He breathed a sigh of relief and laid his head down on the concrete.

Chapter Twenty-Eight

"Eyes up here, Henry," Josh said. They had been in the police station for about an hour. Josh was sitting in a chair across from Henry's desk. Henry had been checking his phone constantly while continuing to ignore Josh. To pass the time, Josh had started counting every time Henry looked at his phone.

Twenty-seven times.

When they had gotten there, Cynthia had been led through the double doors marked Holding Cells, and Josh imagined she was currently locked up. Out of sight and out of mind. Which was good, because as soon as she had been shot, she had become a real pain. Normally, getting shot would garner compassion from him, but when someone knocks you unconscious, rolls your inert body down a flight of stairs and tries to hack you two pieces with a machete, they don't earn themselves a lot of sympathy points.

Twenty-eight.

"Shouldn't you be asking me some questions?" Josh asked. Henry looked up from his phone.

"My shift ended two hours ago. I'm just waiting for someone to take over, 'kay?"

"Shouldn't Mrs. Morgan be in the hospital?" he asked.

Twenty-nine.

The phone came down. "Look, she didn't get shot bad. I only grazed her," Henry said, as if that was how he had planned things. Josh imagined that was more coincidence than any real skill on Henry's part. He had actually fired three times and the two others went completely wild. Josh was a little surprised he and Amber hadn't been hit.

"Paramedics got her all patched up," Henry continued. "And now she's safe and sound in a comfy bunk." The paramedics had also patched him and Amber up. They wanted to take the two of them to the hospital, but Chief Braden had shown up by then, and he had insisted that they all go to the station.

At first, Henry had been razzing Josh about arresting him and how Henry had known all along that this day would come. Josh had been informed of his rights and told he was under arrest for the thefts that had been happening around town for the past several weeks. Knowing that the Chief of Police had been turned, this hadn't come as a great surprise to Josh.

But since getting to the station, Henry had completely lost interest in him. It was obvious he just wanted to go home.

Josh looked around. Sonia was in her usual spot at the front. But the rest of the office seemed dead. There was only one other officer at their desk.

A figure peered into Henry's cubicle and Josh recognized the Chief of Police. Josh shrunk down. He was pretty sure he was safe as long as they were out in the open. But really, who knew? It felt like having someone point a loaded weapon at you. You figured they wouldn't actually pull the trigger, but how could you know?

The chief glanced down at Josh, then up at Henry. "I thought I told you to wait till I got there before going in?" Braden said.

Henry stood up, grabbing his car keys from the desk. "Sorry, Chief. I heard screaming. I had to take action." Josh noted Henry failed to mention that the screams had been coming from him. "And the Morgan bitch attacked me with an ax," he said, holding up his arm to show the bandages. Both he and Amber had prudently neglected to tell Henry that she had been the one holding the ax when it struck him.

The chief put up his hands to stop Henry from talking. "Okay. I get it." He looked down at Josh, who gave a weak smile. "I'm going to want to talk to you. There are some serious charges you're going to have to answer for." Josh nodded, hoping the loaded gun wouldn't fire. After a tense moment, Braden turned back to Henry. Josh resumed his lifelong habit of breathing.

"Send him to my office in a few minutes. I'll question him privately," he said. Josh's eyes widened. He had to get out of there. Being alone with one of those things was definitely not the situation he wanted to be in.

"Uh, yeah, can you take him now?" Henry said. He was actually whining as he spoke. "I was supposed to be done hours ago."

"Just wait two minutes and send him in, okay?" The chief made to leave, then stopped. "How's Cynthia Morgan?"

"Fine, sir. I guess."

"I want her comfortable in her cell. Nobody bothers her. You hear me?"

"Uh, yeah. Sure." Henry said. "She's fine."

"Did you remove all her belongings before she went into the cell? Jewelry, belt. Anything she could harm herself with?"

"Uh...not jewelry. She's got old lady hands, chief." Henry held up his own, curling it into an arthritic claw to demonstrate.

"Okay. Well, nobody goes into the cells, got it?" And with that, the chief walked to his office. Josh watched him as he went into a room with frosted windows for walls and closed the door. Josh thought about being on the other side of those frosted walls, his soul being gobbled up, his skin torn apart, knitting itself back together with some monster inside.

He saw another man was already in the office. The stranger stood up and Josh could see him looking through the glass into the outer office. He felt whoever it was looking at him. The infamous Fred

Morgan, perhaps? Or at least the creature that was taking his form.

He turned back to Henry, frantic. "Henry, you gotta let me go. They're going to…" To what? What could he say to Henry that would make him understand? Let alone believe him.

"Forget it, man. You do the crime, you do the time."

"I told you, I didn't steal anything. They're just saying that to…" He paused, feeling silly, but said it anyway. "To frame me."

"Uh-huh. Whatever. It's probably been two minutes. Can you just go in so I can leave?" Henry said, packing up his stuff and standing.

"Hey guys," Amber said, walking up to the desk. Josh had been so focused on his imminent absorption into the local creature culture, he had mostly forgotten about her. She had been dismissed at Cynthia's house after the paramedics had evaluated her — she had only sustained a number of cuts and bruises on her face and arms. Josh hadn't seen her since.

"You're going to have to leave," Henry said, not even trying to hide his annoyance. "Josh is about to be questioned by the chief for his criminal activity. And I'm leaving. I'm about three hours past my shift," he said.

"Chief of police, huh?" Amber said, looking down at Josh. He tried to express as much panic in his eyes as he could. He mouthed the words, "Help me."

"Yeah," Henry was saying, coming around the desk. "So let's go, Dom Toretto. Chief wants to talk to you."

Josh stood up. "Okay! I'm going, Henry. I can make my own way. It's just across the room. You can head out!"

"Yeah, right. I'll take you there, then I'll head out. I'm not an idiot. Come on," Henry said, and began pushing him toward the door. Josh fought back. It was more involuntary than anything like bravery. He just saw himself being pushed toward the door and his body responded as if he was being pushed toward a cliff's edge. Which he felt like he was. Henry began to push back.

"Stop fighting, freak! He's just going to ask some questions! Don't be such a pansy!"

"Henry, can you show me where the bathroom is?" Amber said, putting her hand on his arm.

"Ask Sonia!" Henry shot back. "Can't you see I'm busy?" He turned his attention back to Josh. "Come on, don't make this a big thing, man."

"No!" Josh shouted. "He's going to..." Josh's panic was starting to take over. "He's going to kill me, Henry! Trust me. Something is going on. Things are—"

"Fuck this!" Henry said, and put his whole body into pushing Josh toward the door. Sonia stood up at her desk across the room.

Josh felt the increased pressure, and that's when he lost all control. Panic took over, and he pushed back, trying to circle around Henry like a quarter-back performing a sneak.

It didn't work. Josh was surprised when Henry proved to be a semi-capable police officer. He grabbed Josh as he was coming around and threw him to the ground, pinning him down with a knee in the small of Josh's back. Josh heard the rattle of cuffs as his face was forced down.

"Guess I should have cuffed you to begin with. I didn't think it would be necessary, but I won't make that mistake a—"

Josh heard a hollow sound like something striking wood, and Henry bucked wildly. Then the officer went limp, falling on top of him. He heard Sonia scream from across the room.

He felt Henry's weight roll off of him, and Amber helped him to his feet. Josh was shocked to see a gun in her hand.

"Shut up!" she shouted at Sonia, waving the gun around. Josh wondered for a second where she had gotten it before he eyed the empty holster lying on Henry's desk and breathed a sigh of relief. Henry had left his gun unattended with civilians around. The world made a bit of sense — at least in one area. Henry was still a bad cop.

Chief Braden's door burst open as the creature that was impersonating him stepped out into view. Josh saw the mysterious figure reappear in the frosted glass of the window.

"Stay back!" Amber said, still waving the gun. "I don't know what the FUCK you Things are, but don't come any closer, okay? We're getting out of here. Leave us alone!

"Come on, Josh!" she said, and they both turned and ran out of the room.

Henry woke up to find the place in chaos. At least, as much chaos as could be created by only four people. His head ached and Josh and Amber were nowhere in sight. He stood up, realizing he had been knocked unconscious. Not for very long, but enough to miss the excitement.

"Ledbetter," the Chief yelled at him. Oh crap. He was in trouble now.

"Yeah Chief," Henry said.

"Can I see you in my office, please?"

Henry sighed. Truth be told, he was a little relieved. He figured he would be suspended, and that just meant a weeklong vacation. Sure, he would miss out on some pay. But the time off would be nice.

He walked into the chief's office, closing the door behind him.

Chapter Twenty-Nine

Josh woke from a daze. He had spent time in this park as a kid, but in the light of mayhem, the nostalgia wasn't quite hitting the same. He and Amber had run from the police station, not sure where to go. They hadn't stopped running until they had come through the clearing and collapsed in the same spot they were at…had that really only been a few hours ago?

The park was deserted. Josh and Amber sat, staring at nothing. They sat that way for a long time. His chest was so tight, Josh could barely catch a solid breath. Fear and worry were clinging to him like a strong odor.

"I've been in police custody two times in the past month," Josh said, breaking the silence. "I've never even had a speeding ticket before this. I haven't even littered."

"Everybody has littered," Amber said.

"Only by accident!"

Silence. "I attacked a police officer," Amber said. "Probably killed him."

"No, he was fine. I checked. Snoring like a baby."

"Figures. I can't even kill a man properly."

"You're pathetic," Josh said. "But I'm a fugitive from the law."

"Thief," Amber chided.

"And you're my co-conspirator!"

Amber rolled her eyes. "Please. You're MY co-conspirator!"

"How did this even happen?"

"Uh, you brought an otherworldly testicle-monster to our small town. Like an idiot."

"I was just doing my job."

"You know who else was, 'just doing their jobs?'"

"Don't say the Nazis," Josh said. "It's disrespectful." His gaze drifted over the downtown section of Osprey. Nothing on the street moved. No cars driving home from a late shift. No teenagers cruising in cars borrowed from their parents. Just utter and terrifying stillness.

A police car could come rolling along any second. They were practically on display.

"You know, we probably shouldn't be sitting here," he said, looking around. "We're really out in the open."

"Yeah. We'll leave," Amber said and yawned. Her eyelids drooped. It had been a busy evening, and the morning didn't show any sign of slowing down.

Josh shifted and shared her yawn.

"Thanks for coming back to get me, by the way," he said.

"Not a big deal," she said. "I pretty much had to."

"Oh? And why is that?"

"Cause right now, I think you're the only one in this crazy town I can trust."

"It can't be that bad," Josh said. "Can it?"

"Can't it? Sure, this Thing couldn't have gotten everyone. But it's gotten someone. Lots of someones, actually. Everybody who's a client at the Home. Probably a lot of people who've been at the hospital in the past few weeks. It obviously got the police chief. And all that was seven hours ago. Who knows who else it's gotten since our little adventure started?" She paused. Josh caught the hesitation in her voice, like she was going to say something, but didn't.

"What?"

"Nothing."

"Come on, tell me. I'm your co-conspirator, remember? You said you can trust me."

"That's just it. Can I actually?"

That shook him out of his daze. "Of course. Why—"

"You've been living with your dad for weeks when he was actually…that Thing. How do I know you didn't get turned? Or, for that matter, you were with that body for three days! How do I know you didn't come back as one of Them? How do I know you didn't, like, start all this? Turned your dad and…" she trailed off.

Josh paused. He hadn't thought of it like that. He was pretty sure he was himself. But she made a good point.

"Look, as difficult as it is, that's not helpful. I can assure you, I'm not one of those Things," he said. "That body was frozen the whole ride—"

"*Most* of the ride."

"Okay, yes, it was pretty thawed when I got here. But I think it was more interested in getting here. I don't think it could have gotten to me if it'd wanted."

"Well, clearly it did get to you."

"What do you mean?"

"You said you were driving in your sleep, right? Ever done that before?"

"...no."

"So whatever that thing is, it was using you. Which means that it took over your brain to do it. I mean, how do we know it didn't...I don't know... do something to you then? Infected you through brainwaves or something."

"I'm pretty sure it needs to touch you or something to—"

"Do you know that? Really? Who the hell knows anything about what's going on? Not me!"

Josh was quiet. He realized that he couldn't be positive she wasn't part of...whatever it was. He thought back to the night he had discovered his dad unconscious in the Home. She said she had been upstairs when that thing had taken over his dad. Cleaning the attic or something. Was she? How could he know?

"I guess," he started, "we have to trust each other. I think we've saved each other's lives enough by now to know we're on the same side. Though it would be nice if there was some way for us to tell who was a monster and who wasn't."

Josh shook his head, trying to clear his thoughts. He got up with a bit more effort than he had expected. "Let's go. We shouldn't be here."

"What?" Amber said. She looked drugged.

"You're right. It did take control of me. Whatever this is has some kind of psychic abilities. It can control people. And it's controlling us right now."

Amber looked around. "No, we're just tired. Fright and stuff is pretty draining on the body. Right?"

"Yeah, but I think it's more than that."

"Huh?"

Josh thought back. "I think whatever these things can do…" he paused, trying to work things out. He held up an index finger, pointing to it. "They took control of me to force me to drive. Granted, I was asleep. That didn't happen when I was awake. So they might not be able to take control of our bodies willy-nilly."

"Okay," Amber said, listening.

Josh held up a second finger. "They send thoughts. I remember having some really weird urges. Like to grab a cop's gun and start shooting. It sounded like my own thoughts at the time, and I chalked it up to being exhausted. But I think it was that Thing sending thoughts into my head."

"Weird," Amber said.

He held up a third finger. "They read thoughts."

"How do you know that?" she asked.

"Cause that thing's been impersonating my dad for weeks and I wasn't aware of it. How can something do that? I would imagine that when it melds with something, it downloads whatever is in their brains. That's probably part of it. But I bet you it's also reading our brains when we're around them. Reading our thoughts and giving us the impression of the person we think they are. Dad was...very accommodating the last few weeks. I remember thinking he was acting different, but not in a suspicious way. More in a 'This is the type of dad I've always wanted' way."

"Okay, I think I get what you're saying," Amber agreed. "You think it knows where we are?"

"I don't know. I hope not. I think we have to assume it doesn't."

"Why?"

"Cause if it does, then there would be no reason for us to even try stopping it. It would pretty much be omniscient."

Amber paused, seeming to think things through. But was she thinking? Or did she just look like she was thinking and was actually one of them, busy transmitting their location to the rest of the—

Stop it! He shouldn't start doubting her! This was going to be tough enough without adding that kind of mistrust into the mix.

"So what does that mean?" she asked.

"We need to find a better place to hide," Josh said. Then he looked around, not exactly sure where they could go and not be found.

"What about Cynthia Morgan?" Amber asked after a while.

"What about her?"

"Where does she fit in?"

Josh shrugged. "I guess she doesn't. She's clearly not one of them."

"So you think it's just coincidence that there happens to be a serial killer living in this town that nobody knew about? Married to the godfather of Osprey."

Josh considered this.

"You said Fred Morgan died in a boating accident while on the lake with his wife?"

Josh nodded. "That was the story, yeah. Now it turns out Cynthia was behind it."

"Makes you think that something might have been going on long before this Thing got here," she said.

"What do you mean?"

"Well...how does such a high-profile woman as Cynthia Morgan hide in plain sight for decades like this? She would either need to be very good at keeping herself secret... or..." she trailed off.

"Or have some powerful people helping her keep the secret," Josh said, finishing her thought.

"Like a chief of police who could steer people away from certain obvious crimes. Or a..." she stopped mid thought.

"What?"

"Nothing," she said. But she had a guilty look on her face, like she was keeping something from him. She looked around. "We should definitely get out of here."

"Right," he said. "But I also think it's time we get some outside help. This is way too big for us," Josh said. "Give me your phone."

"Who are you calling?" she asked as she slapped it in his hand.

"Jim."

"Oh. Mr. Crazy-man? You think he's going to have a change of mind about helping us?"

"We need to try something," Josh said, searching through Amber's recent calls list. "Maybe I can reason with him. If he won't help, we'll start calling whoever we can. Police in another town, maybe? Maybe figure out how to call the army, or..." he trailed off.

"What's wrong? Not picking up? It's the middle of the night, remember?"

"No. There's nothing. I can't get a signal."

"What?" she said, grabbing the phone. "I always have a signal." She looked at the screen. Josh saw there was zero reception.

"That's weird," she said.

"Try calling 9-1-1. I think I heard you can always reach an emergency line. By satellite or something."

She tapped away, then put the phone in her pocket, shaking her head. "Nope. Nothing. We could try moving around."

"Yeah," Josh said. But he had his doubts that they would find a signal anywhere in town.

He held out his hand to her. "We need to find some place to hide. The Home is obviously out."

"How about your place?" she asked.

"No. Dad — or It posing as dad — has been living there for weeks. I'm sure they would look there."

"How about my place?"

He hesitated. He didn't know where she lived and he had known her for over a year. But still, it didn't seem like the smartest place to hide.

"Come on! We don't need to be there long. Just some place to get hunker down for a few minutes and make a plan. I can't think out here," she said, gesturing at the pitch blackness around them.

"Well…" Josh started, unable to come up with an alternative. "Yeah, let's go. What's the worst that could happen?"

"The worst that could happen is it's the wrong move, and we get turned into horrible shape-shifting monsters," Amber said with a smile.

He glared at her as they headed to the main street area, keeping an eye out for anyone that might be watching. They moved quickly, trying not to draw attention to themselves.

As they hurried along the sidewalk, Josh paused beneath the banner that he had watched being strung across the street a few weeks before. WELCOME TO OSPREY! '100 YEARS OF GRANDEUR'.

The rope holding up the right side of the banner had given way and nobody had been around to fix it. The banner hung unreadable, flopping in the wind, lazily smacking the pole of the streetlight.

Not knowing why he did it, Josh undid the rope that held it in place. The banner slipped out of the pulley and settled to the ground, landing partway on the road. Josh looked down at it for a moment.

Then, feeling sad and alone, he resumed walking, following Amber into the darkness of the night.

PART THREE

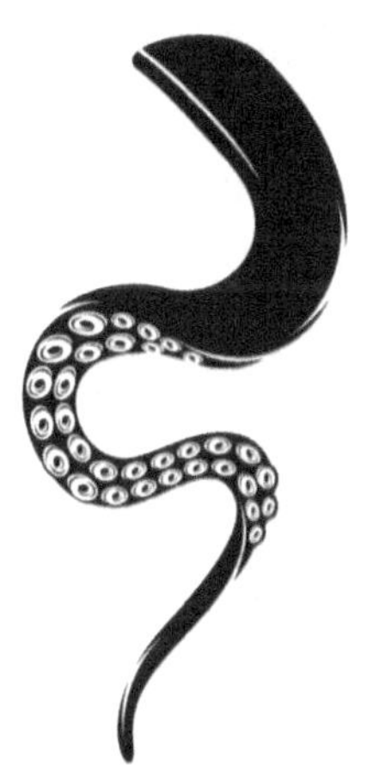

Chapter Thirty

Sonia was way beyond frustrated. She had been at the call desk for almost twenty-four hours and nobody seemed to notice or care. Her shift relief hadn't come in the night before and the only thing the chief had said was that if she could find a replacement, she could leave. Which didn't exactly feel legal to her, but she had never been the type to question authority figures. "Yes, sir," was all she had said, and he'd walked out to God knew where.

Which was strange. As long as Sonia had worked there, Chief Braden had made it a point to always tell her where he was when not in his office, in case there was an issue, and she needed to get a hold of him. He would sometimes even do it when he wasn't on duty. But the past few weeks, he had been in and out of the building, seemingly at random, and she often had trouble contacting him.

Sonia looked at the phone. She was waiting for Jill, one of the other dispatchers, to call back to relieve her. But so far, no Jill. That was another strange thing. The place had been unorganized for the past few weeks. People not showing up for their shifts. Calls being ignored when they were on shift. The whole operation seemed to be falling apart. And when that operation was a police station, that wasn't a good thing. It was a pretty bad turn when one of the most reliable officers was Henry Ledbetter. He at least had seemed his usual asshole self. But his shift ended last night, and she hadn't seen him since he had walked out of Chief Braden's office. He had looked terrible, but she assumed that was probably because he had been suspended, which meant she couldn't rely on him anymore. She just hoped things would turn around with everybody else.

"He didn't stop by his desk," she said. She looked around guiltily when she realized she had spoken out loud. She hoped no one heard her talking to herself.

Then she remembered that the office was deserted. Just her and the chief, who was still locked in his office, out of earshot. What was going on here? She hadn't seen anyone come in for hours.

Her mind turned back to Henry. She stood up and walked around her desk, hesitantly peering into his cubicle, like she was some kind of super spy. And she had been right. There, sitting on his desk, were his car keys. Which was very odd because Henry didn't exactly live close. She had made the mistake of agreeing to go on a date with him several months ago, and they had gone to his place. She was afraid she would have to spend the night brushing off his sexual advances, but instead, he had passed out playing "God of War" while she sat on his couch, watching.

So she knew he lived a good half an hour drive from the precinct. So where did he go?

"Are you still here?" a voice said from behind her. She whirled, startled by the sudden sound in the unbroken stillness of the office.

"Craig!" she said with honest relief. She had never been so happy to see a familiar face. And he had actually noticed her.

"I thought you were finishing up when I left," he said, walking to his desk and setting his gym bag down. "You doing a double?"

"Not intentionally," she said. "Things have been…weird around here."

"Yeah, totally," he agreed, looking around. "Where is everyone?

"That's part of the weirdness. It's just us," she said. "And the chief. He's in his office. There was a bit of excitement last night," she said, thinking about the Warlocke kid and his girlfriend. Another thing for the bonkers pile. She had never had a day that had gone from mind numbingly boring to terrifying so quickly. She couldn't believe the girlfriend had actually pulled a gun on her.

Sonia was about to tell Craig about Cynthia Morgan, who had turned out to be the town's own serial killer. She figured he probably hadn't heard, as his shift finished just before Cynthia had come in. But Sonia was interrupted by the Chief coming out of his office.

"Philips! Perfect. I need you out there looking for the Warlocke kid!"

Sonia saw Craig do a double take. "Warlocke? Josh? Why am I looking for him?" he asked.

"Haven't you heard? He and some female accomplice stole Henry's gun last night and ran away. After pistol whipping him over the back of the head with it. They did us at least one favor, there."

"What?! Why?" Craig said. Sonia was amused to hear his voice go up two registers.

"I told you it was a crazy night," she said. "Two fugitives and a serial killer."

Craig made a face. "Serial killer?" he said, glaring at her. She could tell he thought she was putting him on.

"Never mind Cynthia. She's behind bars. I want Josh and this woman found and locked up, too. Do we have a last name for this Amber person yet?"

"Uh..." Sonia stammered, wracking her brain. "Allen, sir."

"Wait, there is a serial killer?" Craig asked, falling farther behind in the conversation.

"I said never mind Mrs. Morgan! Just go find Josh and this Allen girl."

"Chief, I'm so confused. What did Josh do? Like, BEFORE becoming a fugitive."

"He's the one who's been stealing electronics," Braden said impatiently. "Henry found a bunch in his bedroom yesterday. We arrested him and he pulled a gun."

"Chief, I've known Josh my whole life. He's not the thief."

Braden turned and put his hand on his hip. "Did you miss the part where I said he pulled a gun and knocked out Henry? You can't put your own feelings for suspects ahead of the facts, Craig!"

"Actually, Amber Allen pulled the gun and bashed Henry," Sonia corrected. She was ignored.

"No, that's not what I mean. Whatever is going on is too big for Josh. This can't be just one guy. This theft thing is huge! Some of them had to be inside jobs, like at the university. It's not just some lone wolf, Chief."

"Listen to me," Braden said. He grabbed Craig by the shoulder, then make brief eye contact with Sonia, as if he was checking to see if she was still there. She busied herself at her desk. Then he turned back to Craig. "Craig, they're running around with a loaded gun. Just find him. We'll argue about the case later, okay?"

"Okay. Sorry Chief. Yes, sir." Craig turned and grabbed his duffel bag off the desk. "I'll just get my gear on and—"

"Don't bother with that. Just get out there," Braden said.

"You don't want me in uniform?" Craig said, looking stunned.

"It's not important. Just find him. Radio me when you do. I want him brought to me as soon as you have him. Got that?"

"Yes, sir," Craig said.

Braden nodded and went back into his office.

"Okay, I know I always said I wanted more excitement around here," Craig said, turning to

Sonia. "But this is a bit more than I was expecting."
She barked laughter. She understood what he meant.

"Something is definitely going on around here," he said, looking toward the Chief's office.

"You'd better get out there," she said, looking at him. "If Braden comes back out and sees you still here, he's going to be upset."

Craig looked at her. "You should leave, too," he said.

"I can't. There's no one to cover my shift."

He looked around the room. "There's nobody covering anybody's shifts," he said. "Something's going on and I don't think there will be a need for a dispatcher. Especially if there are no cops to dispatch. Ya know?"

"Yeah. Okay. I'll go as soon as the Chief leaves. I think he's heading somewhere."

"Good," Craig said. He turned, grabbed his bag off his desk and walked out the door, leaving Sonia to listen to the hum of the A/C in the otherwise quiet office.

She started gathering her things, realizing that Craig had been right. There was absolutely no reason she needed to be there.

The door to the chief's office opened and out came Braden. But he wasn't alone. She had completely forgotten in all the chaos. She had seen an older man go in there several hours ago. She didn't know who it was, but he had gone in under his own strength when he had arrived. Now, he didn't look capable of breathing, let alone walking on his own. He had his arm slung around Braden's shoulder and the Chief was helping the man make his way across the room.

Sonia hadn't really gotten a good look at him on his way in, but the impression in her head was of a much younger man than what she was seeing now. He was making his way toward her.

Chief looked around the room. "Craig gone?"

"Yes sir," Sonia said. "Off on the case. Um…am I still needed, sir?" She laughed and looked around the room. "The phone or radio hasn't peeped in hours."

To her surprise, the old man spoke, as if he were in charge. "I think we're done with her," he said. "We need to get going to the quarry. Lots to do there. We'll need all the bodies we can to finish this in time."

Sonia had no clue what that meant. Nor who this old man was. She was about to ask when the chief's hand came down on hers. She jumped, startled. The chief held on.

At first, nothing happened, and she was trying to figure out how to pull her hand away from him without being rude. She briefly wondered if this was considered sexual harassment.

Then she felt something wriggle on the back of her hand. Like his palm was covered in maggots. This was followed by stinging pain. It felt like the skin on her hand was being pulled apart, separating like torn cloth.

She cried out and tried to pull away from his grip. He held on tighter. She began to scream when the Chief's hand began to sink into her own. She pulled furiously, but his grip was iron, and she only succeeded in ramming her abdomen into the desk between them. Desperate, she grabbed a stapler from her desk and began to beat at the Chief's hand.

"Hurry it up, please," the older man said. He turned and began shambling out the door. "I'm going to lie down in the car till we're ready to go. We'll come back for Cynthia when it's time." And with that, the man shuffled slowly out the front door.

Meanwhile, Sonia watched in agony as the skin on her arm began to melt and release a kind of pus that began flowing *UP* her arm, toward her shoulder, neck and head.

"Please!" she screamed. "What is this?! Wha—"

The chief's other hand plunged forward, ramming into her face. She felt his fingers plunge into her eye sockets. Her eyeballs gave way with a sickening pop.

With the sensation of sight gone, it didn't take long for all her other senses to die out, too.

Chapter Thirty-One

Josh pulled back the curtain and peered out the window at the dying town. He had been watching the death cycle for a couple of hours and was so fascinated — and horrified — that he couldn't look away. Nothing about Osprey looked wrong. The sun was coming up, showing all the same beautiful houses. Sure, some of the usually meticulously manicured lawns were getting a bit shaggy, but not so bad that anyone would get fined. Just a few days past prime mowing. But things were definitely wrong.

His eyes moved from house to house, noting several doors hanging open. He knew these houses were now empty, the occupants no longer concerned with keeping their valuables safe.

He watched a small boy, probably six — Josh could never tell kids' ages — moving down the sidewalk. The boy's eyes were vacant, his face dirty.

"Here comes another one," Josh said to himself. He was whispering so as not to wake Amber, who was asleep in her room. He continued watching the scene unfold below, wanting to either turn away or find a way to help. He couldn't do either, so he watched.

The boy veered onto a path leading to a house. He mounted the porch and rang the bell. Josh watched as, moments later, the door opened. A woman looked down at the boy. They were across the street, but at enough of an angle that Josh could see the boy breaking down in tears as soon as the door was open. He couldn't hear them, but he had been watching similar scenes like this unfold all night while Amber slept. He could guess what they were saying. It had become a sick little game that he had been playing. Like putting on a play written by Satan.

"Little Timmy," Josh said in a monotone. "What's wrong?" Across the street, the woman kneeled to the boy's level, peering to the right and left of the door.

"I can't find my mom and dad," Josh replied. The boy put his face in his hands, weeping. "They're not at my house."

"Oh, honey, come inside," Josh said for the woman. "We'll find them." The woman guided the boy inside. She turned and closed the door behind her. There was sudden movement behind the glass of the door. Josh let out a soft moan.

The front door hadn't latched when she closed it and it began to swing back open, slowly revealing the woman, who was pinned against the wall. Little Timmy's arm was plunged into her abdomen, up to his tiny elbow. The woman was convulsing as the dead faced little boy-puppet began to infect her with whatever evil was inside itself. Josh had watched it happen more than half a dozen times on this street and he doubted it was the only place this was happening in Osprey.

He heard Amber enter the room, but didn't turn away. Couldn't turn away. He watched the whole thing. Amber sat down next to him. Josh dropped the curtain back into place, cutting off his view of the scene below.

"What's up?" she asked.

"They're starting to get serious," Josh sighed. "Whatever's happening in this town, it's coming to a head. I guess a chess player would say the end move is coming."

"Is that how chess players talk?" Amber asked, wryly.

"I don't know," Josh said. "I don't play chess." He didn't feel in the mood for banter.

She nodded to the window. "What's happening out there?"

"They're going from house to house."

"Looking for us?" She said, concerned.

"No. Turning people. Any house that looks occupied, someone will show up, knock on the door, and infect the person that answers. Then everyone else that's in the house."

"I guess hiding is done now," she said.

Josh nodded. "After everyone is turned, they all empty out of the house, going somewhere."

"What direction are they going?" Amber asked.

"Nowhere specific. Every direction." He shook his head, trying to bring himself out of the morose, helpless state he was in. He suspected that part of the feeling was the lulling vibes the monsters were sending out, which had given him a groggy feeling that he hadn't been able to shake since the park. He thought of it like the venom some spiders used to paralyze their victims to make them easier to web up and store for food.

But another part was just the reality of the situation they were in. The realization that his hometown was no longer the place he grew up in. That the people weren't all who he thought they were. He lived in a place where a prominent woman was a repulsive killer. The chief of police covered up those crimes. Even his own father was likely...complicit. It was enough to make anybody doubt the world they thought they knew.

He shook his head. He had been doing that a lot. It was easy to give in to the lulling tones in his head that told him not to care. To just sit and give up.

"We shouldn't be here," he said. Amber's place was too obvious. It was only a matter of time before someone came looking here.

"Nobody knows where I live," she insisted. "I've only been here a year and I don't make friends. I collect books," she said, indicating the walls covered in shelves of them. "They're my friends."

"SOMEBODY knows you live here. What about your landlord?"

"She lives in the building, but she's been on some old lady cruise in Florida for the past month."

Josh thought. "What about my dad? You had to give your address to be an employee at the Home."

She made a face. "Okay, confession time. I may not officially be an employee for the home."

"What?" he said.

"Your dad is paying me under the table," she said.

"What?" he repeated.

"Yeah. Cheaper for him and easier for me," she said.

"Well, I guess that's probably not the worst secret I think my dad was keeping from me," Josh said, starting to wonder how well you could really know anyone.

"What do you mean?"

"I've been thinking more about what we were talking about. How there had to be more going on to hide that Cynthia Morgan was a serial killer all these years."

"Yeah..."

"If she was killing people, but no bodies were being discovered, they'd need a place to dispose of those bodies," he said, thinking about the furnace at the Home. It would be the perfect place to get rid of unwanted evidence.

"Yeah, I kind of thought of that, too. But do you think your dad knew the people were murdered?"

Josh hesitated. "I doubt he would have gone along if he outright knew about them," he said. At least that's what he wanted to believe. He thought his dad had at least that much integrity. But he also thought about how his dad would always be looking to earn an extra buck or two. "If he was being paid to look the other way…I doubt he would have asked where the bodies were coming from."

"We don't know that," Amber said, then fell silent. That silence told Josh everything she thought of his dear old dad.

"We need to figure out what we're doing," he said, changing the conversation.

"Well," Amber said. "I need some thinking fuel. You want some tea?"

Josh made a face. "Never touch the stuff. You don't have any coffee?" he asked for the third time since arriving at her place the previous night.

"Why would I have coffee? I told you. I don't drink it."

"It's kind of a staple. You should have it on hand for guests."

"I don't do, 'guests,'" she replied. "Remember? Books! Anyway, my coffee habits aside, don't you think we should talk about the monsters in town?"

"You don't drink coffee! That means you are the monster in town."

"Har, har. I'm glad you're coming out of your funk, but let's get back onto the topic of the people who are dying in town."

"Right. Sorry. Okay, I think we need to start with what we know."

"We don't know squat."

"Well, we don't really know what we know." He looked around. "Do you have a white board?"

"Do I look like a schoolteacher?"

"Paper? Something?"

"Just a second," she said, sighing and getting up. She walked over to a printer, opened the tray, and fished out some blank sheets. She came back holding a black marker. "Here you go. Are we going to write down our wills?"

"No. We're taking stock."

"Meaning?"

"If you ever get stranded on an island or out in the wilderness, the first thing you should do is take everything you have and lay it out in front of you. That way, you know exactly what you have to survive."

"And hope you just happen to have a hatchet with you on your trip?"

"That'd be nice, but I doubt we have a hatchet. Real or figurative." Josh drew a couple of lines on the page, creating a header and columns. "Okay, what do we know?"

"There's a monster in town infecting people, turning them into other monsters," Amber said. "That's about it.

"That's actually more than one thing," Josh said as he began writing. At the top of the first column, he wrote 'What it is…' and in the second column, he wrote 'What it can do…' After a short pause, he wrote in a third column, 'How to stop it…' Then in the first column, he wrote the word monster.

"We know there is something in town. Monster isn't really a helpful word. It's too vague. But something that is taking the shape of Fred Morgan is in Osprey, and is slowly taking it over."

"It doesn't feel very slow," Amber said. "That's about all we know, isn't it?"

"No. It infects people. It makes them like itself." He wrote 'infects' in the second column. "After tonight, I think we're qualified enough to assume that it has to make some kind of physical contact," Josh said, noting that in the middle column.

"But we don't know why," Amber said.

Josh thought. "Well, I'm not so sure. It's not just eating. If it were, then it would be staying the same size. Maybe getting a little larger, but mostly staying the same. This thing isn't just eating. It's multiplying! In that sense, it is getting bigger." He wrote multiplying in the second column, under infecting.

"Okay," Amber said, seeming to pick up the style of what Josh was doing. "We know it infects people. So what?"

"But not just that. It can also control them, as we know it controlled me to get here. I think it's safe to say that it can communicate with each other, too." Josh wrote more words down in the columns.

Amber was quiet for a moment and Josh let her process. "I think you're missing a column."

"How so?"

"We need a 'Why' column. Why is it doing what it's doing?"

"I don't think we know any—"

"Why did it take control of you when you were driving?"

"It wanted to get to the town," Josh said, shrugging.

"Yeah, but you were already headed here. Assuming that here is where it wanted to be at all, why did it matter if you stopped to sleep for a few hours?"

Josh pondered that. "Because it needed to get here faster!" he said, excited. "You're a genius," he said and wrote some more down.

"So that's assuming it cared where it was going. There are people everywhere."

"Yeah, but think about the strange situation that brought it here to begin with. A transfer from a morgue out of nowhere? It had to have set this up."

"We're giving a lot of credit to this thing."

"It can think, it can control. I think we have to assume it's smart enough to have a plan."

"Okay, so it wanted to get here faster to…what?"

"There's something it needs to do. It's either just impatient, or whatever it needs to do has a time frame. A ticking clock."

"Maybe it needs to infect enough people for something," Amber said.

"Something that's happening soon," Josh said, continuing the thought.

"But what?"

And on that point, Josh was stumped. He just gave a frustrated shrug.

"I can't help but notice you've written a lot in the first two columns, but we don't have jack for this one." She tapped the last column that said, 'How to stop it…'

Josh sighed. "Yeah, that one's eluding me."

"Ditto," Amber said, throwing up her hands. "So we're not back where we started! We never left."

A knock on Amber's apartment door startled them out of their thoughts.

"I'm going to assume you're not expecting any-one?" Josh said in a whisper. She shook her head.

The knock came again. "Hello?" a voice said from outside the door. Amber tiptoed over and peered out the peephole. "Ms. Allen?" a man's voice from the other side said.

"Who is it?" Josh whispered when she had joined him by the window.

"I don't know," Amber said. "I mean, he looks familiar. I think I've probably seen him before, but… it's difficult to tell."

"What?"

"He's naked. I'm pretty sure he wouldn't have been naked whenever I saw him before."

Josh walked quietly over to the door and peered out. There was definitely an almost naked man outside Amber's door. Naked except for a pair of boxer brief underwear. Man, things must really be escalating out there. They weren't even trying to blend in anymore.

But Josh recognized the face almost immediately. He made his way back over to Amber.

"It's Lawrence Hardlock. He's a handyman in Osprey. Fixes pretty much anything. Furnaces, A/C units, plumbing—"

"Plumbing!" Amber said, cutting him off. "When I first moved in, the sink was clogged. My landlady called someone to fix it. I'm pretty sure it was Mr. Shrinkydink out there."

"So he, of course, would be the one person who knows where you live," Josh said, not as a question.

"Oops," she replied with a guilty shrug. He waved her off, thinking.

The knock came again. "Ms. Allen? Repair man. Got a call that your refrigerator is out?"

"Maybe he'll leave?" Amber said. Josh shrugged, doubtful. The monsters weren't hiding anymore. There was no reason they wouldn't just force their way—

The door burst inward, splitting down the center.

Wood splinters went flying as the remains of the door hit the far end of the small apartment and embedded themselves in the wall.

Josh grabbed Amber by the back of the neck and pulled her down to the floor, getting low, as if trying to escape a burning building. Amber's couch was between them and the front door and he hoped that thing was hadn't seen them.

Everything Josh had seen indicated they could read thoughts, but he had to hope that they couldn't sense brainwaves in the air like a dog after a scent. If they could, this was going to be a pretty short game of hide and seek. Staying low, he moved to peer around the side of the couch. There was an end table with blankets draped down, so he was pretty well hidden. But Amber grabbed his leg, as if to pull him back.

"Stay calm," he mouthed, looking into her terrified face. He turned back to the doorway.

The creature, who looked like Lawrence Hardlock, entered the room. Its right arm had elongated. The skin of the arm had turned a bright, infected-looking pink. Wrinkles lined the length of it up to the tip. Where a fist would be on a person, hundreds of teeth like claws protruded. The flesh looked hard and calloused. Fascinated, Josh figured that they could change their form for the task at hand. The creature needed a battering ram, so it made one. But the result was a grotesque mockery of living tissue. It looked like some otherworldly appendage. Maybe there was something to Amber's idea that they were aliens.

But that didn't matter. What mattered was that this thing didn't seem to know they were there. Yet. Lawrence Hardlock's head turned and seemed to make eye contact with him. Josh fought the urge to pull back. If he hadn't been seen, any movement would definitely draw the creature's attention. He held his breath.

As the creature's gaze moved on around the room, he could hear it muttering to itself. It was barely audible, and what Josh did hear didn't make any sense. Just random words, separated by pauses, as if it were a radio signal that was cutting in and out.

"...inside...them...think...hunt...close...get Cynthia...things..."

Get Cynthia?

The eyes looked dead and sightless, like the eyes of a shark. But Josh had no doubt it was looking around. Or maybe, more accurately, whatever was taking the form of Fred Morgan was looking around, seeing everything. He was coming more and more to think that was the case with whatever was going on in town.

Josh watched. Amber's apartment was small. The main area here was all one room. A kitchen and living room combo. There were only two other rooms. The bathroom and a single bedroom. The thing could either turn right and inspect the bedroom, or turn left and look beyond the couch. Josh prayed it would turn right, because he had no plan if it looked over the couch and saw them lying on the floor.

The creature turned left and looked beyond the couch into the living room. Its gaze fell directly on the two of them as they lay on the floor.

Amber, who was still grasping his arm, began to let go. Josh was afraid she was going to bolt. He grabbed her arm, hoping the slight movement wouldn't be detected. The room was dark, as the sun was still rising. There was a chance that they hadn't yet been spotted.

He squeezed her arm, and she stayed where she was. Josh kept his eyes on the monster, who hadn't moved since turning in their direction. Somewhere in the apartment, Josh could hear a clock ticking. It was very loud in the stillness.

Watching the creature watch them, Josh started to count the ticks. Twelve. Thirteen. Fourteen.

The dead eyed thing starred directly down at them. The only movement was the steady lowering of Its jaw — as if it were held in place by wax and the heat of the room was causing it to droop.

Twenty-seven. Twenty-eight.

No shifting of its focus. No movement of its deformed arm. Just that drooping jaw.

Thirty-four. Thirty-five.

It had been long enough. This thing wasn't watching them. This might be their only chance to get away. Josh began to shift forward, hoping Amber would take his lead. Crawling on his belly, he moved his hands in the direction of the front door, which, as far as he could tell, was the only way out of the apartment. The creature had taken a couple of steps inside. If they were going to get out, they would have to brush past it.

Amber held him back for one split second. He tugged. She let go and began to follow.

What were they at? Fifty-two? Fifty-three seconds? Still no movement from the Lawrence-thing. It might as well have been a wax sculpture. Just that slowly collapsing jaw.

Ever so slowly, Josh tried raising from his belly onto his hands and knees.

Seventy-five. Seventy-six. Seventy-seven.

They crawled to the doorway. Had the door still been attached to the jam, they would have been blocked from going out. But since it was in splinters in the apartment, they were able to just continue crawling into the outer hall. Josh turned and twisted his body to keep from touching the creature in any way. He was up on his feet but crouched down. He felt like one of those crabs on the beach, sideways walking his way out the door. Josh looked behind him. Amber was right there, back braced against the wall as far from the creature as they could get. Now if he could just—

"Hey Josh! Long time no see." Josh looked back at the creature. The dead eyes were gone. The eyes were human. The face was settled back in place. Lawrence Hardlock had a huge smile on his face, as if he were genuinely glad to see Josh. It was so convincing that Josh felt the immediate urge to return the smile.

Instead, and without any forethought on his part, he kicked out at the creature's leg with all his strength. His back was supported by the door jamb and he used it to give his kick more power.

Josh saw Lawrence's supporting leg give out. He felt the snapping of internal structures giving way. The creature fell, awkwardly tumbling to the side.

"RUN!" Josh yelled, and started down the hall, hoping to hell that Amber was following.

The creature hadn't even finished its fall when it let out an ear-splitting noise. Josh heard scrabbling sounds as they rushed down the hall. He didn't look behind him, but as they rounded the corner, he couldn't help but notice in his peripheral vision that the thing's outer appearance had morphed into something beyond recognition. Its gate was no longer human.

Then it was blessedly blocked from view as they rounded the corner and headed down the stairs. He leaped the steps a few at a time. He had to remind himself to slow down. It wouldn't do either of them any good to fall and break a leg or twist an ankle in their attempt to escape.

Josh expected to be grabbed at any moment from behind and pulled backward down the hall. But so far, he didn't even hear anything coming after them.

They made it to the front hall of the building. Josh burst out the door so fast that he thought he heard the glass panel crack as it slung open. He leaped down the four steps to the outside world, allowing himself a quick glance back over his shoulder. He didn't see any movement beyond Amber, and he thought they were in the clear.

When he faced forward, it became obvious that there was no reason for Lawrence Hardlock to be chasing them. Through the morning gloom, Josh saw dozens of people crowding around, forming a semi-circle outside the front door of the building.

Amber swore as she saw the gathered crowd. They were both out of breath.

A crashing sound came from above, and Josh saw something vaguely spider-like crawling out of a window. It came scampering down toward them in a strangely gravity defying way. Lawrence Hardlock landed in front of them, his body deformed. The same smile lit his face.

"What do you say, buddy? How's the family business treating you?"

Chapter Thirty-Two

As Craig approached his truck, he heard a hissing sound, and assumed one of his tires had sprung a leak. Just great. The tires on the passenger-side looked fine. Must be on the driver-side.

He rounded the corner and had to pinwheel his arms to keep from tripping over the person that was crouched down on the other side.

"Whoa!" he shouted. The kid kneeling down on the ground gave a startled cry and began scooting away from him and the truck. He kicked something, and it skittered over to Craig's feet. Craig bent down and picked it up.

It was a can of neon pink spray paint. He noted that the hissing sound had stopped, and realized what he had heard was the can, spraying onto his truck. He looked at the truck and saw a very familiar painting on his door.

"What the hell, man!" Craig shouted, angry.

"Don't arrest me!" the kid yelled. "I'm sorry. I didn't know this truck belonged to a cop."

Craig studied the kid. He must have been sixteen or seventeen. Dressed in an all white track suit. Not the best outfit for sneaking around at night. But the kid didn't seem to have the best set of brains.

"How'd you know I'm a cop?" Craig asked, gesturing at his clothes.

"Uhhhhh," the kid said, his face going blank. He suddenly stood up and tried to make a run for it. Craig grabbed him by the shoulder and twirled him around, knocking him back down on the curb.

"Okay, I knew it was you, but I'm sorry. Alright? I won't do it again. Just don't tell my mom, okay? She's been in a bugger of a bad mood the last few weeks. I know she'll kill me or something, okay? You want that on your conscience?"

"I won't want graffiti on my town," Craig said firmly as he reached into his duffle bag, searching for his handcuffs.

That's when he saw movement, and turned. The front door of the station opened. He figured it was the chief, finally going…wherever the hell it was he went.

"Please, man! Don't take me in, man!" the kids said, blubbering. "I don't want this on my record—"

"Shhhh!" Craig said, silencing the kid.

He was watching the door and was surprised when the person who came out wasn't the chief, but some old dude who was barely able to shuffle down the steps. Craig didn't even know someone else had been inside. He watched as the bent figure made his way to the bottom. He half expected the man to slip and tumble. He considered running up to help him, but didn't want to run into the chief. Besides, this whole thing was weird. The old guy might have something to do with it.

"Come on, man," the kid cried again. "Don't you cops have something better to do with your time? There are bigger crimes than vandalism, ya know?"

Craig barely heard. Something was going on with these thefts and there was no way it was all Josh's doing, like the chief said. This seemed like something that was being orchestrated by someone with real power. Someone who had pull at the university and hospital. There weren't too many people that fit that bill in Osprey.

The old man made it without falling and Craig relaxed. Then, to his surprise, the old man climbed into the back of car number one, which was parked at the foot of the stairs. The old guy closed the door and disappeared from sight, lying down on the back seat.

Craig continued waiting, his mind swimming with the possibilities. The head of the police department being in on a major crime spree? That was some serious movie level shit. He couldn't believe it, but he thought he should look into it.

"You're right," Craig said, turning to the kid. "There are bigger things going on right now." He opened his door and tossed his bag to the passenger's side. "Get out of here," he said over his shoulder as he hopped in. Turning, he saw the kid was already running away. "And don't spray paint my town again," Craig shouted after him. He turned back to watch the station.

Less than ten minutes later, Chief came out. He expected Sonia would be exiting not long after the coast was clear. As he had said to her, there wasn't much else going on.

He put his truck in drive and followed the chief and the mystery man from a safe distance.

HE HAD NEVER TAILED ANYONE before — only dreamed of it — so this was a learning experience. He kept monitoring his distance and had to hit the brakes more than once to keep himself from getting too close. The cruiser was going painfully slow. A couple of times, the chief seemed to lose control, and the cruiser swerved on the road. What the hell? Was Chief drunk?

As they made their way through Osprey, Craig became convinced he knew where they were headed. He silently congratulated his fine detective skills when they turned under the sign marked Morgan Stone Quarry, Ltd. He held back, not wanting to pull in while they were getting out of the cruiser. He knew the layout of the quarry pretty well, as did most kids in Osprey. School trips to the quarry were common and so were part-time jobs. Craig had worked there one summer when he was in college. It was an industry town, after all.

After waiting ten minutes, Craig drove in. He moved slow, not wanting to run into any rocks. He saw lots of debris along the driveway. Plastic casings for computer monitors, towers, cell phones and other electronics. Clumps of discarded wires and internal computer parts that Craig couldn't have identified if his life depended on it.

But he knew he was on the right track. The chief was definitely in on the thefts.

The main entrance to the quarry was down below, where large trucks and equipment could drive in and out. Craig could see the dirt billowing up as work crews operated down in the quarry. Chief had brought them in through the administration entrance. The main business building, where all the desk jockeys and corporate types, would meet and plan out the work that the laborers would be responsible to actually do.

Craig spotted the Chief's squad car at the edge of the ravine, overlooking the main mining area of the quarry. Both men were outside. Chief standing stiffly at the edge of the ravine, looking down. The old man was seated in a camping chair beside him. Craig could just make out the top of his head. Both men had their backs to him.

He parked his truck and got out, deciding it might be smarter to approach on foot. He walked slowly, moving so that he was coming at them directly from behind. He wanted to get as close as possible before they were alerted to his presence.

The old man was talking. Craig couldn't quite make out what he was saying. His voice was weak, barely audible, even though the morning wind was very light. Craig stepped carefully, not wanting to let his foot fall crunch in the gravel. He was less than twenty feet away and closing in.

"Hello?" Chief Braden said, startling Craig, who froze in place. He was about to answer back, thinking the chief had finally spotted him. But Braden wasn't talking to him. He was still looking out over the ravine.

"Got to be the place," the old man muttered from his camp chair. "Just need to flush them out."

Chief responded with, "Ms. Allen? Repair man. Got a call that your refrigerator is out?"

What the hell? Refrigerator? Were they stealing home appliances now? And who was Braden talking to? Who was Ms. Allen? Craig looked around but didn't see anyone else. Just the Chief and the old guy.

Craig reached the car and crouched down. He had been hoping there would be some kind of incriminating conversation between the two men. Something to prove they were behind the thefts. Craig moved around to the side of the car.

"Okay, we're inside," the old man said. "If we don't find them here, I think we'll just call off the hunt. Things are getting too close. We need to get Cynthia here before things—"

Craig stumbled over a large rock as he was making his way around the car. The old man stopped talking, and the Chief turned.

"Craig!" the Chief said. He turned away from the ravine. "What are you doing here, officer? Shouldn't you be out on patrol?"

Craig stood up, not sure what his next move would be. The old man was craning his neck, trying to see over the hood of the car.

"Is that the boy detective?" he said.

"That's our Craig," Chief said. "Hot on the trail of the bandits." Braden smiled as he spoke.

"Dammit," the old man said. He sounded genuinely disappointed. "I was hoping he would be the one to…oh, the hell with it. Come around here, son," the old man called. "Let's get a look at you." Craig came around and stood next to the Chief. "It's the Philips boy!" the old man said. "You never told me," he said to Braden. "You look just like your father," he said to Craig.

"Uh…do I know you?" Craig said.

"Yes and no. Better leave it at no. It's easier that way. I take it you don't know what's going on here, do you? Just kind of the wrong place at the wrong time?"

Craig didn't know how to respond. He thought he had a pretty good idea of what was going on. "I'm here because it appears you and Chief Braden are involved in some kind of underground stolen electronics ring," Craig said, trying to sound official. He turned. "Sorry Chief. Just, you know. Doing my job."

"There's a bit more than that going on, son," Braden said.

The old man waved him off. "No sense burdening the boy with that, Darrel," the old man said to the Chief. "Come here," he said, calling Craig to step toward the ravine with him. "Come look at your stolen electronics. All accounted for, I believe." He gestured with a grizzled and twisted old man's hand toward the quarry below. Craig stepped forward and peered down.

"What's going on down there?" he asked. The crews were working away. Dozens of men and women — maybe hundreds — were running about here and there, driving loaders, lugging equipment.

In the center of the quarry, behind a newly erected fence, a small group of men, women, and children stood around. They weren't working. Some were lying around, while others watched the work being done around them. They looked like a group of chickens trapped in a pen.

The work was all centralized on the main wall of the quarry.

A large square frame had been erected there on the rock face of the excavating wall. Sparks were flying as workers were attaching various gizmos here and there. Craig didn't know what he was looking at.

The frame was made of four long trusses, like the kind that makes up the frames of a stage — the kind used at rock concerts. But these were much larger. Craig realized after a moment that they were actually the main supports for tower cranes, the kind that were used to build skyscrapers. The frame was almost to the top of the rock wall, which Craig knew to be a couple hundred feet tall.

The massive structure was laced with wires and electronics. Several long cables crisscrossed in the center of the frame, giving the thing the look of the world's largest spider web.

"What do you think?" the old man asked.

"I...this is everything?" Craig asked. There was more here than he had been prepared for. A lot more.

"That's all of it. The university supercomputer and sensors. The hospital scanners. Aaron McDonald's milking machine. Everything. Things I'm sure you didn't even know you were looking for. We had to find some pieces that were outside town, ya know? Can't build something like this without some real specialty pieces of equipment."

"Something like...what?" Craig asked. "What is this?"

The old man chuckled. He didn't look like he was having a lot of fun, but he chuckled none the less. "The end of the world," the old man said. "You're looking at the end of the wor—"

"Hey, Josh!" Chief Braden said. Craig whirled, expecting to see Josh Warlocke in on the crime wave after all. But Josh was nowhere in sight. In fact, nobody was in sight. Chief was looking out at nothing. "Long time no see."

Craig turned back to the old man, looking for answers. "What's wrong with the Chief?"

"I'm afraid you're the last one left," the old man said, giving Craig an apologetic shrug. Then he looked over Craig's shoulder. "Chief Braden? Would you mind escorting our friend here down to the quarry? We might as well make use of him. The end is coming."

Braden turned and began walking toward Craig. Chief's arm reached out, as if he wanted to caress Craig's face. Then the man's arm split down the center, the skin exploding outward. Craig screamed. He was shocked to see not bone in the center of Chief's forearm, but a slithering tongue, bright pink and glistening. The interior of his arm was also lined with hundreds of sharp teeth.

"Uh," the old man groaned from behind him. "Now he's just showing off. Does it always have to be so dramatic?"

Craig turned and ran toward his truck as fast as he could. He looked back over his shoulder and saw the chief coming after him, loping along on three limbs like some kind of animal.

Turning back, Craig saw that he had run right into a circle of towns people who had surrounded his truck while he wasn't paying attention. Some people he recognized. A few were strangers. But all were coming toward him, arms outstretched and distorted.

"What the hell is going on here?" Craig bellowed as they closed in on him.

"What do you say, buddy? How's the family business treating you?" someone said.

Craig began to scream.

CHAPTER THIRTY-THREE

D on't let them touch you," Josh said as deformed creatures closed in.

"Don't take this the wrong way, Josh, but no shit, Sherlock!"

"Right," he said, edging backward toward the building. So far, they hadn't been rushed.

Lawrence Hardlock, reached out with an arm that was half tentacle, half pincer. Josh recoiled, ducking backward. He bumped into Amber, who in turn, tripped over the bottom step of the building. They both tumbled down and Lawrence's arm snapped above Josh's head, missing by inches.

"Up the steps," he said frantically. "Go, go!"

"Going, going," Amber replied equally frantically. They managed to scramble into the main entrance of the building. Josh got the huge metal door closed. He could see the crowd through the wire reenforced glass front. As soon as the door clicked shut, something large pounded into the glass, shattering it. Whatever it was — probably the tooth crowned limb of Lawrence Hardlock — also shattered, splattering the glass with red gore. The creature outside bellowed with rage.

Josh looked around the door. No deadbolt. Instead, he jammed his foot against the bottom and pushed his weight on it, holding the door shut.

"This is not a permanent solution," he said. "Is there a back exit to the building?" he asked.

"Yeah," she said. "But we can't get to it!"

"What? Why not?"

"Cause I don't have my frickin' keys!" she said. Josh turned and remembered there were two doors to get into the building. The main door and the locked door that only residents could open. They were currently trapped inside a room about the size of a walk-in closet. How were they going to get out of this?

Throw Amber into the crowd and run, Josh thought briefly. Oh, great! Now the Creature was in his head.

"If you feel like throwing me in the crowd, please don't," he said.

"You too?" she said.

"Yeah. Thoughts that sound like me. Wants me to abandon you, I guess."

"Mine just told me to stab you in the back."

"Stab me? Wait, you have a knife?" he asked.

"Yeah. I grabbed one from the kitchen as soon as we got here last night. Just in case you turned out to be one of those things."

"Comforting," Josh said. "Well, don't be shy now! Pull that thing out and protect me! I'm no chauvinist!"

"I'd rather take my chances inside the building," she said. "If we can get inside somehow."

"Honestly, there are probably just as many of those things inside as there are outside!" He glanced around the tiny room as he talked, looking for another way out. It was an older apartment building with very few features. An old intercom system with buzzer buttons for each apartment and mailboxes. Beside the mailboxes was a metal panel with a recycling decal. It wasn't huge, but maybe big enough for them to squeeze into.

"Open that," he said, pointing to the chute. As he said it, he heard a click as something from the outside pushed down the door handle. The door began to open, and the rubber soles of his shoes began sliding along the linoleum. He bore down and pushed the metal frame with all his strength. "Open the chute!" he repeated.

She did, looking inside. She shook her head. "No good. We can't crawl in when it's in the open position. Things can only go down when it's closed. And there's no way we'll fit inside when it's closed. Even one at a time."

"Can you pull the door out?" he yelled, feeling the pressure of the creatures pushing from the other side. They started pounding and glass began raining down on him. The wire grid began bulging out toward him.

Amber began pulling on the recycling chute. First straight down, then side to side, trying to lever it out. With an exasperated cry, she slammed it down, trying to break it off. Nothing.

She shook her head, seemingly spent with the effort. "Maybe if I had twenty minutes to beat at it, but I doubt we have twenty minutes."

As if to accentuate this, a section of glass completely broke away, and something began slithering in through a small hole in the top corner. Amber pulled out her knife and made to attack the thing.

"NO!" Josh yelled, pushing her back.

"What?" she cried, looking frantically at the thing making its way in.

"Don't let it touch you, remember?!" he said. "If you cut it, whatever it is will get on you. I don't know if that's enough to infect someone, but I don't want to find out. Just...keep your distance from it!" He turned his head away as the thing began oozing down the glass toward his head. As he did, he looked at the chute.

"Give me the knife!" he said.

"I thought we couldn't stab it!" she said.

"Just — give it!" he yelled. She slapped it in his open palm. "Now hold the door. It's not going to be easy!"

They shuffled around, her foot replacing his as a door stop, all while avoiding the thing that was now forming into a complex matrix of shapes on the glass. It looked like a mossy bed of human flesh was slowly growing on the inside of the door, covering everything. Josh saw that it was even starting to seep in from the edges of the jamb.

He turned, trying to ignore it. He jabbed the knife about an inch into a wooden support beam, and with a quick jerk, broke the tip off.

"Nice job! Now you've broken our only offensive weapon," Amber said between grunts.

He ignored her, but did point over her head. "Duck down some." She looked at where he was pointing. The pink flesh was now covering the top third of the door. She moved down. "They're not pushing as hard," she said. "Maybe they're giving up? This might just be whatever those things bleed."

Josh shrugged and turned back to the recycling chute. The panel was covered in a thick layer of paint. He had to scrap around with the knife to find what he was looking for. Eventually, he found it.

The gray paint chipped away, revealing a screw. Josh had been hoping for a flathead design, as opposed to something more vandal proof. Luckily, it seemed management wasn't too concerned with the safety of the building's recycling. He used the broken tip of the knife to turn the screw. It started to strip at first, but Josh bore down and it began to turn.

After it was out, he worked his way around the panel. He found six screws in all.

"I think they're gone," Amber said from behind him as he was working out the last one. "We might be able to go out the—"

She screamed and Josh whirled. The pink growth on the door was past the halfway mark. Amber had been crouching, keeping her distance. Josh felt a gut punch of repulsion when he saw what had made her scream.

The flesh-moss had sprouted a weird mixture of a face and hand, which was grabbing out from the door blindly. As he watched, more tentacle-like things began sprouting and flinging around wildly. Bubbles began forming on the surface, growing large, like flesh that's being boiled in a furnace, the skin blistering and running. It was what he pictured happening every time they cremated a body at the Home.

Amber had scurried away from the door toward the far wall when the flesh began to flail out. Now, whatever was outside returned to pushing the door. It opened about a foot. Several hands began reaching around.

Josh slid his foot along the bottom of the door. He was practically doing the splits with one foot on the bottom of the front entrance and the other propped against the rear door.

"Little help!" he cried. But Amber was cowering by the wall, staring at the things flailing from the flesh-moss. Josh heard small sounds and turned in time to see the blisters popping, one by one. The inside of each blister had formed a series of tiny eyes, each scanning around randomly. One eye stopped and seemed to focus on him. Then the rest zeroed in and the wild whipping from the strange flesh-tentacles stopped.

"Oh, crap," he said. A tentacle shot out toward his face. He stabbed out with the knife, slicing it in half in mid air.

The tentacle pulled back as if stung. Josh checked his hand to make sure nothing had gotten on him. He made a lunge toward the metal frame of the chute, pulling at the top. Most of his fingernails broke off halfway as he pulled. The thing almost came free. Except for the bottom corner, where the last screw stuck out.

"Help!" he cried to Amber. She finally came to life, leaped up, and put her weight into the metal frame. It came down, missing Josh's crouched body by inches.

The hole left was still small but appeared big enough for them to squeeze through. One at a time.

Without needing to be told, Amber began climbing in. Josh helped her get her second leg into place, and she began to shimmy in. Josh stayed in place.

As she climbed, Josh watched in fascination as the flesh-moss continued to pour in. It had begun to thicken in places and Josh saw a form was taking shape. Something almost humanoid was forming and bulging out. The surface seemed to breathe as it birthed this new thing.

Without making sure Amber was out of the way, Josh lunged toward the hole. Fear and survival instinct had given his body a surprising amount of grace and he leaped in headfirst, striking a diver's pose. His shoulders barely touched the surface of the tight space as he tumbled down the chute to the recycling bin below.

The bin was filled with newspapers and flyers. Nothing sharp that would have impaled them. He climbed out and found Amber peering out a grimy basement window at the street outside.

"Looks clear in this direction," she said. He struggled his way out of the bin and walked up behind her.

"Probably not for long. We should get going now."

"Out of town?" she said.

Josh shrugged. "I don't know. Probably. But I'm wondering if maybe we're missing something."

"Like what?"

"Lawrence Hardlock."

"I don't think I want him along with us," Amber said.

"No, something he said. He was muttering a bunch of randomness. Didn't make any sense. But I did make something out. Sounded like, 'Get Cynthia.'"

Amber made a face. "Cynthia Morgan? She's at the jail. I would imagine she's been turned by them, Josh."

"I don't think so. When I was under arrest, Braden seemed very concerned that she not be harmed. Like he wanted her just the way she was. I think she might be a part of whatever's going on. With whatever it's after. I think maybe we should go to the jail and see if she's still there."

"Hell no!" Amber said. "I ain't going there. It's one of the epicenters of this thing. I think we should go down some back roads and find a way out of town! Get ourselves some help. I think we can do it if we pick the right roads. You know Osprey better than I do. You think you can get us out?"

Josh thought this through. "Yeah, I think so. There are some pretty secluded paths. But…"

"No jail!" Amber said.

"I wasn't going to say that," he said. "It was a stupid idea. But I do have one stop that I think we should make. It's actually not far from here. It might help if we run in to those things again."

He told her what he was thinking.

"That…might be a good idea," she said hesitantly.

Chapter Thirty-Four

This was definitely *NOT* a good idea," Amber said as they walked down the center of a dirt road. They hadn't seen a car driving all morning, and it was just before noon. In fact, there were no sounds whatsoever. Aside from the swishing sounds of their bulky suits, that is.

Josh was willing to admit that maybe it had been a bad idea. After leaving Amber's apartment building, he had led them to the local humane society, where Josh knew they would find the bite suits they were currently wearing.

They were actually anti-bite suits. Outfits with thick material used to train dogs. They allowed the wearer to antagonize the animals into biting them without having to worry about teeth sinking into their flesh. Josh hoped the suits would give them a bit of protection from the creatures, which seemed to need to make direct, skin on skin contact with whatever they were trying to infect.

But the suits were also turning out to be slow, cumbersome, and noisy to wear. The SWISH-SWISH sound their legs and arms made as they walked reminded Josh of kids walking around in large snow suits. And the bulky material didn't exactly give them a full range of motion. They might as well be dressed up in those sumo-wrestling suits.

And lastly, the outfits were hot. Josh was sweating profusely in the midday sun.

"How much farther till we're out of town?" Amber asked. "I don't know how much longer I can keep up this pace."

Josh judged their pace and the distance from the edge of town. "Probably another twenty minutes. Maybe thirty, the way we're walking."

"Might be better if we—"

"Quiet!" Josh said, hearing a vehicle coming toward them from up ahead. "Something's coming." He led them to the right, into a forested area that lined the road.

Once out of sight, Josh watched as three vehicles came over a hill, taking up the entire road. The trio was led by a police cruiser. They went by slowly. It appeared the drivers were having a difficult time staying on the road. They were swerving and jerking as they went. Once or twice, the vehicles even bumped into each other.

"That was painful to watch," Amber said once they had turned onto another road and were out of sight. The turn had been particularly atrocious.

"Yeah," Josh said, thinking. "I bet that whoever — or whatever — is controlling all the creatures is struggling with the enormity of controlling an entire town's worth of them. It's probably bad enough when it's just one or two people. But we're talking tens of thousands. There's no way someone could control all of them at once. That would probably explain why most of them seem to zone out a lot. They're being controlled one at a time."

"They were all pretty lively back at my place," Amber said.

Josh nodded, thinking it through. "Yeah...but by that point, they were aware of us. It was only after Lawrence saw us that he really," Josh paused, grasping for what he was trying to say. "Really perked up. Like he was being controlled by an outside force, and it was having difficulty keeping up. Like a bad signal. But then it found an alternate source to control it."

"Like feeding off our brainwaves, or whatever?" Amber said.

"Right. I don't know about brainwaves, but something about us. It found a battery source and then was able to switch to some kind of autopilot."

"But without an alternate source," Amber continued the thought, "they're left to being controlled by groups at a time." Amber said, pointing in the direction the cars had gone.

"Yeah. Maybe," Josh said. It was all guesses at this point, but that made sense. As much as any of the situation made sense, at least.

"Any idea where they were going?"

Josh looked in that direction. "Well, the police station is right down that road," he said slowly. "I bet you they're going to get Cynthia Morgan."

"Good for her," Amber said, eyeing Josh suspiciously. "You brought us by the one road out of town that happened to pass the police station? Some accident."

"Purely coincidence," he said, smiling.

"Well, the monsters can have that bitch for all I care," she said, then paused. "But I was thinking about the police station. It would be nice to have something more threatening than a broken kitchen knife if we run into more of those things up ahead. Not that I don't appreciate your idea," she said, holding up her arm to display the bulky bite suit.

"Yeah. Maybe we can raid the station for some guns," Josh said.

"*After* they've left with Cynthia Morgan," Amber added. "I'm not gonna risk my life for her. This ain't a movie, Joshy. We don't go around saving the irredeemable killer cause it's the right thing to do."

Heroics wasn't exactly why he had suggested going back for Cynthia, but he saw her point. "Okay! We'll wait for them to leave," Josh said.

"Good. Lead the way," she said, and they walked in the direction of the police station.

THEY MADE THEIR WAY TOWARD the station through dense foliage, staying out of sight of the path. The dirt road they had been on had met up with a paved road that led straight to the rear of the station. Josh had never been back here before, but he imagined it was like the Home. He thought the jail cells were likely accessible from the back in the same way the rear was where they unloaded the removals to get them into the preparation room.

"Well, they'll never excel as valets," Josh said when they got to the edge of the forest. The three vehicles were parked almost on top of each other. The red pickup truck was literally resting in the bumper of the cruiser, and the green sedan had rammed into the driver's door. Josh imagined that the driver of the truck would have had to scoot over and get out of the passenger seat.

"What is going on with these guys?" Amber mused aloud.

Josh had the mental image of a little kid using a remote-controlled car blindfolded. That probably summed up what it was like trying to control these creatures. Now multiply that by fifteen thousand people — which was the rough population of Osprey — and it was amazing anything was getting done these days.

Though, once they had Cynthia Morgan, assuming they were right about these creatures, things would get a lot easier. They would switch over to autopilot — which is how he had begun to think of the different stages of their control. He said as much to Amber as they waited for them to come out of the rear doors and pile into their vehicles.

"So if you're right, they'll be leaving acting normal. Makes sense."

"Yup. But for now, we just have to wait and—

Josh felt something on his back through the thick fabric of the bite suit and whirled around. Amber moved at the same time, so he figured she had felt something, too.

He had a brief moment where he thought they had been caught, but breathed a little easier when he saw it was Sonia, the girl from the dispatch desk at the police station. She was crouched down behind them. If it had been a creature, they likely would have been turned before they'd had a chance to react.

Josh scolded himself. They had been so fixated on the back of the building, they hadn't even heard her coming up behind them. That was stupid. They could have been in serious trouble if it had been one of those creatures.

Sonia was dirty, disheveled, and looked about as exhausted as they felt. Although she looked a good deal cooler than he felt inside the bite-suit. He really should just take the stupid thing off. It was probably doing more harm than good.

"Hey," she said, peering past them toward the station. "Sorry I spooked you. I've been here for hours looking out for these things. You guys trying to stop whatever is going on?"

Amber laughed. "Hardly. We're just trying to keep from becoming one of them. Going to get some hardware from the police station and then get the hell out of town."

"Good plan," Sonia said. "But you'll need me if you want to get something more powerful than a stapler," she said, holding up a chain of keys that were tied to her belt. "I know where the guns are locked up. Mind if I tag along?"

Amber nodded, but Josh hesitated. This whole situation had been happening for a while, but he and Amber had only been aware of it since yesterday. Not very long. So his natural inclination was still to trust people. Especially a friendly face. He didn't know Sonia very well, but he still knew her. It was so easy to assume that what you were seeing on the outside was what you were getting on the inside. But that wasn't the case anymore.

"What are you doing out here, anyway?" Josh asked.

"Same as you guys," Sonia said. "Scoping out the situation. Thinking it might be nice to have some fire power to use if I run into one of these things."

Amber seemed to catch Josh's concern. He saw her shift ever so slightly away from Sonia. "Oh yeah?" Amber said. "Seems like you were probably already inside the building. How come you're out here now?"

Sonia, seeming to notice Amber's shift, gave a nervous laugh. "I left the building at the end of my shift. Those things have been chasing me off and on all night." She looked between the two of them, obviously not liking what she saw. "What the hell? You think I'm one of those things?"

Josh shifted back an inch or two. "What makes you think we're not?" he said. He had dismissed the idea that she was a monster because she hadn't tried to turn them. But now, he thought about how she had come up behind them. She hadn't signaled to them, or tried talking. She had put her hands on their backs. On the bite suits. He looked Sonia in the eye for a moment.

"Run!" he said.

Sonia lunged, taking Amber by surprise before she could move. Amber hit the soft ground with the creature on top of her. Sonia began tearing at the bite suit, trying to find an opening. Very quickly, Josh saw her focus shift to Amber's exposed face. The bite suits also had helmets, but Amber had drawn the line at those, and Josh had agreed. They were more like hockey helmets, with a metal grill for face protection. Good for keeping a dog from biting your nose off, but not so great for a malleable creature like these things that could change their shape and get into tight spaces.

Still, it meant Josh didn't have much time to react. He grabbed a large branch on a dead tree and pulled. It snapped off. He used the momentum of his pull as he swung in an arc. The blunt end of the branch hit Sonia just beneath the jaw.

For a normal human being, that would have been all. She would have flown off, either unconscious or dead.

In this case, the creature had obviously anticipated the strike. The face of the thing separated, flowing in the path of the stick, its neck elongating. The head exploded in a cloud of red.

But the body stayed where it was — on Amber's chest, grabbing at her exposed flesh. Amber had grabbed its forearms with the thick gloves of the suit and was desperately trying to hold it back. Josh saw that the thing's flesh was now crawling along the sleeves of the suit, probably searching for gaps that it could crawl into.

Josh dropped the stick and tried grabbing Sonia from behind.

"Get the hell off her, you--"

Josh had never grabbed a bag filled with coiled vipers before, but he couldn't imagine it being much different. Sonia came off Amber and attacked Josh with tendrils of flesh and gore. Her body wriggled and writhed in his arms, trying to get at his face.

He had picked the body up from behind, but somehow she was instantly facing him, her front melting through her back. Sonia's uniform was now on the woman's body in reverse, as if she had put her clothes on backwards that morning.

He threw the thing as far as he could, which was less calculated and more out of repulsion.

"*RUN,*" he shouted. This time, they both ran out of the line of trees. All thought was gone. Josh was just trying to get away from Sonia and had completely forgotten about Cynthia Morgan and the other creatures who had come to collect her.

Until he literally ran into them, coming out of the police station. The four of them — three monsters and Cynthia Morgan — went flying. They were all taken by surprise. Not one of them made a move for him. Which Josh was sure wouldn't last long.

"Grab her!" Josh said to Amber, who had stopped when she realized Josh wasn't beside her anymore. She turned and ran up to him, obviously doing her best to keep a distance from the monsters that lay sprawled on the pavement.

She helped Josh up, and after making a face of disgust, helped him grab Cynthia Morgan by the arm and haul her to her feet.

The older woman cried out in pain as they both roughly grabbed and tugged her after them.

"Help me," the woman said. "They want to take me. They've come for—"

"Shut up!" Amber replied. "We're helping you, okay?"

"The truck!" he shouted. It was the closest and the passenger door was open. Rather than all trying to pile into the cab, Josh made a quick decision. "The back. Put her in the back," he yelled.

"Wha—?" was all Cynthia could get out as they picked her up and tossed her into the bed of the pickup. She landed hard, crying out in pain. Without hesitation, Amber jumped in behind her, obviously realizing it would take too long for them to both pile into the truck's front.

"Stop right there!" the police chief yelled, still lying on the pavement of the parking lot. They had begun coming to and were all making their way to their feet.

Josh lunged at the passenger door. No thoughts were going through his head. He, like the creatures that were after him, was operating on autopilot. If he had been thinking, he never could have managed the precision movements that helped him to catapult himself into the driver's seat, pull down on the shifter and punch the pedal with his foot. Fortunately, the truck had been left running and roared to life. Josh pulled the wheel to the right. Metal screeched as it pulled away from the police cruiser.

One of the creatures appeared in the open door of the truck, grabbing onto the frame of the passenger's side. It held on as the truck moved away from the other vehicles. The creature was in the act of reaching for Josh when the door closed, bashing into it from behind.

The door snapped closed, cutting off the creature's legs, top of its head and the fingers of the hand that had been holding onto the frame. The rest of it was pushed into the cab like Play-doh being forced into a mold. The remains continued, reaching out for Josh.

"Aaagh!" Josh screamed, jerking the wheel to the left. This was not a calculated move. The truck swerved. The door, which had not latched, flew open, and the creature was carried out of the cab with the momentum. Josh saw it land in a pile on the pavement. It rolled, spraying bits of itself like a watermelon disintegrating as it dragged along the rough surface of the cement.

The door closed, and they drove at manic speed away from the police station. Josh looked behind him, making sure there was nobody in the bed of the truck that wasn't supposed to be there.

A sour faced Cynthia Morgan glared at him as her body tumbled around with the speed of the truck. Amber was also tumbling around, but the padding of the suit would likely keep her injuries pretty minimal.

He focused on the road, trying to figure out where he was going now.

Chapter Thirty-Five

Josh drove hard, pushing the pedal to the floor, something he had never done before — well...at least not while conscious. He wanted to get as much distance as possible.

The window behind him slid open and Amber stuck her head into the cab.

"They're following!" she said. He looked in the rearview mirror to see sunlight twinkling off chrome.

"Great," he said. He also got a glimpse of Cynthia Morgan as she bounced around in the back. She wasn't able to steady herself, as her hands were cuffed. But at least they were cuffed in front, so she was able to protect her face as she slid around, bouncing off the sides of the truck-bed. He definitely didn't have the time to stop and let her into the cab. "Hang on back there," he said to Amber. "I have a feeling this ride is only going to get bumpier. Can you climb in?" he asked, letting off the gas a bit so she could try.

Amber attempted, but the bite suit made it impossible. The hole in the horizontal sliding window was just too small.

"Damn it," she said. "Just a second." Josh focused on the road. A moment later, the sliding window shot into the cab, followed by Amber's foot. It barely missed him in the head. Moments later, Amber came shimmying through headfirst, like some kind of automotive baby being born.

"Where's your jacket?" he asked as she turned herself around in the tight space.

"Tossed overboard. It served its purpose. Now we got wheels!" she said, patting the truck's dashboard.

He wanted to point out that they were far from having escaped town, but let it go. As long as they could stay in the truck, that might be good enough. "Can you help Cynthia in?" he asked, figuring he knew what her response would be.

"In the truck? I'm just waiting till you tell me we need to lighten the load so I can toss her overboard," Amber said.

Josh smiled. "Well, try to contain yourself. I'm not being a hero about her. I don't like having a serial killer as a companion any more than you. But there's something about her. I don't know what it is, but they're after her. She figures into this in some way."

"You mean like she's part of some kind of sacrificial ritual?" Amber said.

That gave him pause. He hadn't known what he was thinking, but even though she had likely meant it as a joke, Amber had probably hit very close to what he was suspecting. Maybe not a sacrifice, but—

WHAM! All three of them went flying forward as they were struck from behind. Josh looked back to see that the much faster police cruiser had caught up and was ramming them. Josh cursed himself for picking the truck. It was probably the slowest vehicle of the three. He pushed the pedal back down to the floor, trying to outpace it.

"Hang on!" he said. Amber grabbed hold of a handle above the passenger side door and did her best. Cynthia was unable to reply as she bounced around in the truck bed.

Josh braked and made a sharp right turn onto a new road and sped back up. In the rear view, Josh saw the cruiser attempt the same turn, but it skidded and rammed into a tree. The other car was forced to stop.

"Yes!" he said, giving the steering wheel a celebratory smack. "This road borders the edge of town," he said, jerking a thumb out his window. A dense line of trees obscured visibility, but he knew it would thin out up ahead. He thought maybe he had done alright picking the truck after all. It was a four by four, which meant of the three vehicles, the truck stood the best chance of not getting stuck if he decided to take things off-road. Which he would as soon as—

"Uh, Josh?" Amber said. The tone of her voice caught his attention. Now what?

He ignored her. He had to concentrate if he was going to be able to pull off this maneuver once the trees were gone. A tight turn, hoping he could jump the ditch, then a short drive over bumpy fields, and they would be out of Osprey. It wouldn't be easy, but—

"Josh!" Amber said more emphatically.

"What?"

Her hand shot in front of his face, pointing out the driver's side window, past the diminishing trees. His eyes followed the line of motion.

The last of the bushes cleared away, revealing a line of people where he knew the town limit to be. They were holding hands, eyes closed. They looked like a group of worshippers. A lot of worshippers. The line stretched backward and forward as far as he could see.

As the truck drove on past them, their eyes opened. Not one by one, but all at the same time. Hundreds of pairs of eyes were following the path of the pickup.

"That is creepy as hell," Amber said. Josh agreed.

Okay, doesn't matter. He could still make it. There's only one line of them. If he could launch the truck over the ditch, he could ram through them—

No! I should head back into town. I might be able to find a place to hide there, he thought. *Someone will come to save us.*

"Should we head back into town?" Amber asked. He could tell she had just had the same thought as him. "We can hide somewhere, and—"

"And someone will come to save us?" he said, finishing her thought.

"Yeah," she said.

"I had that thought, too. Except I don't think it was my thought." He pointed out the window. This time at the line of people.

"Oh," she said.

Josh realized he had missed his chance at taking the field out of town as the line of trees thickened again, cutting off his view of the people. But it didn't matter. They were still there. And his brief glimpse convinced him they must be lining the whole town.

Doesn't matter, there's a bridge up ahead. Maybe he could—

—*ram through the side. It's a pretty powerful river below. We might be able to float the truck out of town.*

What? No. That was a stupid thought. He shook his head. He was very tired. He had to slap himself to keep his eyes open and on the road.

The creature, working through the collective power of the town, must be attempting to control—

— my thoughts. I should get away from this road—

— put some distance between them and the edge of town and —

— find a place to think this through.

He looked at the next road that turned away from the border of town. The quarry was down that way. There wouldn't be anyone working there! Not with the whole town turned into these creatures!

It'd be the perfect place to hide. It would be deserted. He checked his head, trying to decide if that made sense, or if he was being led by the Voice of the Creature. But it seemed to check out. He looked back to make sure they weren't being followed.

The road behind them was empty. No pursuing car. It must have gotten caught up in the wreckage of the police cruiser. They were free and clear.

"Hang on," he said, taking a sharp turn onto the road. He passed a sign which read, 'MORGAN STONE QUARRY, LTD. NEXT RIGHT.'

Josh turned right.

MINUTES LATER, THEY WERE DRIVING into the open area of the administrative building. It looked like he had been right. The place was deserted.

"This looks promising," Amber said. "We can hide in there and maybe get some kind of signal out to someone. A place like this has to have some fancy communication methods. Some kind of direct to satellite telephone or something."

Josh just shrugged. He was looking at the junk strewn around the grounds. Broken computer monitors. Abandoned cell phones. Wires and motherboards in heaps, like cast off detritus from some kind of sci-fi junk vessel.

"The place has gone a bit to seed since I was here last," he said, pointing at the junk. "This place used to be pristinely manicured."

"Looks like a junk yard," Amber agreed. "But as long as there are no creatures, I'm happy. Drive around back. I bet the front is locked up tight, but there might be some kind of loading bay."

He nodded and drove around the building.

"What are we doing here?" Cynthia Morgan said as she popped her head into the cab. Josh jumped.

"Getting shelter," Amber said, keeping her distance from the old woman.

Cynthia looked terrible, and Josh felt a pang of guilt. She was banged and scratched up from rolling around the back of the truck. There were fresh bruises forming on her face and arms.

"Shelter here?" she said, sounding aghast. "Are you stupid, child?!"

"I liked you better unconscious," Amber said. "Can you—"

"This is where it started, you piece of shits!" she yelled. "This is where Fred Morgan heard the Voice!"

"The Voice? What Voice?" Josh said as he rounded the corner. He stopped when he saw a figure sitting off in the distance. At least, he thought there was someone there. It could have just been an empty lawn chair. The sun was setting in that direction and it was difficult to see. The chair was sitting at the edge of the cliff, facing the quarry. Down below was where all the mining was done.

"What Voice?" Josh asked again.

"You are stupid, aren't you? The Voice. Tell me you haven't heard it!" she said. Josh turned to face her. She looked him in the eyes and pointed at him awkwardly with two fingers of her cuffed hands. She pressed firmly into his temple. "It speaks in here."

"Woman," Amber said. "You better get your head out of this truck, cause I am done—"

"What is it?" Josh asked. "What's going on here? What are all these things? What do they want?"

Cynthia looked off toward the quarry. The sun had dipped down below the horizon and Josh could see there was someone in the chair after all. Other figures that had now appeared around it.

"If you want to know, you'll have to ask him."

"And he is?" Amber asked.

"The man who brought me and my brother here and set us loose on this town. And now he's come to collect what's his." Her face was panic stricken. "But I'm not going to give it to him, you see? He's not going to get me." Her head disappeared and Josh felt the truck rock as she jumped out over the side. She landed hard. Somehow, she got herself up and began limping away from the quarry. Away from the man in the chair.

That's when the driver's side door opened and Josh was pulled from the vehicle.

Chapter Thirty-Six

on't worry about her," the figure in the chair said as Josh and Amber were pushed forward. As they approached, Josh saw that the man sitting was emaciated. Shriveled like a mummy in a tomb. "Cynthia will be brought back in short time. A group of my — let's call them minions — will catch her before she reaches the road. They were stationed at the entrance. I watched the three of you coming the entire way, you know."

As they approached the cliff's edge, Josh saw signs of movement hundreds of feet below them. Lights had started turning on. The kind that you see at professional baseball diamonds for playing at night. And there were thousands of people on the ground, working. A large structure was bolted to the far wall. Something Josh didn't remember from any of the tours he had been on as a kid. It looked like something straight out of a Ridley Scott movie. A metal frame with tons of wires and equipment that did God knew what.

Josh saw a group of possibly fifty people in the middle of the quarry. They were penned in. A make-shift cage had been erected around them.

The man attempted to stand. Doing that made him look ancient. Two of the Things grabbed him to keep him from falling back down.

He looked Josh in the eye. "Hello, Joshua."

"Am I supposed to know you?" Josh said.

"You don't recognize me? You brought me here just a few weeks ago."

Josh squinted in the dying light. The ancient skel-etal man in front of him…it couldn't be the Creature he had brought to Osprey. The Thing impersonating Fred Morgan. That Thing had been younger than the Fred Morgan Josh had known. This figure was beyond elderly.

"Why Fred Morgan?" Josh asked after studying the Thing for a minute. "I mean, I know there are bigger questions, and I'll get to those in a second. But answer that first. Why are you impersonating Fred Morgan?"

"You've got it wrong, Joshua," the figure said. He pulled himself free from the grip of the things holding him and fell to the ground. Josh fought the urge to help him up. Instead, he watched as the man struggled closer to him on hands and knees.

"There's no impersonation," he said, coming to within feet of Josh. "I AM Fred Morgan." He bent back on his hunches and looked Josh straight in the eyes. "And I need your help. Come with me. Quick! Hold me up." He reached his hand out.

Josh hesitated, then grabbed the ancient skeleton-man, allowing him to put his arms around the shoulders of the bite suit. No reason not to. There was nothing he could do to escape at this point.

"Quickly, before they return with Cynthia. Because once she's here, everything will move forward and I can't stop it." They moved off into the dark, away from the crowd. Amber followed.

"I know the help you need," Amber said. "You need us turned. We're no good to you as humans."

Fred Morgan turned to face both of them and collapsed. At first, Josh thought his legs had given out on him again. But he landed hard on his knees and Josh became aware that the man was weeping heavily.

"This is my Jonah moment," he said between tears. "The last chance I have at redemption. I...I can't allow this to—" he broke off, sobbing. "I need you to stop the events I set in motion."

"What?" Amber said. "What the hell are you talking about?"

"What do you mean, 'help'?" Josh asked.

"You two have gotten farther than I thought possible. You're so close, Joshua. And there's so much at stake."

"If you want our help, we need to know what you're talking about. What's at stake? If you really are Fred Morgan, what are you trying to accomplish?"

The old guy's tears had begun to subside, and they were now able to hear him clearly.

"When I was young—"

"Here we go," Amber said.

Josh gave her a look, and she quieted.

"It's okay. She has every right to be angry. But please listen, both of you. They have Cynthia, and I'm delaying them as long as I can. But I'm telling you, even I'm not fully in control here."

"Okay," Josh said. "Tell us."

"When I was young," he began again, "my father loved this Osprey. When he died, all I had left of him was this town. But in those days, the quarry was the town. Osprey, it was small and feeble — barely more than a community.

"My father died. My mother remarried, and he took over the quarry. I decided that if I couldn't have the business, then I would be the one to destroy it. I stood out on that ridge," he said, pointing toward the top of the cliff face where the giant frame stood. "I had explosives, and I was going to blow the hell out of this whole damn place. I wouldn't say I was doing the right thing, but I do wish that I had succeeded. At least then, all of this wouldn't have happened," he said, gesturing at the creatures standing a few hundred feet away.

"But instead, I fell. Into a crack in the ground. There're all kinds up there. Cracks in the rock from the explosions. I fell far. Down to hell." He shifted where he kneeled and gave a small, humorless chuckle. "I'm sorry if that sounds melodramatic. A little poetic. But I do mean that literally. At least in a sense. I think the place I landed was Hell. Or at least a place like it!

"I think this quarry is a…I've heard it described as a Thin place. Places that are closer to other realms. That's the best I can do to describe it. These Thin places are where alternate realities, normally separate, rub against each other. If you know where to look, or if you're a stupid kid like me, you can quite literally stumble into them. You can communicate with the other side.

"Osprey is one of those places. And I found God. Or A god. Or THE Devil. I don't know what or who I found. A Voice, a Being, a Force from outside our plane of existence. I've had a lot of time to think about it — decades — but I still don't know what exactly this creature is. What I do know is that it saved my life and promised that it would help me rebuild the town. Save what my father had made. Essentially, it gave me my life, and it gave me what I desired. And all it asked for was an unquestioning loyalty and devotion."

The old man's voice was giving out. Josh leaned in so he could hear better.

"I…I passed out. I actually thought I had died! But when I woke, I was in my bed. My mother had found me lying next to the crevice and gotten me home. Weeks later, her husband disappeared."

"I wonder how that happened," Amber said.

"I have a lot to feel guilty for," he said. "But we don't have the decade it would take for my confession, so I'm going to leave it at that.

"I took over the quarry and made it prosperous. That in and of itself was a bit of a miracle, as I don't think I have a bit of business sense. But, the Voice was very helpful. It told me what to do, and where to dig. What equipment to invest in, what businesses to partner with. It seemed that if I listened to the Voice, I couldn't go wrong. The business and the town grew."

"Apparently Satan makes a good CEO," Josh said. Fred smiled at that. It looked genuine, too.

"And by that time, I was very loyal to It. After all, it had told me how to save everything I loved. One day, I went away on a business trip. When I came back, I wasn't alone," Morgan said.

"Cynthia," Josh said.

"Yes. And her brother."

"Wait," Amber said. "Cecil has something to do with this?"

Morgan looked taken aback. "Yes. I thought you had figured that out. The Porter twins. I was drawn to them and I knew they would have a special place in the plans of the Being. This was the point in my life where I really began to pay for my good fortune. To compromise my beliefs. During a dark ceremony, the Voice, through me, marked both Cecil and Cynthia."

"The brand!" Josh said. "When I picked up Cecil's body at his home. We saw a brand on his arm. A triangle with three lines."

"The sign of power," Fred Morgan said.

"And Cynthia?" Amber asked.

"She was given the sign of control."

"Did you know what they were when you brought them here?" Josh asked.

Morgan hesitated. "...yes. I knew they had certain dark predilections."

"Let's not beat around the bush," Amber said flatly. "You brought two serial killers to Osprey."

"Not at the time, no. That is, they weren't killers when they came here," Morgan said. "They hadn't...uh...consummated their desires. They were little more than two depraved children, killing stray cats and dogs in a trailer park. The Voice found them and commanded me to bring them here. I marked them and set them free to...do what they were called to do."

Josh pondered that for a moment. "So as the town was growing in population, they started killing."

"Doesn't sound like a loving founder," Amber said.

"Why?" Josh asked.

"I didn't know at the time. I wasn't on a conversational basis with this Being. I was just listening."

"You could have said no," Josh said.

Fred Morgan dropped his head. "Yes. But I saw the good that was being done in the community. I knew people were thriving. And this place was becoming a good place in an otherwise dark world. If I let it continue, I figured—"

"It would justify the death you were responsible for?" Amber finished.

"Something like that."

Movement in the distance caught Josh's eye. A large crowd of creatures was moving slowly in their direction. He could just make out Cynthia Morgan in tow, fighting like a wild dog. Josh knew they didn't have much time left.

"Okay, they were killing, and you didn't know why. I imagine you were able to convince people in town to help you make those bodies disappear. The police chief, the local doctor—"

"The local funeral home director," Fred Morgan said, eyeing Josh as he said it. "Yes, even your father was helpful in making the bodies disappear. To keep the killing going."

"I figured. I guess you never really know someone," Josh said, quickly whipping a tear from his eye.

"Anyway, we did our business in the shadows of Osprey for years. Always close to being caught, but God was on our side, as they say. Cynthia and Cecil killed, and—"

"Charged," Josh said, thinking of batteries.

"They were preparing to power the machine," Amber said, nodding into the quarry. "Is that it? Everything has been building to whatever that thing is?"

Fred nodded.

"So everything was going according to plan until Cynthia learned what you were using them for," Amber said. "I bet she didn't like it very much! So she killed your ass, am I right?"

He smiled. "No, she didn't find out. She did kill me. But it was just her nature. An inevitability. Like living with an animal that has a wild streak. It'll eventually turn on you. She is what she is. Cynthia never knew the full scope of what was happening. Just that I served a dark force.

"But she played into the plan. She slit my throat as I stood over the very rift that I had fallen into as a boy. Only this time, when I fell, the Thin place gave way. I fell directly into the other world.

"The Voice remolded me in his image. Made me a new body with parts of itself. I am fully myself. But I'm also fully the Voice. At least, as far as my flesh goes."

"How'd you end up in Hawk Junction?"

"I was sent back here, but I was no bigger than a zygote. I floated on the breeze, killing microbes and bacteria in the air, gaining strength and size. I landed and began to feed and grow. Biding my time until I was ready for my hibernation."

"In Jim's freezer," Josh said. "How did you get me out there to pick you up?"

"How should I know? I was frozen. But controlling events for Its own purpose is what the Being does."

"But why, for crying out loud?!" Josh shouted. "Why the hell is this happening?" He looked around, helplessly trying to piece it all together. He saw the giant structure in the cavern. Sparks flew as the workers continued preparing for whatever would happen. "What is that thing even for?"

"Haven't you guessed?" Fred Morgan asked, surprise on his face. "I assumed you had."

Josh was silent for a moment. "The Voice. The Being or whatever it is. It wants to come here, doesn't it? That thing is a doorway between worlds."

"*Yes!*" Morgan said, raising a fist, looking like a teacher when a stupid student gives the correct answer. "A machine that will melt this thin place away entirely, allowing the Being to breach our world. To be birthed here. To rule."

"Or destroy," Amber said. "You are kind of hazy about its exact intentions, aren't you?"

"I know—"

"Nothing," Josh cut in. "Amber's right. You don't know shit. You're just hoping it won't kill when it arrives. Make you king over Osprey or something. That's what it's been telling you, right?"

Morgan was silent.

"Uh-huh," Amber said, chiming in. "So chatty, but now you don't have much to say for yourself. You feel guilty, so you think you're doing us a favor by telling us everything. But you don't have any intention of stopping this. You say you're not in control, but you could just pull the plug on this whole thing. You have that power, right? But you don't want to. Because in the end, you still want this town all to yourself! You're hoping we can stop it, sure. But short of that, you want to make sure it knows you've been a good little servant boy, and you did all the right things for it."

Morgan looked up, anger in his eyes. "Shut up, bitch. I can see you aren't going to be able to help me. I've done all I can do. You don't know what power this Being has! What it has over me. Well, fine!" He got slowly to his feet as the crowd of deformed things arrived with Cynthia in tow.

Henry was in the crowd. Henry's bandage was gone and the wound Amber had made with the ax was completely healed.

Cynthia was thrown to the ground. A body bag was thrown down beside her. Josh recognized it. It was from the Home. He thought briefly about his dad. Good memories of a father he loved now tainted forever. He couldn't forget the terrible things his dad had done.

"Open the bag," Morgan said. A grotesque creature stepped forward and began pulling back the zipper.

"This must be getting pretty draining for you," Amber said. "Controlling all these creatures. It's all you, right?"

He glared at her. "It's taking its toll on me, yes. But it's easier with you two around," he said. He sounded like a man who could tell you what a thing did, but didn't actually know exactly how it worked.

"So we're the last?"

He shook his head as the body of Cecil was being pulled roughly out of the body bag. "No. There are about fifty or so who haven't been turned." He pointed to the group of caged people in the center of the quarry. "Their time will come. The Master will need as many on this side as It can get.

"Now, I'm done answering questions. I'm very tired, and it appears that I'm going to the end." He walked over to the body of Cecil Porter and kneeled down. A hack saw was placed in his hand.

Morgan pulled Cecil's arm out to the side and, placing the blade carefully above the Brand that had been burned into Cecil's flesh, began to cut.

It should have taken longer than it did. Josh knew from personal experience how difficult it was cutting into a human body. Even one that had decayed so much. Tendon and bone are tough.

But the job was done in a couple of minutes. The arm was removed. Like some kind of sacrificial offering, Morgan handed it to one of the creatures he controlled.

"Take this to the machine and put it in place."

Josh expected the thing to shamble toward the path which wound its way into the quarry. But instead, the Thing stretched, and out its back two large leathery wings sprouted. Then, carrying the arm, it plunged out over the edge of the cliff and down to the base of the machine. It landed softly and placed the arm of Cecil on a metal plate that had hoses and wires coming off it.

The effect was instantaneous. The gray rock visible through the metal frame was replaced with a red glow. No monster. Just that ominous red glow. Josh could just make out Cecil's arm from this distance. It was floating above the plate by a foot or two, vibrating and shaking in place. Powering the machine was obviously very draining, and it didn't look like the arm was going to last forever.

Fred Morgan turned to Cynthia. "Now, I believe you have something of mine."

Josh, deciding he had heard enough, stepped forward while Morgan's focus was on Cynthia, and rammed into him with all his strength. The full padding of the bite-suit kept him from feeling much as he pushed Fred Morgan toward and over the edge of the cliff. At the last second, he went down on his chest to keep from following the old man down into the quarry below.

Morgan hit the ground with a splat, his body exploding.

The creatures around all of them paused. That was what Josh had been hoping for. Like machines after smashing their remote controller. But, of course, who knew? And most remote controls can't put themselves back together after being smashed. Josh had a feeling this one could.

"Run!" he said and piled into another group of the creatures that were standing around Cynthia. They also tumbled, like powered down robots.

The three of them began running toward the truck. Josh tried to remember if he had left the keys in the ignition.

No, I took the keys with me, he thought. *We should keep running on foot.*

"Get to the truck!" he shouted, ignoring his own thoughts.

"I think the truck is out of gas," Amber said, panting. "Maybe we should go on foo—"

"STOP LISTENING TO YOUR THOUGHTS AND GET IN THE TRUCK!" Josh yelled back. Seconds later, he skidded into the driver's side door.

"Toss Cynthia in the back!" He yelled as he ran to the front. He didn't wait to see if she heard. He figured they had already run out of time and would be swarmed any minute.

The key was in the ignition. Halleluiah. He cranked it hard and heard a loud **BANG**.

At first, he thought the truck had backfired. But it was running smoothly. Then he realized the sound had come from outside the cab. It was followed by a quieter THWUMP and the truck rocked and swayed as Cynthia fell in. Seconds later, the passenger's side door opened.

"They shot Cynthia," Amber said.

"Shot?! Since when do monsters use guns?" Josh said.

"Just drive!" she said. Josh saw she was holding her arm. Did she get shot, too?

No time for questions. He put the truck in drive and peeled out of the parking lot. He had no idea where they were going. He just knew it was away from there.

Josh looked in the rearview mirror and saw something was chasing them. It wasn't a mob, as he had expected. What was following them was one big, lumbering creature. And it was moving fast!

"Great," he muttered to himself. "Of course they can combine!"

And put the pedal to the floor.

Chapter Thirty-Seven

ou need to let me out," Amber said as the truck screeched around a corner. Josh didn't hear her. He was busy making sure the lumbering, crashing beast that was behind them stayed a safe distance away. Now and then, he tried to peek in on Cynthia Morgan, who had been shot in the arm. It looked bad. Her arm was covered in blood, which was pooling in the truck bed. She let out a scream at every bump he hit. And given his speed, she was doing quite a bit of screaming.

"Josh," Amber said, more forcefully this time. "You need to let me out!"

"I'm a little busy at the moment," he said, making another turn. Every turn cost them speed. A problem the creature behind them did not seem to have. It was large and wide. When it came to traffic signs, it simply pulled back a limb and whacked them aside. It was even able to knock down utility poles in its mad charge.

"YouNeedToLetMeOutOfTheFuckingTruck NOW!!" This last came out in a flood of panic that finally got through to Josh.

Josh took a quick glimpse to the side and saw again that Amber was holding her arm.

"Did you get shot, too?" he asked. He didn't see any blood, but she was starting to wriggle and convulse beside him.

"Arm," she said between panicked breaths. "They were. Holding onto me...when Fred Morgan was—pushed."

"They were holding you?" Josh said. "Who was—" and that's when it dawned on him. The creatures that were surrounding them. They had been holding both him and Amber. He had broken away to shove Fred Morgan, but he had been wearing his full bite suit, so Morgan hadn't been able to infect him. But it seemed he could still infect Amber on his way down.

She was starting the process of becoming one of Them. And from personal experience, Josh knew that did not take long to happen.

"Oh no," Josh whined. "No. God, please no!" He had picked up her panic. What could they do? They had been running from this thing for more than a day, but he had never stopped to wonder what they could do to stop the infection if one of them started to turn. In a movie, he could just take an ax and lop her arm off and that would do it. But he didn't have an ax, nor did he have the time to stop and look for one. And he didn't really think it worked like that, anyway. This Thing spreads so quickly, he thought that maybe it was through the body before he could even—

Amber screamed. He screamed with her.

"The Voice," Amber said. "It's in my head. Stronger than…stranger than before…loosing my. Self!"

Josh looked around. He couldn't stop without that Thing behind them catching up. But he couldn't just leave her to turn on her own. He needed to do SOMETHING!

"I can't stop, honey," he said, tears starting to well in his eyes. He wanted nothing more than to reach out and grab her. To take her in his arms. Maybe to suck the Infection out of her, like they said you were supposed to do with snake venom. "I can't do—"

She surprised him by getting up on one elbow and turning toward him. His first thought was maybe that the change had finished, and she was about to reach over and jam her hand into his skull, infecting him, too. Which wouldn't be that bad. He doubted they were getting out of this thing alive. Maybe going out together was the way to do it.

Instead, she continued twisting around, exposing her mutating arm to him. He could see the grotesque way it was wriggling and writhing. It was like each individual muscle fiber had been replaced with maggots, and they were trying to pop out of her skin.

She reached her arm out of the window toward the creature. "Hey, Mr. Spooky Voice!" she shouted through the back window. Josh could hear the pure rage driving each of her words. "Back the FUCK OFF!"

The effect was as instant as it was surprising. The creature that was following them exploded outward. Body parts flew from the center of the creature as if it had swallowed a brick of plastic explosives. There was no sound over the rushing wind of the truck, but Josh saw bits of it smacking into the sides of houses and mailboxes along the road.

She flopped back in her seat. "Now, stop the truck," she said in an exhausted voice.

He slammed on the brakes. The last sound he heard was a thump as he assumed Cynthia's body struck the rear of the truck bed. He didn't hear a cry from her, which meant she had either passed out from blood loss, or...

"Get out of here," Amber said. "I would, but I don't think I can walk right now!" She ended in a scream. When she broke off, gasping for air, she continued.

"You'd better take the witch, too. You were right, Joshy. They need her. She's a big part of it. AH!" Amber cried out in fresh pain. "This friggin' hurts like hell!"

"Maybe we can—"

"Shut up, Josh! I think I'm holding the change back, but it's taking a lot of—" she grunted, obviously working her way through pain. She looked like a woman in labor. Josh briefly mused how accurate that thought actually was. Though instead of birthing something, she was becoming something. "If you can get Cynthia away...ennnn...hide long enough. Morgan will burn up! Cecil's arm will disintegrate. Everything will be...alright."

"How do you—" Josh began.

"Shhhh," she hissed more than said. "The Voice! I'm stealing...thoughts. Go! It's sooooooo-aaaaaghhh-"

She cut herself off with a loud, guttural scream. Josh, hearing the pain she was going through, turned to leave the truck at quickly as possible. He realized he was causing her even more pain by staying.

Before he could fully open the door, her screams stopped.

"Wait!" Amber said as Josh stood with the door open. He turned halfway out of the truck. She had a half smile on her face and a look of wonder. "I think I beat it," she said.

"Beg pardon?" Josh replied.

She was silent for a moment. "I think I won. I held out long enough and beat the infection. Look!" she said, holding up her arm. It was no longer transforming. For the briefest of second, Josh allowed himself to hope that it was true. That holding out was really the way to beat it.

But then he saw the clean and unblemished flesh of her arms and face. The scrapes and bruises she had received while being flung around in the back of the truck were gone. Each one of them was magically healed.

Josh put his other foot down and slowly backed away from the truck.

"Joshua. What's wrong honey?" Amber said. "It's me. I—"

Josh slammed the door shut. The window exploded in a star pattern as something from the other side pounded into it. A loud wailing screech of rage sounded inside the cab. Josh got two steps away before he remembered Cynthia Morgan.

He turned and, with one fluid motion that only panic could grant him, reached over the side and grabbed the woman by the cuffs. The arms came up in a sickening popping of dislocated joints. He ignored it as he pulled with all his might. The un-conscious — OR DEAD — body of Cynthia Morgan came flying out of the back. He threw her over his shoulders, fireman style, and began retreating down the dark road.

Something reached out from the back window of the cab and tried to grab hold of him. He heard tearing material, and the collar of the bite suit, which was held together with velcro, gave way. Josh did not waste time looking back to see if the thing that had once been Amber was able to get out of the truck. He kept running, wondering where the hell he was going to be able to hide out with an entire town of creatures looking for him.

Chapter Thirty-Eight

The best place to hide, it turned out, was the utility shed at the back of Craig's house. Josh used the keys from the truck to open a Master Lock on the shed and dumped Cynthia Morgan down between a push mower and some bags of mulch. He thought that he could prop her up on the mulch to keep her more comfortable.

Then he got a look at her face. A streetlight shining through a window high up in the shed was all Josh needed to confirm the obvious signs of a dead body. He had checked on her after escaping Amber. She had been unconscious, but alive. Somewhere between there and here, she had died in his arms. He was not turning out to be very good at rescuing people. He collapsed on the other side of the mower with a deep sigh.

It's okay. He was hiding somewhere nobody would think to check. At least not without a thorough town search. And as Amber had said while she was stealing thoughts from whatever this Being was, then there wouldn't be enough time for Fred Morgan to search for him. Josh could just wait things out and all the creatures would just explode when Morgan disintegrated from all the raw power of this otherworldly creature. Right?

Except, a part of him wasn't so sure. He didn't know if he could trust anything that came from this otherworldly creature. Even if it was stolen from it, like trinkets in the night. And while Josh thought he could trust that Amber was herself up to the end, those trinkets could be deceptions.

Plus, he had no reason to believe that the bodies of the infected would just stop existing once Fred Morgan died. For all he knew, when Morgan's control slipped, those things would be cut loose to go out and infect the world. It was still part of this Being, after all. The plan might fail, but if those things continued infecting, then the creature would still win. Right? Or if not win, at least go out sticking its middle finger up at the world.

Who knew? Not him, that was for sure. If Josh had been given a rule book for this whole thing, he had dropped it around the time his dad had first tried to kill him in the funeral Home. This was out of anybody's expertise.

Okay, so where did that leave him? With Cynthia Morgan's corpse, of course. Did it matter that she wasn't alive? Cecil hadn't been, and all Morgan had to do was lop off the arm with the brand and chuck it into the machine. Like some kind of mutilated Energizer Bunny. The brand was the important part. It was what was powering the Rift — or whatever Fred Morgan had called his giant, cosmic gizmo. Fred had said he had marked both the brother AND the sister.

Josh looked down at Cynthia's cooling body and made a face. It wasn't like he had never undressed a corpse before in his years at the Home. That was one of the main reasons he had loved the modern trend toward cremation that society had been turning to. To the world, it meant spending less on coffins and tombstones and even gravesites. To Josh, it meant fewer naked corpses he had to shimmy into respectable clothing on a daily basis.

Reluctantly, he picked up her arms and checked the upper area, just beneath the armpits, where Cecil's brand had been. Nothing on the right or left. He did a quick check of both legs. She was wearing a dress, so it was easy to verify. No brand on either leg.

At least, nothing below her dress.

"Oh, come on, God. Don't make me do this." He picked up her hands, which had fallen into her lap, so he could lift the hem of her dress. That's when he saw the shine of her wedding band. He remembered that Chief Braden had asked Henry about her jewelry, and Henry had said he had tried to remove it, but it wouldn't come off.

Fred Morgan hadn't said Cecil and Cynthia had both been branded. He had said they had both been marked. Cecil's brand had obviously been his mark, but maybe…

Josh turned the ring around on Cynthia's finger. The woman's knuckles were knobby from a bad case of arthritis.

In the faint light coming through the shed window, he was just able to see some kind of inscription on the inside of the band. It looked similar to Cecil's brand.

Josh's mind wandered back to the image of that large, lumbering creature exploding behind their escaping truck. That, he felt fairly confident in saying, was not part of the Being or Fred Morgan's plan. So what was it? A fluke? A freak accident?

Josh's thoughts were cut off by a noise from outside. Had they gotten around to checking Craig's house already? He tried to remember if there was a back exit in Craig's yard and couldn't.

With as little noise as he could manage, Josh stood up and peeked his head out the bottom corner of the window. A figure was coming out of the sliding door of Craig's house with a large rolling suitcase in hand. Josh saw with surprise that it was taking the form of Craig! Why was it holding a suitcase? The creature didn't even appear to be searching for him. It slowly closed the sliding door, then patted down its pockets, as if it were searching for keys. Josh looked down at the keys in his hand, then back up.

Faintly, Josh heard, "Ah shit," as it seemed to realize it had no way to lock the door behind it. Josh smiled to himself and moved to stick his head out the door.

"Craig?" he asked as the man passed him on his way to the gate in the yard.

"Whoa!" Craig said, startled. He dropped his suitcase and Josh was suddenly looking down the barrel of a very large and oddly shaped gun. It took him a second to realize what it was.

"Is that a paintball gun?"

"Warlocke? Is that you?" Craig asked, the gun dipping down.

"Yeah."

"What are you doing in my shed?" Craig asked, sounding terribly confused.

"Hiding out from those things," Josh said. At the mention of the creatures, Craig brought the gun back up in his direction. Not feeling particularly threatened, Josh looked at the suitcase Craig had dropped. "What are you doing?"

"Getting out of town. How do I know you aren't one of those mutant things?" he asked. "Those dudes have some pretty sick superpowers, but they're also scary as f—"

"You can trust me, Craig. I'm not one of them. What's in the case?" Josh asked, curious. Something about Craig had put him more at ease, more comfortable, but he couldn't figure out what. Maybe just the sense of a fellow human being that he could trust. But how did he know he could trust Craig? He is a pretty unique guy and all, but as Craig had said, those things do have some pretty sick superpowers.

Then it occurred to Josh what eased his mind and a few things clicked into place.

"Your head," Josh said, noticing a gash that ran along the side of the other man's head. "Where did you get the cut?"

"Oh, am I still bleeding?" he said, touching his head. He winced. "Yeah, I got cornered at the quarry earlier today when I went to check out the thefts. Dude, you should see it. All the stolen stuff is there! They built some kind of super Star Trek level portal device or something in the side of—"

"The cliff face," Josh said. "Yeah, I was there."

"Ah. Well, anyway, they knocked me out. Put me in this cage with a bunch of other people. Just had us stand around for hours. Wouldn't feed us or give us water or nothin'. We finally made a run for it when some old dude did a nosedive off the top of the cliff."

"I was there for that, too."

"No way!" Craig said, sounding impressed. "Old dude totally exploded into guts and stuff. All the other super mutants just kinda stood there for a few minutes. Bunch of us took off running. Not everybody got away. They started rounding us up again."

"Well, I'm glad you got away," Josh said. And he was shocked at how much he meant that. It was good seeing a face he could trust.

"So how do I know I can trust you?" Craig asked again.

"Well, I know I can trust you. You are Craig. You're kind of hard to imitate," Josh said, smiling. Craig broke out in a big grin at that. "As for me... those things don't bleed. Did you notice? Not one of them had a cut or bruise? Like Henry. I saw his arm get chopped up earlier today. Bloody thing. Amber actually hit him with an ax!"

"No way!"

"But when I saw him tonight, the arm was healed. No bandages, no cuts. Those things don't bleed and their bodies heal right away." Josh held up his hands and pointed to his face, which he knew was still covered in cuts and bruises from his tumble down Cynthia Morgan's stairs.

"Okay," Craig said. "Makes sense."

"So where are you headed?" Josh said, pointing to the suitcase.

"Out of town. I got a buddy in the military. He's pretty friendly with people on the base where he works. I figure something like this should be fought by someone with a little more authority, ya know? So I'm going to find him and tell him all about it. I got a bit of video on my phone," Craig said, holding up his cell. "Figured they would want to see some proof."

"Clever," Josh said, honestly impressed.

"Yeah. You wanna come with?" Craig asked, picking up his suit case. "I think I know a way to get out of town without being seen."

Josh thought it over. Getting someone in authority involved seemed like a good plan. Let someone else figure things out. On the other hand, Amber had said he should lie low and wait for this whole thing to just blow over. That seemed like a safe bet, too. If he left now, Craig might get them caught, and the whole thing would be over.

But he didn't trust that plan, either. Too risky to the rest of the world if Amber happened to be wrong. No, he had an idea of his own. It was also pretty risky and would mean a quicker end if he was wrong. For everybody. But he thought he might be onto something.

"No," Josh said. "I think I'm going to hang out here. I've got an idea about how I might be able to stop these things for good."

"You need help, dude?" Craig said without hesitation and Josh smiled. "The more the merrier!" Craig added. Josh's smile faded as he considered Craig's last words.

"Yeah, more hands make light work," he said.

"Damn straight," Craig said. "You can't do it all yourself!" He moved toward Josh.

"Thanks man. But no, you go find your buddy. We might need the army here after all. Especially if I'm wrong." Craig nodded. "Right. Okay, my man. You take care. And don't get yourself caught by these super-mutants, okay?"

"Same to you, buddy." And with that, Craig picked up his suitcase and turned to leave. "What's in there, anyway?" Josh asked.

"Clothes, bro. Never leave home without a change of undies."

Josh shook his head. "You should probably go without the case. It'll just slow you down and be more likely to get you caught. You can just buy a change of clothes on the outside, right?"

"Right!" Craig said, dropping the case. "Smart. Thanks, bro. You're always thinking, man. Always the man with the plan. Take care." And with that, he disappeared down the dark street. Josh hoped Craig would make it out of town safely.

He went back inside the shed and looked around for the tools he would need. It was going to be a long night, and he wanted to make sure his plan went off without a hitch.

CHAPTER THIRTY-NINE

He crept toward the tin shack in the quarry, which was off to the side of the entrance. Josh had made his way across town, stopping often to avoid being spotted. It seemed like the whole town was out looking for him. Obviously, Morgan wanted Josh before the old man's time ran out.

Now, approaching the shack marked with the symbol for explosives, he pulled out the bolt cutters he had grabbed from Craig's shed. He snapped the lock and carefully opened the door, hoping he wasn't heard. The door squeaked. He peered inside the tiny room and saw boxes of dynamite neatly arranged. He moved to pick up one of the boxes, looking for instructions. He had never worked with dynamite and doubted he would be able to set it up properly. The Star-Gate, as he had begun thinking of Fred Morgan's machine, was huge. And he figured it would take a lot of well-placed TNT to take it down.

"Looking for something?" said a voice. Josh whirled around. Fred Morgan stood behind him, flanked on either side by dozens of creatures. The fall had not been kind to him, it seemed. The man had been able to pull his body together, to a degree. But the effort had obviously taken its toll on him. A fair bit of his insides were now outside, collected in a heap on his lap. He was being rolled around in a wheelchair.

Josh, expecting something like this to happen, quickly hooked the road flare out of his pocket and struck it to life. The light blazed. He grabbed a stick of dynamite and held it close to the flare.

"Make a move," Josh said, looking Morgan in the eye, "and I'll close that doorway for good! Daddy won't be coming through."

"I don't have time for games," Morgan said. "Or anything else. Cynthia's body was found. Her left hand ring finger is missing. You've become quite the ghoul, Mr. Warlocke. Give me the ring. Or I'll send someone in to grab it." He gestured to the former townspeople standing all around him.

"Not likely," Josh said.

That's when Amber stepped out of the crowd. Josh was struck still. She didn't turn into any terrifying creature. She just walked up and put her hand on the glove holding the flare. Josh looked past her at the creatures. He saw all the people from his town. People he recognized.

Josh's gaze stopped on his dad, and his stomach lurched. Pain welled up, bringing tears to his eyes.

Amber took the flare from his hand. He was barely aware she was doing it. It would have been hopeless for him to blow up the door, anyway.

"Very good," Amber said. Josh heard Morgan muttering the same thing behind them, like an ancient ventriloquist. "Now give me the ring." Amber held out her hand.

Josh sighed and reached into his shirt, revealing the ring. It hung on a length of twine around his neck.

Before he could move, Amber's hand shot out and grabbed it, breaking the rope.

"Ow!" he said, rubbing his neck as she walked away. Amber dropped the ring in the old man's outstretched hand. Morgan had decomposed so much, Josh thought it looked like the ring might be too much for him — that he would collapse with the minuscule weight. Wouldn't that be fun to see?

But the ring landed and Morgan closed a fist around it with glee. So much for the man who wanted them to stop him. He held his fist high in the air and cheered in a soft guttural cry, which was picked up and repeated by the creatures closest to him. The sound grew outside the shed, spreading into a gigantic roar. He stepped outside, and saw illuminated by the flood lights, the creatures, in the form of most of the towns people, standing at the top of the cliff face, and in the valley itself. Fifteen thousand creatures strong, if the last Osprey population numbers could be believed.

Morgan lowered his arm, opened his hand, and began to place the ring on the pinky finger of his right hand. Josh saw the old man was shaking, but couldn't be sure if it was from decomposition, or from excitement.

Morgan was just putting the ring to his bony knuckle when Josh saw his chance. He grabbed a handful of TNT and pushed the two creatures flanking him, and made a break for the machine. The flame from his flare burned brightly, lighting his way.

Josh had only made it a couple of steps before he was grabbed by half a dozen creatures. He was pulled back and plopped down rudely at Morgan's feet. Josh looked up at the aging man.

"I think you've done enough for the day."

"I'm not going to stop fighting this," Josh said.

"Oh, I think you will," Morgan said, reaching down and grabbing Josh by the face. The only part of him not protected by the bite suit.

"NO!" Josh yelled, trying to pull away. But he was held in place and couldn't move. Josh felt a wriggling feeling of worms as they burrowed into his flesh. Morgan pulled his hand away, but Josh knew that the damage had been done. The pain tore through his body. He felt his bones shifting and expanding. He felt the meat of his body begin fighting itself. He wasn't able to hold in the screams.

"Don't worry," Morgan said. "You'll come around to the changes soon. In the meantime, you get to enjoy the show. You're about to bear witness. The birth of a new lord into this world. Behold!" He said, holding up the hand with the ring over his boney finger.

And nothing happened. Josh, in his agony, turned toward the doorway. Nothing flickered or changed.

"It's leverage you need," Josh said, holding in the pain. The man turned toward him. Josh thought of Amber holding the change back. Holding onto her humanity for as long as possible. Could he do what she had done?

"What?" Morgan said, looking at the door. Then at the ring, and finally to Josh.

"Leverage," Josh grunted. "This Being you love is huge, right? And it needs something big on this side. In fact, I think it needs part of itself on this side. Like a helping hand, to pull it through. That's why the town needed to be bigger. That's the first thing it told you to do, right? Increase the size of the town? It needs leverage to pull itself through. Well, fifteen thousand town residents now turned into living breathing Mini-Beings, acting and moving as one? That might be enough, right? And all you need to do is open the door and invite it in." Josh said.

"What did you do with it?" Morgan said, pulling the ring off his hand and holding it in the light. Josh knew he was looking for the inscription. He also knew he wouldn't find it. The ring was plain when Josh had picked it up from the jewelry store that he had broken into on the way over here. It was such a simple ring, he was surprised how difficult it was to find one just like it.

In a fury, Morgan threw it into the gathered crowd of monsters. "Give it to me, now!" he said, "Where is it?!" His body was collapsing in on itself even as his rage burned bright on his face.

"Oh," Josh said, pulling the glove off his left hand. "Are you looking for this?" He showed them the ring that he had put on his pinky finger shortly after coming up with his plan. He hadn't enjoyed cutting off Cynthia Morgan's finger to get it, but knew it had to be done. "Looks like I've got the upper hand now. Pun intended."

"Get the ring!" Morgan said.

Things slowed down as Josh tried to concentrate through the pain of his changing body. So far, things had gone according to plan. But this was the part that was all guess work. He figured that only the Being would be able to open the portal with the ring. So he knew he had to let himself get infected. But once infected, would he be able to control it while he still retained his mind? That was the question. There was another question. Once the portal was open, would he even be able to do what he wanted to do? Or was he just rolling out the red carpet for whatever lay beyond?

Before anybody could move to grab him, Josh closed his eyes and concentrated on what he wanted.

Everyone stopped as blinding red light flashed. The portal, already open when Cecil's branded arm had been thrown onto the plate, turned a darker shade of crimson. The color of another world. A moment passed where nothing moved. Then, a form moved out of the portal, reaching in through our world. Tentacles flowed out, stretching, grasping as they went. As it moved, the rock wall around it began disappearing, the worlds melding into one.

The world also seemed to be absorbed. To be infected by the Being.

Fred Morgan shouted with joy, screaming and laughing.

"Okay," Josh said to himself. "It's now or never." Fred Morgan didn't even notice he was there. It seemed all his holy talk about not wanting to doom the planet was a load of horse shit, because he looked like a kid on Christmas day. Josh guessed he really believed he was going to be given some kind of reward for his part in birthing this Thing into their world. But looking at the vague shape coming through the portal and the world that lay beyond, he had his doubts that this thing — whatever it was — was the promise keeping type. Josh got the impression it was out for its own gratification.

Josh turned his mind back to the task at hand, not sure what he was doing, but trying anyway. He glanced around the quarry. Everybody in town was there. All fifteen thousand residents — or the forms of them, anyway — were there. Good. Now to dig deep and reach out.

Josh reached with his mind for the portal that had opened. Hot wind gusted around him. Debris and sand smacked him in the face.

He mentally avoided the thing that was coming through, feeling that connecting with it in this state would have very bad consequences.

Josh focused on the quarry — on the entire town. He grabbed hold of everything, every memory and emotion of the place where he had grown up and slammed the door between the worlds, shutting off the connection.

Everything went black.

Chapter Forty

Josh opened his eyes and fixed them on a strange, dead world. The place gave the appearance of desert at first glance. It even had the eerie quiet that deserts were supposed to have, devoid of even wind. A calm place.

But the mountains in the distance looked too large. Higher up than the clouds. Or at least what passed for clouds in this world.

The mountains seemed to defy physics, being narrower in places at the base than they were near the top. No snow-covered peaks. Just black monoliths scraping the sky.

Josh appeared to be standing on sand, but each individual grain was larger than it should have been. Larger than any sand he had ever seen. And it had the shape of shark teeth, or perhaps lizard scales. They looked sharp. As if rolling around in them would tear your flesh in gushers of blood.

And speaking of blood, the air had the deep red appearance of looking through a window bathed in the stuff. Like the world seen through a film gel. Josh looked up, expecting a red sun. But though the light given off was indeed red to his eye, he saw a strange pale blue orb in the sky. He couldn't tell if this orb was a star or a moon. He couldn't even be sure it was floating in outer space. It looked like maybe it hung in this strange planet's atmosphere.

All this he saw in the blink of an eye. He then became aware of a figure in the distance. Perhaps two hundred yards away. It was in his peripheral vision, and he knew all he had to do was flick his eye in that direction, and it would come into focus. But he flicked, and it was no clearer.

"Josh?" a voice said. And though the voice sounded as if it were right next to him, he could have sworn it came from the figure in the distance. "What's going on? Where is this place?"

Josh knew the voice. He turned his head and the figure in the distance morphed. Not unlike the creatures that had infected his town. But though those things changed shape, this figure changed distance. All at once, like she was made of elastic, she was pulled through time and space, traveling distance at unknowable speed. Then Amber was standing right next to him. He had only to lift his hand slightly to take hers. And so he did.

She jumped, startled, at his touch. Obviously, she experienced something similar to him.

Josh smiled, because he knew this was Amber. Not a monster in Amber's skin.

"What's going on?" Another voice said. Josh turned from Amber. He was slightly fascinated by the way she returned to her previous spot, this time with his own arm trailing behind like a streamer. That weird time and space displacement thing happened again, and he was now standing next to a woman holding a little girl. And he saw many others; townspeople that he knew or at least recognized. They were zipping in and out of his vision. Far, then close.

"Where are we?" someone asked. Josh was very happy. Everyone was back. All fifteen thousand of them and not a monster in sight.

"We're on the wrong side," Fred Morgan said. Josh saw him a mile away but heard him as if he were standing in front of him. Josh turned his head, and there he was. The man who had caused all the trouble. All the turmoil. When looking head on, he appeared to be ten feet from Josh. He turned and made eye contact.

"I guess you stopped me after all," the man said. Then he fell to his knees. "And now all of us are going to pay the price." He began to weep.

Josh started to ask Morgan what he meant, but then the screaming started.

It came from the back and spread around the crowd.

"What the hell is that?" a man yelled. Josh turned in the direction of the speaker, but it was too disorienting. Figures flew about in elastic horror, hands thrown over faces, or pointing into the sky. Elongated limbs were everywhere, and crying faces distorted beyond recognition as he tried to look where everyone else was looking. It was nearly impossible, as the slightest movement of his head changed so much.

"Mommy!"

"Oh my god, what is that thing!"

The shouts came from all around. The people were freaking out. And then they began running. And falling. Blood welled up around each person that came down on the strange sharp things that Josh thought of as sand. He turned behind him and looked up.

And up. And up. All the way to the top of the globe of this strange world. It was so high that the atmosphere blotted out the uppermost parts of... whatever it was.

A Giant. A Being. A Force. Josh wasn't sure how else to describe it. The Voice. It stood, towering over this strange world's mountains like they towered over our own.

You have failed me, came the thought from his head. But no more pretense that these were his own thoughts. That time had passed, apparently.

"NO!" Fred Morgan yelled. He pointed in Josh's direction. "I did everything that you asked. He is the one who—"

Anger. Noise. Sound that was louder than anything Josh had ever felt before. And this noise was felt, not heard. It was beyond hearing. It shook him and threatened to burst him apart. Molecule by molecule.

I gave you what you wanted. But you failed me. Failed my young. For that...

The world shook. Josh looked around, trying to locate the source of the shaking. After a moment, he caught sight of Fred Morgan just as he was being pulled into the ground of this world. And his guess had been right. Torrents of blood gushed up as he was slowly pulled down through the sharp objects covering the surface. Josh saw a tentacle looking thing coming up from below, wrapping itself around the elderly man's legs.

"Aaaarrghh," Morgan screeched as he was pulled down. His body stretched and elongated as Josh watched, and Josh realized that it wasn't just some optical illusion. This was how the world worked. That stretching wasn't always instantaneous. This pulling, this torture. Josh knew this could go on forever, if that's what the Being that towered over them wanted.

"Stop it!" Josh yelled. He tried to yell at those around him. "Stop running!"

He felt a tug on his arm. Amber was yanked from him by a limb from the ground. She was tossed up in the sky and something swooped down, catching her in its large jaw. Some kind of flying insect, he thought. He watched as she screamed and reached out for him. Then the creature bit down and her body was sliced in half, cutting off her screams.

"NO!" he cried, but survival instinct kept him from running in her direction. Instead, he looked toward the Being, tears streaming down his face.

"What do you—"

Do not speak to me, his mind thought, and darkness enveloped him.

He came to seconds later. His legs were bound by the tentacle things from the sand, and he was hovering five feet above the ground. His mind had given out from the direct mental contact with It. He looked down and the tentacle which held him had burst apart a mound of the sand stuff. Josh saw that what he was looking at wasn't ground. It was the Creature of this world. The sand could have been flakes of dead skin. The detritus of this thing's body.

They weren't standing on a world. They were standing on the creature itself.

You have kept me from my nourishment, it said from inside his head. *My rightful feast. And for that, you will suffer. Your suffering shall be greater than these. And when I'm done, you will help me find my way to your world. To my feast!*

Josh was held aloft as the towns people were slowly massacred. He saw the mother and her child fall and both spill open like over ripe melons. He saw creatures burrow up from below, grab people two at a time and begin peeling their skin off with barbed like limbs.

It went on and on that way. So long that exhaustion took him, even through the screams of the people he knew and loved. Blackness settled in on his mind.

You will breach for me, so that I can finally feed.

EPILOGUE

Chris drove his truck along the quiet streets of Osprey, headed home in the early morning light. This week, he was working the night shift. He hated the night shift. He always felt like a vampire whenever his two weeks were done and he ended up having to sleep all day and work all night. Never seeing his kids. Missing out on hanging with the guys.

But either way, he always enjoyed his commute, which took him from his hometown of St. Timothy, through this quaint community. Osprey was probably the most beautiful city he had ever seen, and he never failed to bring his family there for at least one of their yearly festivals. The soothing drive through the streets always calmed him after a hard night working in the factory.

But tonight, the town seemed different. It wasn't the lack of people. There was hardly ever anyone out when he drove through so early in the morning.

Chris had never seen the town looking so…ignored. There was garbage thrown in the streets. Old computers and electronics lay strewn about. And doors were hanging open. Not just a couple, but every other house seemed to have another door swung in the breeze, like an open invitation. It looked like people had fled and were in too much of a hurry to lock up after themselves.

"What's going on here?" Chris said, observing the normally put together neighborhood. He was so busy looking around, he almost didn't notice the body sprawled in the middle of the road. He braked hard, coming to within a foot of crushing the man's head under the front tire of his truck.

"Hey!" he shouted, getting out. "You okay, man?" He reached the figure and rolled him over. It was a young guy, probably in his early twenties. He had obviously been in some kind of fight or something. His face was bruised and battered so badly, Chris figured he wouldn't have recognized him if he had been his own brother.

He felt the kid's neck and found a strong pulse.

"Buddy!" he said, shouting right into the kid's face. He realized he probably shouldn't be moving him, but it was too late for that now. "Wake up! You okay, man?"

"Huh?" the kid said, his eyes fluttering open. "Is it over?" he asked, eyes bleary.

"Yeah," Chris said, reassuring him. He didn't have the slightest clue what the kid meant, but he just wanted to keep things mellow. Chris looked around, hoping someone might come along to help. He realized his phone was in the truck. He should probably go grab it and call 9-1-1.

"How did I get here?" he asked. Chris laughed.

"Beats me, kid. I just found you lying in the street. I don't know what kind of partying you did to get you here." He shifted, trying to pull the kid into a more comfortable position. Something tinkled onto the pavement. That's when Chris saw the kid's right arm was burned, the skin charred and crispy.

"Oh, shit!" he said. "We gotta get you to a hospital, kid. Those look like some serious burns." He tried to pull the kid up into a standing position to get him in the truck, but he fought back. He kneeled down and picked something up from the road with his unburned hand. Chris thought it looked like half a charred ring. He could see bits of gold where it hadn't been burned black.

"Sorry, kid. The ring's seen better days."

"Yeah." He looked up, surveying the town. "Looks pretty empty around here."

"Yeah, I was thinking that, too," Chris said. "Osprey doesn't seem like it normally does. Something going on here that I oughta know about?"

The kid seemed to think that over. Then he shook his head. "Nope. Nothing special about this place anymore." He turned to Chris. "Hey, you think you can give me a ride?"

"Sure. You look like you need a hospital. There's one just up the road there."

"No!" the kid said quickly. "Not there. Just… let's just start by getting out of Osprey. I'll figure out where I'm going after that."

"Okay," Chris said, not really sure how to argue. He thought closer would be better if he wanted medical help, but the kid seemed to be doing alright. "I'm Chris," he said as he helped the kid over to the passenger side of his truck.

"Thanks. I'm Josh."

FROM THE AUTHOR

Thank you for picking up this book. If you read it (instead of skipping straight to this page - heavens knows why you would), I hope you liked it. Please consider heading to your online retailer of choice, and leaving a review. It helps others who might be interested find the book! Plus, I always enjoy seeing what did (and did not) resonate with people.

If you would like to read more of my work, you can go to www.HatMakerPress.com/chuck to sign up to my mailing list and get the latest info.

Acknowledgments

Many people helped bring this book into a reality, and I just know I'm going to forget someone. Thank you my editor, Karmen Wells, for taking the raw form of this story, and helping shape it into something a little less embarrassing.

There were several super stars that helped with proofing the manuscript to catch any last minute errors. Thank you to Chandra Marie, Lori Nunis, Kate Forsman and Emma Miska. Your keen eyes were a blessing.

And finally, thank you to my family, especially my beautiful and patient wife, for allow me to put time into creating stories. I ignored plenty of dishes as I tried to get this past the finish line. I love you all!

ABOUT THE AUTHOR

Charles Howard is the pen name used by Seth Wilks when writing horror fiction. Seth is an illustrator and writer. He writes all ages novels and comics under his own name, and works in the animation industry when he's not making up stories. He lives in southern Ontario with his wife and two sons.

www.ingramcontent.com/pod-product-compliance
Lightning Source LLC
Chambersburg PA
CBHW030928120726
47906CB00002B/526